H

Of

Evil

by

Wendy Cartmell

Published by Costa Press
This edition published in 2025

Copyright 2025 by Wendy Cartmell

The right of Wendy Cartmell to be identified as the author of this work has been asserted in accordance with the Copyright Design and Patents Act 1988.

All rights reserved.

All characters and events in this book are entirely fictitious. Any resemblance to actual events or locals or persons living or dead is entirely coincidental

CONTENTS

Contents

CHAPTER 1

CHAPTER 2

CHAPTER 3

CHAPTER 4

CHAPTER 5

CHAPTER 6

CHAPTER 8

CHAPTER 9

CHAPTER 10

CHAPTER 11

CHAPTER 12

CHAPTER 13

CHAPTER 14

CHAPTER 1

The Unwanted Gift

Alex Morgan was drowning again.

It always began the same way: sunlight fractured through green water, tiny bubbles streaming from his nose and mouth like silver coins, a distant voice calling his name as if from the wrong end of a long tunnel. Then the crushing pressure in his chest, the desperate need to breathe, and finally, that moment—that terrible, wonderful moment—when something changed.

When he stopped being alone in the water.

Alex jerked awake, gagging on phantom lake water, sheets twisted around his legs like grasping hands. The red numbers on his nightstand clock burned 3:17 AM into the darkness. It was always 3:17. As if whatever dreams were, they at least had the courtesy to keep a schedule.

"Goddammit," he muttered, pressing the heels of his hands against his eyes until phosphenes bloomed behind his eyelids. Sleep, what little he'd managed to get, was over for the night.

In the merciless fluorescent light of his bathroom, Alex looked like what he was: a thirty-four-year-old man clinging to the ragged edge of his life. Dark circles under bloodshot eyes. Three days of stubble that couldn't decide if it wanted to be a beard. The fine white scar at his temple, a souvenir from his last month on the force, seemed especially prominent this morning.

He fumbled for the orange prescription bottle in the medicine cabinet. He dry-swallowed two. Dr. Keppler would disapprove, but then, Dr. Keppler didn't have to live inside Alex Morgan's head.

His apartment told the same story as his face. Once upon a time, Alex had been a rising star in Boston PD's homicide division. Three citations for outstanding detective work. A corner office waiting for him. Now he had a studio apartment where the heat worked when it felt like it, walls thin enough to hear his neighbor's television, and a stack of past-due notices on the kitchenette counter.

The one good thing about 3:17 AM was that it gave him time for a run before the day started. Running was the only thing that quieted the noise in his head, the whispers that weren't quite there, the shadows that moved when they shouldn't. Five miles minimum, preferably ten. Cheaper than therapy. Almost as good as whiskey.

Today he managed seven miles before the dizziness started. It was happening more frequently now. Like the headaches. Like the moments when the world seemed to... stutter... and he'd catch glimpses of things that couldn't possibly be there. Things like the old woman who stood on the corner of Harrison and Pike every morning, transparent as tissue paper, watching commuters with empty eye sockets. No one else ever looked at her. No one else ever noticed when she opened her mouth and dark water poured out.

You're just tired, he told himself, stretching against a lamppost. *Or the meds are screwing with your head. Or you're finally going crazy, like Dad did.*

None of those explanations were particularly comforting.

Back in his apartment, showered and dressed in his one decent suit (slightly shiny at the elbows but passable), Alex reviewed his current caseload. Two insurance investigations, the kind he could do in his sleep. An infidelity case he was considering dropping because the husband was starting to make him uncomfortable with his increasingly specific questions about evidence gathering. And a missing teenager who had almost certainly run away to New York with her boyfriend, no matter how many times her mother insisted she would never do that.

The rent was due in five days. His checking account could cover it, barely, but only if he didn't eat much this month. Or turned down the heat. Or—

A sharp knock interrupted his calculations.

The woman at his door was the kind of wealthy that doesn't need to advertise. Her wool coat probably cost more than three months of Alex's rent, but it wasn't showy. Her blonde hair was drawn back in a simple chignon that nonetheless looked professionally done. When she removed her sunglasses, her eyes were red-rimmed, but her makeup was flawless.

"Mr. Morgan?" Her voice had the faintest trace of a Back Bay accent, old Boston money trying not to sound like it. "I'm Katherine Bishop. I need your help finding who killed my sister."

Rich people problems, Alex thought. But he managed a professional smile and invited her in, making a mental note to move the stack of bills into a drawer before she could see them.

"The police said it was an overdose," Katherine continued, sitting ramrod straight on his secondhand couch. "They said Elizabeth—Eliza—had a history of experimentation. But I know my sister, Mr. Morgan. She was careful about everything, especially what she put in her body. She wouldn't have made a mistake like that."

Alex nodded, taking notes more out of habit than necessity. He'd heard this story before.

Grieving relatives unable to accept the messy reality of how their loved ones died. Sometimes they were right. Usually, they weren't.

"Ms. Bishop, I understand how difficult this must be,"

"I don't think you do," she interrupted, opening her designer handbag and removing a check. She slid it across his coffee table. "This is my retainer. Twice your usual rate, according to your website. There will be another payment like this when you tell me what really happened to Eliza."

Alex glanced at the check and managed not to let his expression change. It was enough to cover his rent, utilities, and still have a decent cushion left over. The drowning sensation from his nightmare seemed to return, pressing against his lungs.

"I'll need all the information you have," he said, already reaching for the check. "Police reports, autopsy findings, access to her apartment. And I should warn you, sometimes the truth isn't what we want to hear."

Katherine Bishop's smile was thin and didn't reach her eyes. "I'm not paying you for what I want to hear, Mr. Morgan. I'm paying you for the truth."

As she handed him a manila folder containing Eliza Bishop's death certificate and police report, their fingers brushed briefly. The sensation was like grabbing an electric fence.

A white-hot jolt of something, surged up Alex's arm and detonated behind his eyes, bringing with it a flood of images that couldn't possibly be his memories:

A circle of candles in a dark room. A knife with an ivory handle. Blood dripping onto polished wood. A woman's voice chanting words in a language that made his teeth ache. And underneath it all, the certainty that whatever killed Eliza Bishop had never been human.

The headache hit with the force of a sledgehammer. Alex dropped the folder, papers spilling across the floor. When he pressed his hand to his head, it came away wet. A nosebleed. Perfect.

"Mr. Morgan? Are you alright?" Katherine was looking at him with what appeared to be genuine concern.

"Fine," he managed, pinching the bridge of his nose to stop the bleeding. "Low blood sugar. Happens sometimes."

He bent to gather the scattered papers, avoiding looking directly at the crime scene photos. He didn't need to see them. He'd already seen worse in that flash of... whatever it was. His hand trembled slightly as he reopened the folder.

"I'll take the case," he said, not because he wanted to, but because the rent was due, and because the alternative was admitting that he was losing his mind. Again.

On the elevator ride down, Katherine Bishop's cell phone rang. She answered with a single word: "Yes." Then: "He's exactly what we're looking for. The reaction was immediate. Much stronger than the others."

And finally, with a smile in her voice that didn't match her grieving sister persona: "Of course I'm sure. He's a Morgan. You can see it in his eyes when the gift takes hold. He just doesn't know it yet."

She hung up as the elevator doors opened to the lobby, once again the picture of elegant grief as she stepped out into the January morning, leaving a faint scent of expensive perfume and something older, earthier. Like freshly turned soil.

Back in his apartment, Alex dry-swallowed another pill, knowing it wouldn't help. The whispers were starting again. Soon the shadows would begin to move.

Running wouldn't fix this. Whiskey wouldn't fix this. Nothing ever fixed it completely.

But maybe, just maybe, finding out what really happened to Eliza Bishop would quiet the voices long enough for him to sleep through the night. Just once.

It was something to hope for, anyway.

CHAPTER 2

The first whisper.

The scene of Eliza Bishop's death wasn't what Alex had expected.

He'd read enough overdose reports in his police days to know what they usually looked like: squalid apartments with blackened spoons and needles, cheap motel rooms with their sad little bottles lined up on bathroom counters, occasionally the homes of the wealthy where everything was meticulously cleaned except for that one telling detail; a razor blade in a designer purse, a hollowed-out book on an antique shelf.

Eliza Bishop's apartment in Beacon Hill looked like a museum. Or maybe a temple.

"Ms. Bishop had a very um specific aesthetic," said the building manager, a nervous man named Pratt who kept checking his watch as if Alex's presence was causing him physical pain. "We'd ordinarily have cleared the unit by now, but her sister paid for three months in advance. Said she needed time to decide what to do with the belongings."

Three months to preserve a crime scene, Alex thought. *How convenient.*

"I'll take it from here," Alex said, and the relief on Pratt's face was almost comical.

"I'll be downstairs if you need anything. But please try not to need anything."

The moment the door closed behind Pratt, the air in the apartment seemed to change. Alex's ears popped as if he'd descended rapidly in an airplane. The temperature plummeted at least ten degrees. And underneath it all, a persistent hum just below the threshold of hearing, like a dentist's drill in the next room.

Great. The pills aren't working anymore.

Alex forced himself to be methodical. He started in the hallway and worked inward, the way he'd been trained. The apartment was immaculate. Too immaculate for a place where someone had died just eleven days ago.

Eliza Bishop had been thirty-two years old, unmarried, and a curator at the Museum of Fine Arts, specializing in esoteric antiquities, according to her personnel file. Her living room contained no television but instead featured floor-to-ceiling bookshelves filled with volumes in at least five languages. Ancient history. Anthropology. Mythology. And on the bottom shelf, tucked almost out of sight: books with titles like Necromantic Practices of Ancient Mesopotamia and The Threshold Between Worlds.

Light reading.

"What the hell were you into, Eliza?" Alex muttered, pulling out a particularly ominous-looking tome bound in what he hoped wasn't human skin. The pages were filled with intricate diagrams. Circles within circles, strange alphabets, anatomical drawings that weren't quite right.

As he flipped through it, vertigo hit him like a physical blow. The room tilted sideways. For a moment he could have sworn the book was bleeding, dark fluid seeping between his fingers, but when he looked down, his hands were dry.

Get it together, Morgan.

He slid the book back onto the shelf and made his way to the bathroom, where Eliza Bishop had been found face-down on imported marble tiles. According to the report, the medical examiner had identified a cocktail of high-end designer drugs in her system: MDMA, ketamine, and something called DTX-5, which Alex had never heard of.

What the report didn't mention was Eliza Bishop's medical alert bracelet. Alex found it in a small jewelry box by the sink. The engraving was clear: ALLERGIC TO KETAMINE, PENICILLIN, SULFA DRUGS.

"Well, that's interesting," he murmured. "Either you didn't know your own allergies, or, someone gave you something they knew would kill you."

Back in the bedroom, Alex began the careful process of searching for anything the police might have missed. He found nothing of note in the closet, nothing under the mattress, nothing taped to the bottom of drawers. Eliza Bishop had been either very clean or very careful.

He was about to move on when he noticed a faint discoloration on the underside of the antique writing desk by the window. Kneeling, he examined what appeared to be a symbol scratched into the wood. It wasn't obvious; you'd have to be looking for it to find it. A circle bisected by a vertical line, with smaller marks he couldn't identify, radiating outward. It reminded him of something, but he couldn't place what.

As he ran his fingers over the marking, the vertigo returned, stronger this time. The room temperature plummeted further. His breath clouded in front of him. And with that breath came a sound. So faint he almost missed it.

A whisper.

"Not... what it... seems..."

Alex jerked back from the desk, heart hammering. The voice had been right behind him. Right in his ear. But when he spun around, the room was empty.

You're losing it, Morgan. The meds are screwing with your head. Or you're not taking enough of them.

He forced himself to keep searching. In Eliza's walk-in closet, he found outfits organized by color, shoes in pristine rows, and at the very back, a small safe hidden behind a rack of evening gowns. It was open, and empty.

So either Eliza left it that way, or someone got here first.

Alex's money was on the latter.

In the kitchen, he found nothing but expensive organic food and a collection of herbal teas with names like Clarity and Dream Walking. No alcohol. No cigarettes. No signs of recreational drug use. The toxicology report seemed increasingly at odds with the woman who had lived here.

He was examining a calendar on the refrigerator when it happened again. The temperature drop. The strange pressure in his ears. And this time, when he turned around, he wasn't alone.

A woman stood in the kitchen doorway. Slender, pale, with long dark hair and eyes that seemed too large for her face. She wore a white dress that moved slightly in a breeze Alex couldn't feel. For a moment, he thought it was Katherine Bishop, there was a family resemblance, but this woman was younger. And there was something wrong with her. Something about the way the light passed through her at certain angles.

"Hello?" Alex said, reaching instinctively for the gun he no longer carried. "This apartment is,"

She opened her mouth and no sound came

out. But Alex heard it anyway, not in his ears but directly in his head, like a radio station caught between frequencies:

"You... see me?"

Then she was gone, leaving nothing but a lingering chill in the air and the faint scent of something floral. Lilies, maybe. The flowers of funerals.

Alex braced himself against the counter, breathing hard. This was bad. Hallucinations this vivid weren't just side effects anymore. They were symptoms of something worse. His father had started seeing things right before the end. Right before they found him in the garage with his wrists open, having written THEY'RE COMING THROUGH on the wall in his own blood.

It's the stress. The lack of sleep. You just need to get through this case, get paid, and then maybe see Dr. Keppler about adjusting your medication.

A logical plan. A sane plan. Alex clung to it as he finished searching the apartment, finding nothing else of note except a business card tucked into a book on ancient Sumerian burial practices. The card was cream-colored, expensive stock, with only a name THRESHOLD WELLNESS and an address in the Back Bay.

He slipped it into his pocket along with his notes about the medical bracelet and the strange symbol. As he was leaving, he noticed a dark sedan parked across the street, a familiar figure sitting behind the wheel. Detective James Rivera from Boston PD, watching the building with the practiced stillness of a career surveillance officer.

Their eyes met briefly. Rivera made no attempt to hide or look away. His message was clear: I see you.

Alex Morgan had been a cop long enough to know when he was being warned off a case. And he'd been a private investigator long enough to know that warnings like that usually meant he was onto something.

He was halfway down the block when the nosebleed started. Just a trickle at first, then a steady flow that splattered onto his shirt collar before he could find a tissue. When he finally managed to stem the bleeding and looked at his reflection in a storefront window, he froze.

For just a second, less than a heartbeat, his eyes had changed. The irises had expanded, pushing out the whites until his eyes were solid, depthless black. The eyes of a deep-sea creature. The eyes of something that had never seen sunlight.

Then they were normal again. Just ordinary, bloodshot eyes in the face of a man who hadn't slept properly in weeks.

Alex Morgan turned away from his reflection and walked faster, hunching his shoulders against the January cold and the persistent feeling of being watched. Not just by Rivera in his sedan, but by something else. Something whose attention he very much did not want.

Behind him, in a window on the ninth floor of Eliza Bishop's building, a pale face pressed against the glass. Watching. Waiting. Its mouth opening and closing like a fish gasping for air. Trying to tell him something important, if only he would listen.

But Alex Morgan didn't look back. If he had, he might have seen the word the ghost was trying to form:

RUN.

CHAPTER 3

*Some lies we tell others. The worst
lies we tell ourselves.*

By the time Alex Morgan made it back to his apartment, he had almost convinced himself that what happened in Eliza Bishop's kitchen was nothing more than a stress-induced hallucination, amplified by too little sleep and too many pills. A trick of the light combined with an overactive imagination. Perfectly explainable. Perfectly rational.

He'd worked eighty-six homicides during his time with Boston PD. He knew dead people stayed dead.

The bottle of Jack Daniel's called to him from the kitchen counter, promising temporary relief. Alex ignored it. Instead, he spread the contents of Eliza Bishop's case file across his desk, forcing himself to look at the world through the lens of evidence and procedure rather than... whatever the hell had happened in that apartment.

The photos from the scene showed Eliza's body exactly as described in the report:

face down on the bathroom floor, one arm outstretched toward the toilet. No signs of a struggle. No defensive wounds. Just the vacant stare of someone whose spirit had already departed.

Spirit. Jesus, now you're thinking like one of those psychic scam artists.

Alex turned his attention to Eliza's background. Museum curator. PhD in Anthropology from Harvard. Her bank records showed a comfortable but not extravagant lifestyle. Until three months ago, when she'd suddenly withdrawn nearly $50,000 in cash. No explanation in the police report for where that money had gone.

Her phone records were similarly unremarkable. Calls to her sister Katherine, to colleagues at the museum, to take out restaurants. And then there was Martin Prentiss.

Over a six-month period ending two weeks before her death, Eliza had called Prentiss 157 times. Sometimes multiple calls in one day. He'd called her back almost as frequently.

The police had interviewed Prentiss, identified as Eliza's ex-boyfriend, exactly once. His statement claimed they'd broken up amicably after differences in lifestyle priorities.

That's a fancy way of saying 'we fought about something, Alex thought.

The address on Prentiss's statement was in Jamaica Plain. Not far. Alex checked his watch, just past 4 PM. Still time to catch him before dinner if he was home.

As he reached for his coat, a splitting headache crashed through his skull like a lightning bolt. The pain was so sudden and intense that Alex dropped to his knees, hands pressed against his temples. The edges of his vision darkened as the pain intensified, pulsing in time with his heartbeat.

And with each pulse came a whisper:

"Behind... you..."

"Behind... you..."

"Behind..."

Alex whirled around, half-expecting to see the pale woman from Eliza's apartment. The room was empty. Of course it was empty. But the headache remained, a vise grip tightening around his skull. He staggered to the bathroom and fumbled in the medicine cabinet for the prescription bottle.

"Just... make it... stop," he gasped, swallowing two pills dry.

He slumped against the cool porcelain of the sink, waiting for the drug to take effect. In the mirror, his reflection looked ghostly, skin waxy and pale except for the dark circles beneath his eyes. As Alex watched, a thin trickle of blood began to seep from his right nostril.

"Perfect," he muttered, tilting his head back and pressing a wad of toilet paper against the bleed. "Just goddamn perfect."

By the time the nosebleed stopped, the headache had receded to a dull throb. Alex changed his bloodstained shirt and headed for Jamaica Plain, determined to talk to Martin Prentiss before the next wave of whatever was happening to him hit.

Prentiss lived in a renovated Victorian that had been divided into condos. Upscale for the neighborhood but not ostentatious. The kind of place a successful young professional might buy as an investment. Alex rang the bell three times before a voice crackled through the intercom.

"Go away." Male, late twenties or early thirties, with the distinct edge of someone nursing a hangover.

"Mr. Prentiss? My name is Alex Morgan. I'd like to talk to you about Eliza Bishop."

A long pause, then the unmistakable sound of a security chain being removed. The door opened to reveal a man who looked like he'd been through hell recently and was planning a return trip. Unshaven, bloodshot eyes, wearing what appeared to be the same clothes he'd slept in. A half-empty tumbler of amber liquid dangled from his fingers.

"You a cop?" Prentiss asked.

"Private investigator. Eliza's sister hired me."

"Katherine." Prentiss spat the name like it tasted bad. "Of course she did." He stepped back, gesturing for Alex to enter. "Welcome to the wake. Party of one."

The inside of Prentiss's condo was sleek, modern, and currently in a state of profound disarray. Empty bottles littered the coffee table. Take-out containers formed a small city on the kitchen counter. The air smelled of stale beer and unwashed male.

"Sorry about the..." Prentiss waved vaguely at the chaos. "I haven't been great since, you know."

"I understand," Alex said, though in truth he'd seen this particular brand of grief-drinking before and knew it masked something else. Usually guilt. "I just have a few questions about your relationship with Eliza."

Prentiss collapsed onto the couch, spilling a bit of his drink on his wrinkled oxford shirt. "What's to tell? We dated for a year. It was good, then it wasn't. We broke up. She died. The end."

"The phone records suggest you two were still in regular contact after the breakup."

"Yeah, well." Prentiss drained his glass. "Breaking up is easy. Staying broken up is harder." He reached for a bottle on the coffee table and refilled his glass without offering Alex anything. "I loved her. Even after."

"What happened? Why'd you split?"

Prentiss barked a laugh with no humor in it. "Have you met her sister? That whole family is... They're not like regular people. They've got ideas about themselves. Who they are. What they're entitled to."

"And Eliza?"

"Eliza was different. At least I thought she was." Prentiss took another long swallow. "Until she got involved with their little club."

Alex leaned forward. "Club?"

"That wellness center. Threshold something. Started out with yoga classes, meditation. Then it was all special retreats, secret meetings. She changed."

"Changed how?"

"Started talking about 'the other side' and 'the veil between worlds.' Crazy stuff. Said she'd found her true purpose." Prentiss's face darkened. "Then she started seeing this woman. Marsh. Dr. Evelyn Marsh. Supposed to be some kind of spiritual guide or something."

"A relationship?"

"No. Not like that. More like a guru. A cult leader." Prentiss reached for something on the table. A photograph in a silver frame, which he handed to Alex. "That's us. Before."

The photo showed Prentiss and a dark-haired woman on a beach, arms around each other, squinting into the sun. Eliza Bishop looked happy, normal. Nothing like the pale apparition Alex had seen, or thought he'd seen, in her apartment.

As Alex's fingers touched the glass covering the photo, the room... shifted. The air grew thick, difficult to breathe. A high-pitched whine filled his ears. And suddenly he wasn't looking at a photograph anymore but through it, like a window opening onto another time.

Eliza and Prentiss in this same living room, screaming at each other. Her face contorted with rage as she hurled accusations, "You're holding me back!" and "You've never understood what I'm capable of!" Prentiss grabbing her arm, shaking her. "They're brainwashing you! Can't you see that?" Eliza breaking free, slapping him hard enough to split his lip. Blood on his chin. Murder in his eyes. "If you go back there," Prentiss was saying, "we're done. Forever." "We've been done since the day you tried to drown my potential in your neediness," Eliza replied coldly. "You're just too pathetic to admit it."

The vision, if that's what it was, ended as abruptly as it had begun. Alex found himself back in the present, still holding the photograph, while Prentiss watched him with narrow eyes.

"You okay, man? You look like you're about to pass out."

Alex set the photo down carefully. "I'm fine. Just, didn't eat lunch." He paused, deciding to take a risk. "The police report says your breakup was amicable."

Prentiss snorted. "Yeah, well, that's what I told them. Didn't seem smart to admit I was the angry ex-boyfriend of a dead woman. Not with my history."

"What history?"

Prentiss had the grace to look uncomfortable. "I've got a record. Bar fights mostly. One domestic with an ex before Eliza. Nothing major, but enough to make me look bad."

That explained why the detective handling the case had flagged Prentiss as a person of interest before concluding he had no involvement in Eliza's death. Classic red herring suspect. Violent history, bad breakup, no alibi. The only thing missing was motive.

"Did you see Eliza in the days before she died?"

Something changed in Prentiss's eyes, a flash of fear quickly masked. "No. Not for weeks before."

Alex knew a lie when he heard one. "Mr. Prentiss, please."

"Look, I've got nothing else to say, okay?" He stood abruptly, swaying slightly. "I didn't kill Eliza. She got herself into something dark. That Threshold place changed her. I tried to warn her, but she wouldn't listen. Now she's dead, and I'm drinking myself stupid because I couldn't save her."

From outside came the sound of a car engine starting and then idling. Alex glanced through the window blinds to see a dark sedan parked across the street.

Rivera. Still watching.

"One more question," Alex said. "Does this symbol mean anything to you?" He showed Prentiss a quick sketch he'd made of the marking under Eliza's desk.

The change was immediate and alarming. All the color drained from Prentiss's face. The glass slipped from his fingers, shattering on the hardwood floor.

"Get out," he whispered. "Get out now. And if you're smart, you'll drop this case and leave town."

"What is it? What does it mean?"

"It means you're already dead. You just don't know it yet." Prentiss was physically pushing Alex toward the door now, panic making him stronger than his inebriated state should have allowed. "Don't come back here. Don't call. Just forget about Eliza Bishop if you want to keep breathing."

The door slammed behind Alex with such force that it rattled the hallway light fixtures. From inside the condo came the sound of multiple locks being engaged.

Alex stood there for a moment, processing. Whatever that symbol was, it had terrified Prentiss. And terrified people made mistakes. He'd circle back tomorrow when Prentiss was sober and more vulnerable.

Outside, Rivera's sedan was gone. But the feeling of being watched remained, an itch between Alex's shoulder blades that he couldn't scratch.

Back in his apartment, Alex added his notes from the Prentiss interview to the case file. The prescription medication had worn off, and the headache was returning, a low throb at the base of his skull. He knew he should eat something, but the thought of food made his stomach turn.

Instead, he found himself once again staring at the autopsy photos of Eliza Bishop. Something wasn't right about them. Something beyond the inconsistency with her medical alert bracelet. It took him nearly an hour of scrutiny before he saw it.

According to the medical examiner, Eliza Bishop had died at approximately 2:30 AM. Her body was discovered at 6:45 AM by a housekeeper with a key. The apartment temperature was a steady 72 degrees, according to the thermostat.

But the liver temperature recorded at the scene was 85 degrees. Far too warm for someone who had been dead for over four hours in that environment.

Either the ME had made a mistake in the time of death, or something had kept Eliza Bishop's body warm after her heart stopped beating.

Alex was still puzzling over this discrepancy when exhaustion finally claimed him. He fell asleep at his desk, case files spread around him like the remnants of a shipwreck.

In his dreams, he was drowning again. But this time, Eliza Bishop was in the water with him, her long hair floating around her face like seaweed. Her mouth moved, forming words he couldn't hear. When he tried to swim toward her, something grabbed his ankle, pulling him deeper.

"Not what it seems," said a voice in the darkness below. "Nothing is what it seems."

When Alex Morgan jerked awake at 3:17 AM, Eliza Bishop was standing at the foot of his bed, water streaming from her hair and clothes to pool on his floor. Unlike in the apartment, he could hear her clearly now, her voice like ice cracking on a frozen lake.

"It wasn't human," she said. "What killed me wasn't human at all."

And then she was gone, leaving nothing but the lingering scent of lilies and a puddle of water that shouldn't have been there at all.

CHAPTER 4

There comes a point in every nightmare when you stop trying to wake up and start trying to survive.

For Alex Morgan, that moment arrived at 3:18 AM as he stood barefoot in a puddle of impossible water, staring at the empty space where a dead woman had been seconds before. The rational part of his mind—the detective, the skeptic, the man who'd built his life on evidence and procedure, was offering increasingly desperate explanations. Hallucination. Waking dream. Psychotic break.

The rest of him knew better.

"Jesus Christ," he whispered, voice unsteady in the darkness. "This is really happening."

He fumbled for the bedside lamp. Light flooded the small apartment, chasing away shadows but not the certainty of what he'd seen. The puddle was still there, glistening on his worn hardwood floor. Alex knelt and touched it with trembling fingers. Cold. Real. Wet.

Without thinking, he reached for the orange pill bottle, then stopped himself. If he was finally losing his mind like his father had, no amount of medication would help. And if he wasn't and if what was happening was something else entirely, then numbing himself would only make things worse.

Instead, he did what any good detective would do. He gathered evidence.

He took a sample of the water with a kitchen measuring cup. He photographed the puddle with his phone. He checked the ceiling for leaks (none) and the windows for entry points (all locked from the inside). By 4 AM, he had eliminated every rational explanation except the most obvious one: Eliza Bishop's ghost, or whatever it was, had been in his apartment.

And she had told him something important.

"It wasn't human. What killed me wasn't human at all."

Like a mantra, those words repeated in his mind as he paced the small confines of his apartment. Not human. Not human. But if not human, then what?

Alex returned to the case file, flipping to the autopsy photos with new eyes. The ME had documented a small puncture wound at the base of Eliza's skull, dismissed as unrelated to the cause of death. But now Alex noticed something odd about it. The wound wasn't ragged like a needle mark. It was too precise. Almost surgical.

Eliza's toxicology report had shown ketamine in her system. A drug she was severely allergic to according to her medical bracelet. An allergy like that would cause anaphylactic shock within minutes of exposure. Yet the ME had found no signs of anaphylaxis. No swollen airways. No distended blood vessels.

As if the ketamine had entered her bloodstream after she was already dead.

The liver temperature discrepancy suddenly made more sense. What if Eliza Bishop had been killed elsewhere, her body kept somewhere cool, and then returned to her apartment hours later? What if the drugs had been administered post-mortem to disguise the real cause of death?

What if the killer wasn't human?

"I'm going insane," Alex muttered, pressing the heels of his hands against his eyes until he saw stars. But even as he said it, he knew it wasn't true. This wasn't the disjointed paranoia of a mind coming unhinged. This was a pattern. Evidence. A case taking shape.

A case he couldn't possibly share with anyone else without sounding completely deranged.

As dawn broke over Boston, painting his grimy windows with pale golden light, Alex made a decision. He would follow this wherever it led. Not because he believed in ghosts, he wasn't ready to go that far, but because something was very wrong with Eliza Bishop's death, and solving it was his job.

The fact that he was taking investigative leads from a hallucination was a problem for another day.

He showered and changed, avoiding his reflection in the mirror. Some truths you weren't ready to face first thing in the morning. He made coffee, strong enough to strip paint, and tried to plan his next steps like this was any other case.

The symbol under Eliza's desk. The Threshold Wellness Center. The inconsistencies in the autopsy report. And now, the puncture wound that no one had properly investigated.

He needed expertise he didn't have. Medical knowledge. Information about symbols and their meanings. Someone who could tell him if he was chasing shadows or something worse.

The business card in Eliza's book had given him the address for Threshold Wellness, but he couldn't just walk in there without knowing what he was dealing with. Especially if they were somehow involved in her death. He needed background first.

He needed the one thing the PI handbook said never to trust: the internet.

Two hours of intensive searching gave him precious little. Threshold Wellness had a sleek, minimalist website that offered, transformative experiences, and, passage to enhanced awareness, without ever specifying what those things actually entailed. Their staff page featured Dr. Evelyn Marsh, the guru Prentiss had mentioned. A striking woman in her forties with steel-gray eyes and credentials from medical schools Alex had never heard of. The other practitioners all had similarly vague qualifications in, energy work and transitional therapy.

What the website didn't have was customer reviews, prices, or any concrete description of services. Just an application form for prospective clients that asked questions like "Have you ever experienced moments of unexplained awareness?" and "Do you sometimes feel you can perceive what others cannot?"

Alex was about to give up when he found a single post on an obscure forum dedicated to cult awareness. The author claimed to have attended a Threshold introductory session and described it as the most terrifying experience of her life. They wrote about tests to identify special individuals, and, talk of a coming transformation. The post ended abruptly with a promise to share more details later.

There were no further posts from that user.

Alex printed the forum page and added it to his growing case file. Then he turned his attention to the symbol from Eliza's desk. An hour of image searching yielded nothing exact, though he found similar designs in ancient Sumerian artifacts and medieval grimoires. Always associated with transitions, doorways, or passages between worlds.

The headache was back, a dull throb behind his eyes. He'd been expecting it, just as he'd been expecting the odd flickers in his peripheral vision. Shadows that moved when they shouldn't, shapes that disappeared when he tried to focus on them. Without the medication dampening whatever was happening to him, the symptoms were intensifying.

Or maybe, whispered a voice in the back of his mind, *they weren't symptoms at all. Maybe they were signs.*

Alex was contemplating his next move when his phone rang. Unknown number.

"Morgan," he answered, professional by habit.

"This is Katherine Bishop," came the coolly elegant voice. "I was hoping for an update on your investigation."

Alex hesitated. What exactly was he supposed to say? *Your dead sister visited me last night and told me her killer wasn't human*?

"I'm making progress," he said carefully. "Following several leads."

"Excellent. And have you experienced any... unusual occurrences during your investigation?"

The question sent a chill down Alex's spine. It was too specific. Too knowing.

"Nothing out of the ordinary," he lied. "Why do you ask?"

"No reason," Katherine replied smoothly. "Eliza's apartment has some quirks. Old wiring. Temperature fluctuations. I should have warned you."

"Right." Alex's knuckles were white on the

phone. "Ms. Bishop, I wonder if you could answer a question for me. Did your sister have any connection to an organization called Threshold Wellness?"

The silence that followed lasted just a beat too long.

"I believe she attended some yoga classes there," Katherine said finally. "Why do you ask?"

"Just following all possible connections." Alex kept his voice neutral, steady. "One more thing. Did Eliza ever mention someone named Dr. Evelyn Marsh?"

This time the pause was even longer.

"I don't recall that name," Katherine said, each word measured. "Is she relevant to the investigation?"

"Possibly. I'm still gathering information."

"I see." Katherine's tone had cooled several degrees. "Well, I won't keep you from your work. Please let me know when you have something concrete to report."

She hung up before he could respond. Alex stared at the phone for a long moment. Katherine Bishop had just lied to him. The question was, why?

His coffee had gone cold. As he stood to reheat it, a wave of vertigo hit him so hard he had to grab the edge of his desk to stay upright. The room tilted sideways, gravity shifted, and suddenly he wasn't in his apartment anymore.

He was somewhere else. Somewhere cold

and dark, with stone walls slick with moisture and air that smelled of earth and decay. A basement, maybe, or a tunnel deep underground. Candles provided the only light, arranged in a circle around a stone table where something or someone, lay motionless.

Figures in dark robes moved around the table, their faces hidden by deep hoods. One of them held something that gleamed in the flickering light. A knife with an ivory handle.

Alex tried to move closer, to see the person on the table, but he couldn't control his movements in this... vision? Memory? A voice was chanting in a language he didn't recognize, the words guttural and ancient. The air seemed to thicken, to pulse with energy.

Then one of the robed figures turned, looking directly at him, through him, into him. The hood fell back, revealing Dr. Evelyn Marsh. Her eyes weren't gray anymore but solid black, like pools of oil. She smiled, showing teeth that were too sharp, too numerous.

"We see you," she said, her voice layered with other voices, older and darker. "We've been waiting for you, Morgan."

The vision shattered like glass. Alex found himself on his knees in his apartment, gasping for breath. Blood streamed from his nose, splattering the case files spread on the floor around him. His heart hammered against his ribs like it was trying to escape.

They knew his name. They knew he was investigating. And somehow, impossibly, they had reached into his mind and shown him. Shown him what? A warning? A threat? A glimpse of what had happened to Eliza Bishop?

Alex staggered to the bathroom and washed the blood from his face with shaking hands. In the mirror, his reflection looked haggard, pale with shock, eyes too wide. But they were his eyes. Human eyes.

For now.

He needed answers. Real answers, not internet speculation or half-remembered visions. There was only one place he could think to look.

The bookstore.

The strange symbol from Eliza's desk had reminded him of something, and now he knew what. A sign he'd once noticed above an antiquarian bookshop in the historic district. A place he'd walked past dozens of times but never entered. A faded wooden sign with a circular symbol bisected by a vertical line.

The Threshold Between Worlds. That's what one of Eliza's books had been called. Maybe it wasn't just a title.

Alex grabbed his coat and keys, then paused. After a moment's hesitation, he retrieved his old service weapon from the locked box under his bed. He hadn't carried it since leaving the force, but suddenly the weight of it against his side felt necessary. Comforting.

What had Eliza said? *It wasn't human.* If that was true, if any of this was true, then Alex Morgan was no longer investigating a simple murder.

He was hunting something much worse.

The bookshop was tucked between a coffee place and a vintage clothing store on a narrow street in Boston's oldest district. Shadowed by taller buildings, it seemed to exist in perpetual twilight. The sign above the door was indeed the same symbol Alex had found under Eliza's desk, though here it was surrounded by additional markings that made it look more like an astronomical chart than an occult symbol.

MORGAN'S RARE BOOKS, read the faded gold lettering on the window. Established 1898.

The name was a coincidence. Had to be.

A small bell jangled as Alex pushed open the door. The interior was exactly what you'd expect from a centuries-old bookstore; towering shelves, rolling ladders, the comforting smell of paper and leather and dust. Late afternoon sunlight filtered through grimy windows, catching motes of dust that danced in the air like tiny spirits.

"Be with you in a moment," called a voice from somewhere in the maze of bookshelves.

Alex wandered deeper into the shop, drawn to a glass case near the back that contained a display of ancient-looking artifacts. Small statues with too many limbs. Daggers with inscriptions along the blades. A tarnished silver mirror that reflected nothing.

"Looking for anything in particular?"

Alex turned to find an elderly man watching him with mismatched eyes—one brown, one a startling pale blue. Despite his age, he stood perfectly straight, his white hair neatly combed, his cardigan and bowtie giving him the air of a retired professor.

"Just browsing," Alex said. "Interesting collection."

"Interesting customers." The old man smiled, showing teeth that were too perfect to be original at his age. "What brings a private detective with a gun under his coat to my humble shop?"

Alex tensed. "How did you?"

"The way you stand. The bulge under your left arm. And the business card sticking out of your pocket." The old man pointed to where Alex's PI license was indeed visible in his breast pocket. "I'm observant, not psychic. My name is Morgan. Caleb Morgan. This is my shop."

"Alex Morgan." He offered his hand automatically, then froze as the implication of their shared name registered. "No relation. I hope."

Morgan's smile widened fractionally. "Everyone's related if you go back far enough."

He didn't take the offered hand. "Now, why don't you tell me why you're really here, Detective Morgan?"

Alex hesitated, then decided the direct approach was best. He pulled out his sketch of the symbol from Eliza's desk.

"I'm looking for information about this."

Morgan's mismatched eyes narrowed. He plucked the paper from Alex's hand with fingers that were gnarled with arthritis yet moved with surprising grace.

"Where did you see this?"

"In an apartment where a woman died. Scratched into the bottom of a desk."

Morgan studied him for a long moment, his gaze unsettlingly penetrating. "And the woman's name?"

"Eliza Bishop."

Something flickered across the old man's face; recognition, and perhaps sorrow. He set the sketch down carefully.

"Come with me," he said. "We should talk somewhere more private."

He led Alex through a maze of bookshelves to a door marked PRIVATE, which opened onto a small office cluttered with books, papers, and oddities similar to those in the display case. Morgan gestured to a worn leather chair, then locked the door behind them.

"Before we continue," the old man said, "I need to know how much you've seen."

"Seen?"

"Don't play coy, Detective. You've been experiencing things, haven't you? Visions. Voices. Glimpses of what others can't perceive." Morgan leaned forward, his mismatched eyes intent. "Perhaps a visit from Ms. Bishop herself?"

Alex felt the floor tilt beneath him. Not vertigo this time. Just the sudden, sickening realization that he was in far deeper than he'd imagined.

"What the hell is going on?" he demanded. "How do you know about—"

"Because I've been watching for someone like you," Morgan interrupted. "A Watcher, we call them. Someone with the gift. Or the curse, depending on your perspective."

"I don't have any gift. I have hallucinations. Migraines. Possibly a brain tumor."

"Is that what you tell yourself?" Morgan's voice was gentle. "Despite the evidence of your own eyes? Despite the dead woman who visited you last night?"

Alex stood abruptly. "I never said anything about—"

"You didn't have to." Morgan remained seated, unnervingly calm. "It's written all over you. The way you keep glancing at shadows. The nosebleed you recently had—there's still a spot of blood on your collar. And most telling of all, the fact that you've stopped taking whatever medication was suppressing your ability."

"This is insane," Alex muttered, but he made no move to leave.

"Sanity is relative in a world where the dead speak and ancient entities hunger for human vessels." Morgan opened a drawer in his desk and removed what appeared to be an old photograph. "Here. Look at this."

The photo showed two people standing in front of the bookshop. An earlier version of Morgan, perhaps thirty years younger, and a woman with dark hair and intense eyes. She held a small child in her arms, a boy of perhaps three or four with a solemn expression.

"Your mother," Morgan said quietly, "and you."

Alex stared at the photograph, a cold knot forming in his stomach. The woman's face triggered something; a faint memory, a sense of recognition that had nothing to do with family resemblance and everything to do with the eyes looking back at him. Eyes that had seen what others couldn't.

"That's not possible," he said hoarsely. "My mother died when I was five. Car accident in Cincinnati. My father raised me."

"Is that what Joseph told you?" Morgan shook his head sadly. "Your father was many things, but truthful was not among them. Your mother didn't die in any car accident. She was murdered by the same people who killed Eliza Bishop. The same people who've been searching for you ever since."

"Why?" The word came out as barely a whisper.

"Because of what you can do. What you've always been able to do, even when you were suppressing it with chemicals and denial." Morgan tapped the photograph gently. "Your mother called it threshold sight—the ability to perceive beings caught between worlds. She had it. You have it. It's part of your birthright, along with the Morgan name."

Alex sank back into the chair, his knees suddenly too weak to support him. It was too much. Too bizarre. Too impossible. And yet, deep in some primal part of his brain, something was clicking into place. The drowning dreams. The voices he'd been hearing since childhood. The glimpses of things no one else could see.

"Let's say, just for the sake of argument, that I believe any of this," he said carefully. "What does it have to do with Eliza Bishop?"

Morgan's expression darkened. "Everything. She was one of them. A member of the Threshold coven. But she wanted out. She discovered what they were really planning, what Dr. Marsh is really planning, and it horrified her."

"Which is what, exactly?"

"A crossing. An opening of the barrier between our world and somewhere else. Somewhere inhabited by things that were once human but haven't been for a very long time.

Things that want to return."

"And they need people like me to do that?"

"Not like you." Morgan's voice was grim. "They need **you** specifically. The last of the Morgan bloodline. The strongest Watcher born in three generations."

As Morgan spoke, something strange was happening to Alex's vision. The office seemed to shimmer, reality thinning like tissue paper. Behind the old man, Alex could see, or thought he could see, another figure superimposed over Morgan's. Taller, with antlers sprouting from its head, its form constantly shifting like smoke in a breeze.

Alex blinked hard, and the image vanished. But the certainty that they weren't alone in the room remained.

"When I touched Eliza's necklace," he said slowly, "I saw something. A memory, I think. A stone table. Robed figures. A ritual of some kind."

Morgan nodded. "Psychometry. Another aspect of threshold sight. You can perceive impressions left on objects, especially those connected to death or strong emotion."

"And the drowning dreams? What are those?"

A shadow crossed Morgan's face. "Not dreams. Memories. You almost died when you were four years old. Fell through the ice on a frozen lake. Clinically dead for six minutes before they revived you."

Alex's mouth went dry. "How is that—"

"Your mother saved you. Used her own life force to pull you back." Morgan's voice was heavy with old grief. "It's what made you so strong, so sensitive to the threshold. And it's what marked you for them."

"For who?"

"The Threshold. The coven. Dr. Marsh's little cult of personality, devoted to bringing something ancient and terrible back into our world." Morgan's mismatched eyes held Alex's. "They've been looking for you for twenty-nine years. And now, thanks to Eliza Bishop's murder investigation, they've found you."

"How? I've been careful. I haven't told anyone about..." Alex gestured vaguely, unable to put words to the strangeness he'd been experiencing.

"You didn't have to. The moment you stepped into Eliza's apartment, you activated the trap she left behind. A psychic beacon. A way to identify anyone with the sight." Morgan looked grim. "You've been broadcasting your presence to them ever since."

"Jesus." Alex ran a hand through his hair. "So, what do I do now? Go to the police? Tell them I'm being hunted by a cult because I can see ghosts?"

"The police can't help you. Not with this." Morgan stood, moving to a bookshelf behind his desk. "But I can. I promised your mother I would, if you ever found your way back to me."

He removed a leather-bound volume from the shelf and set it on the desk between them.

The book had no title, just the now-familiar symbol embossed in faded gold on its cover.

"This was hers. Your first lesson in controlling what you can do. In protecting yourself." Morgan's voice softened. "She wanted you to have a normal life. That's why she hid you away, changed your name, made Joseph promise never to tell you about your heritage. But normal was never in the cards for you, Alex Morgan. Not with what you are."

Alex stared at the book, feeling the weight of decision pressing down on him. He could walk away. Go back to his apartment. Take enough pills to silence the voices and blot out the visions. Pretend none of this was happening.

But Eliza Bishop would still be dead. Her ghost, or whatever it was, would still be trying to tell him something important. And the people who had killed her would still be out there, planning something worse.

Slowly, reluctantly, he reached for the book.

"Tell me what I need to know," he said.

Morgan smiled, but there was more sorrow than triumph in it. "Everything. But first, let me show you how to control the sight. Before it controls you."

Outside the bookshop, darkness had fallen over Boston. In that darkness, something watched the lighted windows of Morgan's Rare Books with patient, hungry eyes. It had been waiting a very long time for the last Morgan to come home. It could wait a little longer.

Soon enough, the crossing would begin.

CHAPTER 5

Knowledge is power. But some knowledge changes you in ways you can never undo.

Alex Morgan turned the pages of his mother's book with careful fingers, the leather binding warm to the touch, as if the volume retained some trace of the woman who had once owned it. The contents were not what he had expected. No spells or incantations. No arcane symbols beyond the now-familiar threshold mark. Instead, page after page of meticulous observations, written in a tight, elegant script that somehow felt familiar despite being entirely foreign to him.

June 12, 1988 – First confirmed sighting of a Drifter near the harbor. It appeared to be recently deceased, still maintaining human form and awareness. Subject J. McCreedy, dead of apparent heart attack three days prior. Able to communicate limited information about his death before dissipating. Note: No physical residue this time. Improving control.

September 3, 1988 – Encountered what C.

believes to be an Ancient at the museum gala. Disguised as curator R. Phillips, but the eyes were wrong. Vertical pupils, reflective in certain light. Phillips found deceased in his home two days later, completely desiccated. C. says this confirms his theory about their feeding patterns. I remain skeptical.

December 24, 1988 – Alex saw something in the hallway tonight. Only four years old and already the sight is manifesting. C. says this confirms he carries the stronger strain of the bloodline. Joseph doesn't understand why I'm terrified rather than proud. How can I make him understand what this means for our son? What they will do if they find him?

Alex looked up from the journal, his throat suddenly tight. "She knew. She knew what was happening to me even then."

Across the cluttered desk, Caleb Morgan nodded gravely. In the two hours since Alex had agreed to hear him out, the old man had prepared tea (which Alex hadn't touched), locked up the shop, and drawn heavy curtains across the windows of his office. Now he sat with his mismatched eyes fixed on Alex with an intensity that was becoming increasingly uncomfortable.

"Your mother was an extraordinary Watcher," Morgan said. "The most talented I'd ever encountered. She could not only see spirits, but communicate with them, direct them sometimes. And her psychometry..." He shook his head in admiration. "She could touch an object and tell you its entire history. Who had owned it. Where it had been. What darkness or light it had witnessed."

"And that's what I can do?" Alex asked, still struggling to align this new reality with what his rational mind insisted was impossible. "What I've been experiencing?"

"In essence, yes. Though every Watcher manifests differently. For some, the threshold sight is primarily visual; they see spirits, entities from the other side. Others hear voices or experience physical sensations. Your mother's abilities were comprehensive. From what I've observed of you, yours may be even stronger."

"Lucky me," Alex muttered.

Morgan's expression softened. "I understand your reluctance. For thirty years you've believed yourself mentally ill, damaged, possibly doomed to the same fate as your father. And now I'm telling you that what you thought was a curse is actually a gift."

"Gift?" Alex laughed bitterly. "The headaches, the visions, seeing things that shouldn't exist... how is any of that a gift?"

"Because it makes you one of the few who can stand against what's coming." Morgan's voice dropped, becoming deadly serious. "The Threshold isn't just a wellness center or a cult, Alex. It's the current incarnation of something much older. An organization that has existed in various forms throughout history, always with the same purpose: to open the way between worlds."

"You mean like a portal? A doorway?"

"More like a veil, a membrane that separates our reality from another place. A place where things exist that were once human, or never human at all. Things that want very much to return."

"And they need me for that? Specifically, me?"

Morgan's mouth tightened. "Not just you. They need a sacrifice of specific bloodlines. Those with the sight, whose essence can be used to thin the veil. Your mother realized they were tracking her, collecting others like her. That's why she hid you away, changed her name, yours, everything."

"But they found her anyway."

"Yes." The single word carried the weight of old grief. "They found her. Too late to use her for the ritual, but not too late to eliminate a powerful obstacle to their plans."

Alex rubbed his temples, trying to process everything. "And Eliza Bishop? Where does she fit into all this?"

"Eliza was part of the Threshold, one of Dr. Marsh's inner circle. But unlike most of the members, Eliza had real ability. Latent, untrained, but genuine. She could glimpse beyond the veil occasionally, sense things others couldn't." Morgan sighed heavily. "I believe that's what got her killed. She saw something she wasn't meant to see. The true nature of what they're planning. Or perhaps the true nature of Dr. Marsh herself."

"Which is what, exactly?"

Morgan hesitated, choosing his words carefully. "Dr. Evelyn Marsh isn't human, Alex. Hasn't been for a very long time, if she ever was. She's what we call a Vessel. Human form occupied by something ancient and powerful from the other side. Something that has existed in many bodies over many centuries."

"A possession? Like in horror movies?"

"More complex than that. More symbiotic. The entity sustains the human host, preventing aging or death by natural causes. In return, it gets to experience our world, gather followers, work toward the ultimate goal of bringing more of its kind across the threshold."

Alex thought of Dr. Marsh's photograph on the Threshold website. Attractive, professional, with nothing to suggest she was anything other than a successful wellness entrepreneur. Nothing except those steel-gray eyes that had turned solid black in his vision.

"How do you know all this?" he asked.

Morgan's smile was thin and without humor. "Because I've been hunting them for longer than you've been alive." He gestured to his mismatched eyes. "This isn't a birth defect. This is the result of looking too deeply into the other side. Some marks can't be hidden, only borne."

He reached for Alex's mother's journal, turning to a page near the back. "Here. Look at her final entries."

March 19, 1990 – C. has confirmed my worst fears. The Threshold has accelerated their timetable. They've identified at least seven bloodlines with the potential they need. Morgan, Weber, Chin, Okafor, Bishop, Nazari, LaChance. All families with histories of the sight. All under surveillance.

March 20, 1990 – Joseph still doesn't fully believe, but he's agreed to the plan. Tomorrow we leave for Ohio. New names, new identities. Alex will be safe there. They don't know about him yet. C. will remain here, maintaining the shop, watching for signs. We've agreed on the signal if it's ever safe to return.

March 21, 1990 – Last night I dreamed of the lake again. Water dark as night. Something moving beneath the surface. Alex standing on the ice, his small face turned toward me in trust. I pray this decision is the right one. I pray that one day he'll understand why we had to leave, why we had to lie. Most of all, I pray that he never has to face what's coming.

The final entry was dated April 17, 1990. The handwriting was different, blockier, masculine, and Alex recognized it with a jolt as his father's.

Catherine is gone. They found us despite everything. I did what she asked, made it look like an accident, took Alex and ran. He doesn't remember. It's better that way. I'll keep him safe. Keep him dosed with the medication C. provided. Keep him from becoming what they want. But God help me, I don't know how to raise a son who sees things I can't. Who might one day become what his mother was. What they wanted her to be.

If you're reading this, Alex, I'm sorry. For the lies. For the pills. For not being strong enough to tell you the truth. Your mother loved you more than life. She died protecting you. And one day, I fear, you'll have to protect yourself from the same people who took her from us.

Alex closed the journal carefully, his hands shaking. The weight of revelation pressed down on him, reshaping his past, his memories, his understanding of who and what he was.

"My father knew," he said, voice hoarse. "All those years, all those doctors, all those medications—he knew exactly what was happening to me."

"He was trying to protect you the only way he knew how," Morgan replied gently. "Joseph Morgan wasn't a Watcher. He couldn't understand what you were experiencing. But he knew what had happened to your mother, and he was terrified the same fate awaited you."

"So he medicated me into oblivion instead? Let me believe I was going crazy?"

"He did what he thought was right." Morgan's mismatched eyes held no judgment. "Just as your mother did. Just as you must now."

Alex took a deep breath, forcing down the anger, the confusion, the sense of betrayal that threatened to overwhelm him. There would be time to process all of that later. Right now, he had a case to solve and a dead woman's ghost waiting for justice.

"Eliza Bishop," he said, bringing the conversation back to its starting point. "You said she was part of the Threshold but saw something that got her killed. What exactly did she see?"

Morgan rose and moved to a filing cabinet in the corner of the office. From a locked drawer, he removed a thin manila folder, which he placed on the desk.

"Three months ago, Eliza Bishop came to this shop. She was frightened. More than frightened, terrified. She'd been part of the Threshold for years, drawn in by promises of enlightenment, spiritual awakening, the usual cult recruitment tactics. But recently she'd been promoted to the inner circle, allowed to witness certain ceremonies."

He opened the folder, revealing photographs that made Alex's stomach lurch. They showed what appeared to be a ritual in progress. Hooded figures surrounding a stone altar, a body sprawled across it, Dr. Marsh standing with arms raised at the head of the gathering. The photos were grainy, clearly taken in secret and from a distance, but detailed enough to show the chalk markings on the floor. Elaborate versions of the threshold symbol.

"Eliza took these at great personal risk," Morgan continued. "She believed she was documenting a symbolic ritual, a spiritual ceremony. Until she saw this."

He slid forward the final photograph. This one showed Dr. Marsh with her hood thrown back, caught in mid-transformation. Her face elongated, teeth too numerous and too sharp to be human, eyes solid black. And hovering around her, visible as a kind of distortion in the air, was something else. Something with too many limbs and a shape that hurt the eye to follow.

"Jesus Christ," Alex whispered.

"Nothing so benevolent," Morgan replied grimly. "Eliza realized what Dr. Marsh really was. What the Threshold was really working toward. She tried to leave, to escape with what she'd discovered. But they found her."

"And killed her. Made it look like an overdose."

"Yes. But not before she managed to hide copies of these photos and reach out to me. She knew of the shop, of the symbol we share with them, though ours is a warning, not an invitation." Morgan's expression darkened. "Unfortunately, she didn't live long enough to make it here in person."

Alex studied the photos, detective instincts kicking in despite the supernatural context.

"Where was this ritual held? Some kind of underground chamber?"

"The sub-basement of the Threshold Wellness Center. The building was constructed in 1892 as a Masonic temple. The original ceremonial spaces are still there, though they've been repurposed."

"And what exactly were they doing in these photos? The ritual?"

"A rehearsal," Morgan said quietly. "A dry run for what's coming. The true ceremony requires specific participants, specific timing. The seven bloodlines I mentioned, all represented. The proper alignment of stars. And most importantly, a primary vessel of suitable strength."

"Vessel? Like Dr. Marsh?"

"More powerful. More pure. A perfect conduit between worlds." Morgan looked at Alex steadily. "Someone like you, Alex. The last pure Morgan, with threshold sight stronger than any Watcher in generations."

The implication hung in the air between them. Alex tried to process it, to fit it into any framework that made sense. He'd started the day investigating a suspicious death. Now he was being told he was the key to some occult apocalypse.

"This is insane," he said finally. "Even if I believe any of this, and I'm not saying I do, what am I supposed to do about it? I'm a PI with a drinking problem and a history of mental illness, not some chosen one."

"Not chosen," Morgan corrected. "Born. As your mother was. As her mother was before her. The Morgan bloodline has always stood at the threshold, watching, guarding. It's in your very name."

"So what? I'm supposed to just accept all this and... what? Morgan the Threshold Wellness Center with my gun blazing? Call the cops and tell them Dr. Marsh is possessed by an ancient evil? I'd be locked up faster than you can say 'psychiatric evaluation.'"

"What you're supposed to do," Morgan said with unexpected gentleness, "is learn to control what you are. To use the sight as it was meant to be used. To finish what your mother started."

"And how exactly do I do that?"

In answer, Morgan reached across the desk and placed his palm against Alex's forehead. The touch was like an electric shock. Not painful, but overwhelming, a surge of energy that flooded through Alex's body from crown to feet.

The world... shifted.

Suddenly Alex could see **everything**. The dust motes in the air glowed like tiny stars. The books on the shelves pulsed with memories of those who had written them, read them, touched them. And Morgan himself was transformed. His human form still visible but overlaid with something else, something ancient and powerful, with antlers branching from its head and eyes that contained galaxies.

"What are you?" Alex gasped.

"A guardian," Morgan replied, his voice unchanged despite his altered appearance. "One of the few who can stand in both worlds without being consumed by either. As you must learn to be."

He removed his hand, and reality snapped back to normal. Alex slumped in his chair, exhausted but also strangely exhilarated, as if he'd been carrying a weight he hadn't known existed and had briefly set it down.

"That," Morgan said, "is the first step. Controlled sight. The ability to see without being overwhelmed, to perceive both worlds simultaneously."

"You could have warned me," Alex muttered, rubbing his temples.

"Some things can't be explained, only experienced." Morgan leaned back in his chair, suddenly looking every one of his considerable years. "We don't have much time, Alex. The spring equinox is in three weeks. If the stars are right, if they've gathered all they need..."

"Then what?"

"Then Dr. Marsh and her followers will attempt the ritual. They'll sacrifice those with the sight to thin the veil. And if they succeed, what comes through will make everything that came before look like a child's nightmare." He fixed Alex with his mismatched gaze. "You have three options. Run, though they'll find you eventually. Submit, though what they'll turn you into is worse than death. Or fight, though the odds are very much against us."

Alex thought of Eliza Bishop's ghost standing at the foot of his bed, water streaming from her spectral form. *It wasn't human. What killed me wasn't human at all.*

He thought of his mother's journal, her desperate attempts to protect him. Of his father's guilt-ridden confession.

He thought of Dr. Marsh's black eyes in his vision, the way she had looked directly at him across an impossible distance and said: *We see you.*

There was really only one choice.

"Teach me," he said.

Morgan's relief was palpable. "We'll start with the basics. Protection first. How to shield your mind from their influence. Then how to control what you see, what you hear. How to communicate with those caught on the threshold. And finally, how to use the sight as a weapon."

"Will that be enough?"

"Against what's coming?" Morgan's smile was grim. "Probably not. But it's where we begin."

Outside the bookshop, snow had begun to fall on Boston, fat flakes drifting down from a sky the color of bruises. Detective James Rivera sat in his unmarked sedan, watching the darkened storefront of Morgan's Rare Books. He'd been there for hours, recording Alex's arrival, making notes, occasionally speaking quietly into his phone.

His latest call was to a number few people possessed.

"He's found the old man," Rivera reported. "Been inside for almost three hours. No sign of leaving anytime soon."

The voice on the other end was female, cultured, with the faintest hint of an accent that wasn't quite placeable. "As expected. Morgan's bloodline always finds its way home eventually."

"What do you want me to do?"

"Nothing for now. Observation only. Let the old man begin the training. It will save us considerable effort."

"And after?"

"After," said Katherine Bishop, "we bring Detective Morgan the rest of the way home. Where he belongs. Where he has always belonged."

She ended the call and turned to Dr. Evelyn Marsh, who sat across from her in the elegantly appointed office of Threshold Wellness. Marsh's steel-gray eyes reflected the dim light like an animal's.

"Everything is proceeding according to plan,"

Katherine reported. "The Morgan bloodline has awakened."

"Excellent." Dr. Marsh's smile was too wide for her face, exposing teeth that no human mouth should contain. "The final piece comes into play. After all these years of waiting."

She rose and moved to the window, looking out over nighttime Boston with the air of someone surveying what would soon be theirs.

"Begin the preparations," she said, her voice layered with other voices, older and darker. "The crossing approaches."

Back in the bookshop, oblivious to the watching eyes of both friend and foe, Alex Morgan turned another page in his mother's journal and continued his first lesson in a war he hadn't known existed until today. A war he had been born into. A war he was only beginning to understand.

The real education was about to begin.

CHAPTER 6

It's one thing to be told the world isn't what you thought it was. It's another thing entirely to see it for yourself.

Three days after his first encounter with Caleb Morgan, Alex stood across the street from Threshold Wellness Center, trying to look like just another pedestrian enjoying the unseasonably warm February morning. The building itself was unremarkable—six stories of honey-colored stone and gleaming windows, its original Masonic architecture softened by modern renovations. Nothing about its tasteful exterior suggested it housed a cult dedicated to opening doorways to other dimensions.

Then again, what had he expected? Pentagrams in the windows? Black-robed figures patrolling the rooftop?

Focus, Alex reminded himself. *You're here to observe, not engage.*

For three days, Caleb Morgan had drilled him relentlessly in the basics of threshold sight. How to access it voluntarily rather than having it thrust upon him without warning. How to maintain it without succumbing to the nosebleeds and vertigo that had plagued him for years. The training was exhausting, and sometimes terrifying, but Alex couldn't deny the results. The headaches were gone. The random hallucinations had stopped. And when he did choose to see beyond the ordinary world, the experience no longer felt like being hit by a truck.

It felt like power.

Part of him wondered if this was how addiction started. The discovery of a hidden ability, the rush of controlling it, the temptation to push further with each success. Another part of him, the detective, the skeptic, continued to question whether any of this was real or just an elaborate shared delusion.

But deep down, where truths couldn't be denied, Alex knew. He'd always known. The world was wider and darker than most people ever suspected. And he was one of the few who could see it all.

Across the street, the doors of Threshold Wellness swung open. A stream of people emerged, mostly women, mostly wealthy-looking, dressed in designer yoga clothes and carrying expensive water bottles. Their expressions shared the same beatific quality, a kind of mellow contentment that reminded Alex of prescribed medication. Not happiness, exactly, but its pharmaceutical approximation.

Among them moved staff members in simple earth-toned uniforms, guides, according to the brochures Alex had studied. They smiled and chatted with the departing clients, but their eyes remained watchful, scanning constantly. Looking for threats. Or opportunities.

Alex adjusted his sunglasses, took a steadying breath, and did what Caleb had taught him. He focused his attention on a point just beyond what ordinary eyes could see, relaxed his perception, and... shifted.

The world changed.

The building's façade remained the same, but now Alex could see what lay beneath it, a shimmering network of energy, like bioluminescent veins running through the stone. Dark, pulsing currents that wrapped around the structure like constrictive vines. And above it all, hovering over the rooftop like a storm cloud ready to burst, something vast and amorphous that hurt the eyes to look at directly.

Protections, Caleb had called them. Wards designed to hide their activities from those with the sight. But once you know what to look for, they acted as beacons rather than shields.

More disturbing were the guides. With threshold sight, Alex could see that some of them weren't entirely present. Their human forms were intact, but something was missing. A hollowness where a human soul should be. Walking shells with black voids behind their eyes.

Jesus Christ. Alex forced himself to keep breathing normally, to maintain his casual posture. *What the hell have they done to these people?*

Only once had he encountered something similar, a homeless man who'd wandered into the precinct during Alex's rookie year, docile and blank-eyed, speaking only when directly addressed. The department psychologist had called it dissociative fugue. But now Alex wondered if it had been something else entirely. Something that had hollowed the man out and left a vacant space for something else to inhabit.

Alex's focus was interrupted by the arrival of a sleek black Tesla that pulled up to the curb in front of Threshold Wellness. The driver remained behind the wheel as a woman emerged from the passenger side.

Katherine Bishop. Alex recognized her immediately, the elegant blonde who'd hired him to investigate her sister's death. Now he knew she'd been working for the other side all along, setting him up, watching his progress as his abilities awakened.

The surge of anger that rose in him was hot enough to briefly disrupt his threshold sight. By the time he regained control, Katherine was already halfway to the building's entrance. Alex made a split-second decision. He'd come here to observe, but opportunities like this didn't come often.

He followed her.

Maintaining a careful distance and the relaxed demeanor of someone with legitimate business, Alex trailed Katherine into the building. The lobby was a study in understated luxury; marble floors, reclaimed wood accents, a wall of live plants creating a natural privacy screen. The reception desk was staffed by a young woman with the same hollow-eyed look as the guides outside.

"Welcome to Threshold Wellness," she recited, her voice pleasant but oddly mechanical. "Do you have an appointment?"

"I'm here about the introductory session," Alex said, using the script Caleb had prepared for him. "A friend recommended your transformative experiences."

The receptionist smiled without it touching her eyes. "Of course. We have an opening at 2 PM with one of our guides. May I have your name?"

"David Weber." Another of Caleb's suggestions, using the name of one of the bloodlines the Threshold was seeking, to pique their interest without revealing his true identity.

Something flickered across the receptionist's vacant expression, a hint of actual awareness, quickly suppressed.

"Weber," she repeated. "Any relation to the Boston Webers?"

"My grandfather was from Boston," Alex

replied, the practiced lie rolling easily off his tongue. "I never knew him well."

"I see." The receptionist tapped at her computer, then handed him a sleek electronic tablet. "Please complete this questionnaire while you wait. It helps us customize your experience."

Alex accepted the tablet and settled into one of the lobby's plush chairs, positioning himself where he could see both the front entrance and the elevator bank. Katherine Bishop had disappeared down a corridor to the right, but he needed to maintain his cover before following.

The questionnaire started innocuously enough, basic health information, stress levels, sleep patterns. But as Alex scrolled further, the questions became increasingly bizarre.

Do you ever see things others cannot see?

Have you experienced moments when reality seems to thin or shift?

Do you ever hear voices or whispers when no one is present?

Have you ever survived a near-death experience? If yes, please describe.

Alex answered carefully, following Caleb's coaching. Yes, to the unusual perceptions, but attributing them to stress and overwork. No to the near-death experience. Just enough to flag him as sensitive without setting off alarm bells.

When he finished, he returned the tablet to the receptionist, who scanned his responses with that same vacant expression.

"Thank you, Mr. Weber. Please feel free to explore our public spaces while you wait. The meditation garden and juice bar are on this floor. Treatment rooms are on floors two and three. Floors four through six are for members only."

Where they keep the real action, Alex thought. *The sub-basement that doesn't appear on any floor directory.*

"Thanks," he said aloud. "I think I'll check out the juice bar."

Instead, as soon as the receptionist turned her attention elsewhere, Alex slipped down the corridor where Katherine had disappeared. It led to another elevator bank, this one requiring a keycard for access, and a discreet door marked STAFF ONLY.

Alex hesitated, weighing his options. He lacked the keycard for the private elevators, but the staff door might yield to more conventional methods. Glancing around to ensure he was unobserved, he tried the handle. Locked, as expected.

Time for the skills he'd learned before all this supernatural business entered his life.

From his pocket, Alex retrieved the small lock-pick set he'd carried since his days on the force. Most PIs used them for legitimate investigations, retrieving items from locked vehicles when authorized by the owner, accessing apartments when a client was locked out. Some used them for less savory purposes.

Either way, the thin metal tools were the next best thing to having an extra key.

Within thirty seconds, the lock yielded with a satisfying click. Alex eased the door open just enough to slip through, then closed it silently behind him.

He found himself in a service corridor, dimly lit and utilitarian in contrast to the public spaces. The walls were bare concrete, the floor industrial tile. Pipes ran along the ceiling, occasionally dripping condensation. The air was noticeably cooler here, with an underlying smell of damp stone and something else. Something metallic and vaguely organic, like old blood.

Alex moved cautiously down the corridor, alert for any sign of security cameras or personnel. The passage eventually branched, with one direction leading to what appeared to be maintenance rooms and the other sloping gradually downward. He chose the latter, instinct telling him it might lead to the sub-basement Caleb had mentioned.

The corridor descended in a gentle spiral, the lighting growing dimmer with each turn. Alex's footsteps echoed despite his attempts to move quietly. The smell of damp stone intensified, joined now by the unmistakable scent of incense. Something heavy and exotic that reminded him of his vision in Eliza Bishop's apartment.

After what felt like hundreds of feet, the corridor ended at a heavy wooden door reinforced with iron bands. Ancient-looking symbols were carved into the wood—variations of the threshold mark, surrounded by writing in a language Alex didn't recognize.

This door had no conventional lock to pick. Instead, a modern keycard reader had been incongruously mounted beside it, glowing red in the dim light.

End of the line, Alex thought. *At least for now*.

He was about to retreat when he heard voices approaching from behind, multiple people, moving quickly. Trapped in the dead-end corridor with nowhere to hide, Alex made a desperate decision. He pressed his palm against the carved door and reached for the threshold sight.

The effect was immediate and shocking. The symbols blazed with cold blue fire, burning without consuming. The door itself became translucent, revealing what lay beyond—a large circular chamber with a stone altar at its center, unoccupied now but bearing dark stains that needed no explanation. The walls were lined with more symbols, and strange objects hung from the ceiling. Things that resembled dreamcatchers made from bone and sinew.

More disturbing were the figures that moved about the chamber. Some were human, robed cultists performing what appeared to be preparatory tasks for some ceremony. Others were not. Shadowy forms that shifted between human and something else, their features constantly in flux, their limbs too numerous and oddly jointed.

And standing at the altar, her back to the door, was Dr. Evelyn Marsh. Even without seeing her face, Alex knew it was her. Something about the way she held herself, the aura of ancient malevolence that surrounded her like a cloak. She was speaking to someone Alex couldn't see, her voice a multilayered hiss that seemed to come from multiple throats simultaneously.

"The Morgan bloodline has awakened," she said, the words reaching Alex through the wooden barrier as if it wasn't there. "The old man has begun the training. Soon he will be ready."

"And if he resists?" asked the familiar voice of Katherine Bishop.

"Resistance is merely a state of incomplete understanding." Dr. Marsh turned slightly, revealing a profile that wasn't quite human anymore, the angles too sharp, the proportions subtly wrong. "Once he sees what we offer, what we can make him, resistance becomes irrelevant."

A cold certainty settled in Alex's gut. They were talking about him. Planning for him. Waiting for him to complete his training with Caleb before making their move.

The approaching voices were almost upon him now. In seconds, he would be discovered, a trespasser at the very heart of the Threshold's operation.

Alex pulled his hand from the door, breaking the connection. The symbols stopped glowing; the door became solid once more. He looked desperately for any place to hide, any escape route.

There was none.

The voices rounded the final curve of the corridor, three people deep in conversation. Two men in the earth-toned uniforms of guides, and between them, a woman Alex recognized from his research. Emma Nazari, city councilwoman and rumored financial backer of Threshold Wellness. Also, if Caleb's information was correct, a descendant of one of the bloodlines the Threshold sought.

Alex did the only thing he could think of. He straightened his posture, adopted an expression of mild confusion, and walked directly toward them as if he had every right to be there.

"Excuse me," he called, voice steady despite his racing heart. "I think I took a wrong turn looking for the meditation garden. This building is like a maze."

The trio stopped abruptly, faces registering varying degrees of surprise and suspicion. The guides recovered first, their expressions smoothing into that same vacant pleasantness he'd seen at reception.

"Sir, this is a restricted area," said the taller of the two, a broad-shouldered man with dead eyes.

"You'll need to return to the main lobby."

"Of course, sorry about that." Alex smiled apologetically. "Like I said, wrong turn. If you could point me in the right direction..."

Emma Nazari was studying him intently, her dark eyes narrowed. "You look familiar. Have we met?"

"I don't think so," Alex replied, maintaining his friendly confusion. "First time here. A friend recommended your programs."

"What's your name?" she asked, still staring at him with unsettling intensity.

"David Weber."

Something changed in Nazari's expression, a flash of recognition that had nothing to do with having met him before and everything to do with that surname.

"Weber," she repeated. "Interesting. And what brings you to Threshold Wellness, Mr. Weber?"

"Stress management, mostly," Alex said with a self-deprecating shrug. "My job can be intense."

"And what is it you do, exactly?"

The conversation had shifted from casual redirection to interrogation, and Alex knew he was in dangerous territory. These people weren't just going to point him back to the lobby and forget about him.

"I'm in private security," he lied. Close enough to his actual profession to sound authentic if they checked, different enough to obscure his real identity for now.

"Private security," Nazari echoed, her tone making it clear she didn't believe him. "How fascinating. Perhaps you should join us for the new member orientation. I think you'd find it illuminating."

It wasn't a suggestion. The two guides had subtly repositioned themselves to block any retreat back up the corridor. Behind Nazari, the heavy wooden door was the only other exit, and it led directly into the ritual chamber where Dr. Marsh was conducting whatever blasphemous preparations were underway.

Alex was trapped.

"That sounds great," he said, forcing enthusiasm into his voice. "Lead the way."

Nazari smiled, a predatory expression that didn't reach her eyes. "Excellent. I think Dr. Marsh will be particularly interested in meeting you."

The taller guide produced a keycard and approached the wooden door. As he reached for the reader, Alex made his move.

With a quick pivot, he drove his elbow into the guide's solar plexus, doubling the man over. In the same fluid motion, he grabbed the keycard and shoved the second guide into Nazari, creating momentary chaos in the narrow corridor.

Then he ran.

Behind him, Nazari's voice rose in fury: "Stop him! He's one of them!"

Alex sprinted up the spiraling corridor, feet pounding against the stone floor. He could hear pursuit, multiple sets of footsteps, shouted commands. His only advantage was knowing the layout ahead of them, having just traversed it minutes earlier.

At the first branch, he took the turn toward the maintenance rooms instead of continuing toward the staff entrance. A gamble, but one he hoped might confuse his pursuers long enough to find another way out.

The maintenance corridor led to a series of storage rooms and what appeared to be a staff break area, currently empty. Beyond that was another corridor that presumably connected to the building's service areas. Alex tried door after door as he ran, finding most locked.

Finally, one yielded, a janitor's closet barely large enough to hold a mop sink and shelves of cleaning supplies. Not an exit, but maybe a hiding place until the immediate search died down.

Alex slipped inside, pulling the door shut as quietly as possible. In the darkness, he controlled his breathing, listening for sounds of pursuit. They weren't far behind, footsteps and voices, growing closer.

"Check every room," ordered a voice he didn't recognize. "He can't have gone far."

"What if he gets out?" asked another. "He's seen the lower chamber."

"Then we hunt him down," came the chilling reply. "Dr. Marsh wants him alive if possible, but she'll settle for dead if necessary."

Alex pressed himself further into the closet as footsteps approached. A shadow passed beneath the door, paused, moved on. He allowed himself a silent breath of relief.

Which was when he felt something cold and wet drip onto his shoulder from above.

Alex looked up slowly, threshold sight activating involuntarily in response to his fear. In the darkness of the closet ceiling, something moved. Something that shouldn't have been able to fit in the small space between the ceiling tiles and the floor above. A sinuous, multi-limbed shape that reminded him of an octopus, but with too many appendages and a central mass that pulsed with sickly bioluminescence.

A Watcher, it whispered directly into his mind, its voice like nails on a chalkboard. *A Morgan. The last Morgan. She will be so pleased.*

Alex bit back a scream as one of its limbs, cold and slick as wet leather, brushed against his face. He fumbled for his gun, forgetting in his panic that he'd left it at home, unwilling to risk being caught armed in what was supposed to be a simple reconnaissance mission.

No escape, the thing whispered, its many limbs beginning to descend around him like a cage. *No running from what you are, what you will become.*

In desperation, Alex reached for what Caleb had taught him, not just the passive sight, but the active use of it as a weapon. He focused his fear, his revulsion, his anger into a concentrated point of psychic energy and pushed.

The creature recoiled as if burned, its limbs withdrawing with a sound like sizzling meat. It emitted a high-pitched keening noise that Alex felt more than heard, a psychic wail of pain and surprise.

How? it hissed. *Too soon. Too strong. Not possible.*

Taking advantage of its confusion, Alex burst from the closet and ran blindly down the corridor. Behind him, an alarm began to sound. A wailing klaxon that would bring every Threshold employee running. He had minutes, maybe seconds, to find a way out.

At the end of the service corridor, he found what he was looking for, a fire exit with a push bar and the familiar "Emergency Only" warning. Setting off the fire alarm was the least of his concerns now. He slammed into the bar with his shoulder, and the door burst open onto an alley behind the building.

Alex ran as if all the demons of hell were after him, which, for all he knew, they might have been. He didn't stop until he'd put six blocks between himself and Threshold Wellness, ducking into the crowded Public Garden to lose himself among tourists and lunchtime office workers.

Only when he was certain he wasn't being followed did he slow to a walk, breathing hard, mind racing with what he'd seen. The ritual chamber. Dr. Marsh's inhuman profile. The creature in the closet ceiling. They were real. All of it was real. And they knew who he was, or at least, they suspected.

His phone vibrated in his pocket. A text message from a number he didn't recognize.

Get somewhere safe. They're watching your apartment. Rivera

Detective Rivera. The cop who'd been surveilling him, who worked for the Threshold. Except, why would he be warning Alex if he was on their side?

Before Alex could process this new complication, his phone rang. Caleb Morgan.

"They found you," the old man said without preamble. "I've been watching."

"How do you—"

"No time," Caleb interrupted. "Get home. Now. Take a circuitous route. Use the threshold sight to spot watchers. Trust no one."

The call ended abruptly. Alex stood in the bustling park, suddenly aware of how exposed he was. He took a deep breath, centered himself, and activated the sight just enough to scan his surroundings.

Most of the people around him were just that, people, ordinary humans going about their day, unaware of the horror that lurked at the edges of their reality. But there, at the park entrance. And there, near the pond. Figures that looked human at first glance but revealed their true nature under threshold sight. Hollow ones, their eyes empty, their movements too coordinated to be natural.

They were hunting him.

Alex Morgan moved casually toward the opposite park exit, maintaining the relaxed posture of a man without a care in the world. Inside, his mind raced with the implications of what he'd discovered. The Threshold wasn't just a cult, it was an army, with soldiers, human and otherwise, preparing for a war most people didn't even know was coming.

And somehow, he had become the most valuable piece on the board.

When he reached his home an hours later, a circuitous journey involving multiple cab rides, a brief stint on the T, and a walk through back alleys, Alex approached cautiously. From across the street, he studied the building, using the threshold sight to see what Caleb had warned him about.

The warders were visible immediately, dark, pulsing lines of energy that wrapped around the structure like hungry vines. And at his third-floor window, something waited. A shadowy presence similar to what he'd encountered in the janitor's closet, but larger, more substantial. A sentinel, watching for his return.

Alex retreated to a safe distance and called Caleb again.

"I see it," he said when the old man answered. "Can't go home. What now?"

"Come to the shop," Caleb replied. "Take another indirect route. The protections here will hide you for now."

"And after that? They know who I am, Caleb. They know what I am."

"Yes." The old bookseller's voice was grim. "The game has changed. We must adapt accordingly."

"This isn't a game," Alex snapped. "There's a... a **thing** in my apartment. Waiting for me. They've taken over my home. My life."

"Welcome to the war, Alex Morgan," Caleb replied softly. "The one your mother tried to keep you from. The one you were born to fight."

As Alex made his way through Boston's twilight streets, constantly checking for pursuit, he felt something fundamental shifting within him. The last threads of his old life, the skeptical detective, the man who believed in evidence and procedure, were falling away, revealing something older and stranger beneath.

Something that had been waiting all along for him to remember what he truly was.

A Morgan. A Watcher. A guardian of the threshold between worlds.

And as the sun set over Boston, painting the sky in shades of blood and bruise, something else was watching. Dr. Evelyn Marsh stood at the window of her private office at Threshold Wellness, her form flickering between human and something far older, her eyes fixed on the city below as if she could see one specific figure moving through its streets.

"Run, little Morgan," she whispered, her voice a chorus of ancient hunger. "Run home to the old man. Learn what he can teach you. Grow strong."

She smiled, revealing teeth that no human mouth should contain.

"The stronger you become, the brighter you'll burn when we finally consume you."

In the reflection of the window, her face shifted completely, revealing what truly lived behind Dr. Evelyn Marsh's human mask. Something ancient. Something patient. Something that had waited centuries for this moment, this alignment, this final Morgan to complete its long-delayed crossing.

The hunt had begun.

CHAPTER 7

Sometimes knowledge is a burden. Sometimes it's a weapon. The trick is knowing which is which.

Night had fully descended by the time Alex reached Morgan's Rare Books, taking a route so convoluted that even he would have had trouble retracing it. The shop's windows were dark, the CLOSED sign prominently displayed, but the door opened at his approach as if sensing his presence.

Caleb Morgan waited inside, his mismatched eyes gleaming in the dim light from a single reading lamp. The bookshop felt different at night; the towering shelves casting long shadows, the ancient volumes seeming to whisper among themselves, the very air heavy with accumulated knowledge and secrets.

"You're safe," Caleb said. Not a question, but a statement of fact. "No one followed you."

"How can you be sure?" Alex asked, his voice rough with exhaustion.

"Because nothing crosses my threshold without my knowledge." The old man gestured toward the shop's entrance. "Some wards are for keeping things out. Others are for alerting those within."

Alex collapsed into a worn leather armchair, the events of the day catching up to him in a rush of fatigue and delayed adrenaline. His hands were shaking, he realized. Not from fear, but from the prolonged effort of maintaining vigilance, of keeping the threshold sight active enough to spot pursuers without triggering the headaches and nosebleeds that came with overuse.

"Here," Caleb said, pressing a tumbler of amber liquid into Alex's hand. "Medicinal purposes only."

The whiskey burned going down, but the warmth it spread through his chest was worth the sting. Alex took a second, smaller sip before setting the glass aside.

"They know who I am," he said flatly. "They were waiting for me. Watching my apartment. And there was something in the closet at Threshold Wellness, something that recognized me, called me by name."

"A Lurker," Caleb nodded grimly. "One of their scouts. Nasty things. More sensation than intelligence, but effective at what they do."

"Which is what, exactly?"

"Finding those with the sight. Particularly those with bloodlines they're interested in."

Alex leaned forward, elbows on knees. "I need

answers, Caleb. Real answers. Everything you've told me about Watchers, bloodlines, this war, it's all abstract. Until today. Today I saw what we're up against. I saw Dr. Marsh, or whatever she really is. I saw those hollow people. And I can't go home because something is waiting for me there."

Caleb studied him for a long moment, his mismatched eyes unnervingly penetrating. Then he sighed, suddenly looking every one of his considerable years.

"You're right. The time for half-truths is past." The old man rose stiffly. "Come with me. There's something you need to see."

He led Alex to the back of the shop, past the private office where they'd talked before, to a door Alex hadn't noticed during his previous visits. Unlike the other entrances, this one bore no markings, no threshold symbols. It was simply a door. Unassuming, unremarkable, and somehow more ominous for its ordinariness.

"What's down there?" Alex asked, a chill running up his spine.

"History," Caleb replied. "Yours. Mine. The world's. The parts no one remembers because remembering would drive them mad."

He placed his palm against the center of the door, and it swung open silently to reveal a stone staircase descending into darkness. Caleb retrieved an old-fashioned oil lamp from a shelf beside the door, lit it with practiced ease, and started down the steps without looking back to see if Alex followed.

After a moment's hesitation, Alex did.

The stairs spiraled downward, far deeper than seemed possible given the building's location in Boston's historic district. The air grew cooler, damper, with that distinctive smell of earth and stone that suggested very old places undisturbed by modern ventilation.

"How far down does this go?" Alex asked, his voice echoing slightly in the enclosed space.

"Far enough," Caleb replied enigmatically. "Some thresholds are vertical rather than horizontal."

After what felt like hundreds of steps, they reached level ground. A circular chamber hewn from solid bedrock, its walls lined with bookshelves that sagged under the weight of ancient-looking tomes. At the center stood a large table covered in maps, scrolls, and what appeared to be astronomical charts.

But what drew Alex's eye immediately was the far wall, where dozens of photographs had been pinned to a massive corkboard. Some were faded with age, others more recent. All showed people, men and women of various ages and ethnicities, their images connected by a web of red string that created a complex genealogical chart.

At the very top of this visual family tree was a daguerreotype so old the image had nearly faded away. A stern-faced man in 19th-century clothing, standing in front of what Alex recognized as a much newer version of Morgan's Rare Books. The name beneath it: Ezekiel Morgan, 1842-1901.

"The first of us," Caleb said, following Alex's gaze. "Or at least, the first to understand what we were. What we were for."

Alex's eyes traced the branches of the family tree, following the red strings through generations, watching the faces change while certain features remained consistent; a particular set to the jaw, the shape of the eyes. His throat tightened when he reached a photograph he recognized from Caleb's desk upstairs. His mother, younger than he ever remembered her, with a solemn-faced toddler in her arms.

And beside her, another face he knew. His father, Joseph, looking far happier than Alex had ever seen him in life.

"My family," he whispered.

"One branch of it," Caleb corrected. "The Morgans have never been numerous, but we've been persistent. Despite their best efforts to eliminate us."

"Their?" Alex tore his gaze from the family tree to look at Caleb. "You mean the Threshold?"

"The Threshold is merely the current incarnation. They've had many names through the centuries. The Order of the Eternal Gate. The

Brotherhood of the Veil. The Seekers of What Lies Beyond." Caleb's mismatched eyes were distant with memory. "Always the same purpose, though. Always the same hunger for what exists on the other side."

Alex moved to the central table, studying the maps spread across its surface. They weren't ordinary geographical charts, he realized, but something far stranger. Maps of invisible currents, of energy flows, of what appeared to be tears or weak points in the fabric of reality itself.

"What exactly are they trying to do?" he asked. "You said they want to open a doorway, but to where? And why?"

Caleb joined him at the table, tracing a gnarled finger along one of the marked ley lines. "To understand that you need to understand what the threshold truly is. Not just a metaphor, not just a poetic name for the barrier between life and death. The threshold is a membrane. A permeable boundary between our reality and others."

"Other dimensions? Like in science fiction?"

"If that framework helps you comprehend it, yes. Though the truth is both simpler and more complex." Caleb tapped a particular spot on the map—Boston Harbor. "There are places where the membrane is naturally thinner. Places where, under certain conditions, crossing becomes possible. For thoughts. For energies. Occasionally, for entities."

"Like ghosts? The dead people I've been seeing?"

"The recently deceased are the most common crossers—they haven't fully transitioned, so they exist in a state of in-between. What your mother called Drifters in her journal. But there are older things. Things that were once human but have existed on the other side for so long they've changed. And things that were never human at all."

Alex thought of Dr. Marsh, of her face shifting between human and something else, of the many voices that had spoken through her. "And these things want to cross over. To our side."

"Some do. The ones that remember what it was to be flesh, to feel sensation, to experience the physical world." Caleb's voice darkened. "They hunger for it. For embodiment. For life. But their original forms are long gone, so they need vessels. Human bodies specially prepared to contain them."

Understanding dawned, cold and terrible. "The bloodlines. That's what they're for. Vessels."

"Not just any vessels. Perfect matches. Humans with certain genetic predispositions. Sensitivity to the threshold. The ability to perceive both sides simultaneously without going mad." Caleb met Alex's gaze. "People like you, Alex. Like your mother. Like all the Morgans, going back to Ezekiel."

"And the ritual they're planning? The crossing?"

"A coordinated effort to thin the membrane enough for multiple entities to cross simultaneously. To establish a permanent foothold in our world rather than the temporary incursions they've managed in the past." Caleb's expression was grim. "If they succeed, it will be the beginning of the end. Not in fire and brimstone, nothing so dramatic. But a quiet apocalypse, as humanity is gradually hollowed out and replaced from within."

Alex sank into a chair, trying to process the enormity of what he was hearing. This wasn't just about solving Eliza Bishop's murder anymore. It wasn't even about understanding his own abilities. This was about the fate of everything.

"Why me?" he asked finally. "Why are they so focused on the Morgan bloodline?"

Caleb hesitated, then moved to one of the bookshelves and removed a slim volume bound in faded red leather. He handled it with reverence, as if it might crumble at any moment.

"Because of this," he said, carefully opening the book to a hand-drawn illustration that depicted a circular symbol Alex now recognized. The threshold mark, but surrounded by additional glyphs. "Ezekiel Morgan didn't just discover what we were. He discovered how to use it. How to not only see across the threshold, but to close breaches. To strengthen the membrane. To push back against incursion."

"He was a guardian," Alex said, remembering Caleb's words from before.

"The first of many. And with each generation, the ability grew stronger. More refined." Caleb turned several pages to another illustration. A human figure surrounded by a nimbus of light, facing what appeared to be a tear in reality itself. "The Morgan bloodline doesn't just perceive the threshold. It can repair it. Seal it. Prevent crossing."

"Which makes us their natural enemies."

"And their most valuable prizes." Caleb's voice was heavy with meaning. "What better way to ensure successful crossing than to neutralize those who could prevent it? Or better yet, to convert that power to their own use?"

A cold certainty settled in Alex's gut. "They don't just want to kill me. They want to turn me. Make me one of them."

"Dr. Marsh—or whatever entity currently wears that name—has been searching for the last Morgan for decades. After your mother died, after Joseph hid you away, they lost track of the bloodline. Until now." Caleb fixed him with those mismatched eyes. "Do you understand what that means? Why they've been watching you, testing you, waiting for your abilities to fully manifest?"

"They want to use me to open the door instead of to close it."

"Precisely. The same power that can seal the threshold can be inverted to tear it wide open. Especially from someone with your potential strength." Caleb closed the ancient book carefully. "That's why they killed Eliza Bishop when she discovered the truth. That's why they'll stop at nothing to acquire you, willing or otherwise."

Alex stood abruptly, pacing the confines of the underground chamber. The weight of revelation pressed down on him, reshaping his understanding of everything. His parents, his 'illness', his entire life leading to this moment.

"So what do we do?" he asked. "How do we stop them?"

"We prepare," Caleb replied simply. "We train your abilities. We find allies. And we disrupt their ritual before it can be completed."

"Allies? Like who? The police?" Alex laughed humorlessly. "I can't exactly walk into my old precinct and tell them I'm fighting a cult of interdimensional body-snatchers."

"Not that kind of ally." Caleb moved to a wooden cabinet against the wall and removed what appeared to be a metal lockbox. "But first, there's someone you need to speak with. Someone who's been trying to reach you."

Before Alex could ask what he meant, the door at the top of the stairs opened. Footsteps echoed on stone as someone descended. Someone whose tread was too heavy to be anything but an adult male.

Alex tensed, reaching instinctively for the gun he still didn't have. "I thought you said no one followed me."

"No one did," Caleb replied calmly. "He was already here. Waiting."

The figure that emerged from the stairwell was the last person Alex expected to see. Detective James Rivera, the cop who'd been watching him for days. The man who supposedly worked for the Threshold, yet had warned Alex about the trap at his apartment.

"You," Alex snarled, taking an aggressive step forward.

Rivera raised his hands in a placating gesture. "Easy, Morgan. I'm not here to take you in."

"Why are you here, then? Last I checked, you were working for the people trying to kill me."

"Appearances can be deceiving," Rivera replied evenly. "Especially in our line of work."

"Our line of—" Alex broke off, looking from Rivera to Caleb and back again. Understanding dawned. "You're working together. You're a Watcher too."

Rivera's smile was humorless. "Not exactly. I'm what you might call independent contractor. I keep an eye on the Threshold's activities for Caleb, feed them just enough information to maintain my cover, and occasionally extract people they've targeted."

"He's been watching you since you took

Katherine Bishop's case," Caleb added. "Making sure you found your way here when the time came."

Alex's mind raced, reevaluating everything he thought he knew. "The sedan outside Eliza's apartment. Outside Prentiss's place. That was you, deliberately visible. You wanted me to see you."

"Had to nudge you in the right direction," Rivera confirmed. "Get you curious enough to start digging, but not so panicked that you'd run."

"You could have just approached me directly. Told me what was happening."

Rivera and Caleb exchanged a glance that spoke volumes.

"Would you have believed me?" Rivera asked softly. "A stranger telling you that you had supernatural abilities? That a cult was hunting you for those abilities? That the headaches and visions you'd been suppressing all your life were actually glimpses of another reality?"

He had a point. Alex wouldn't have believed it—not without experiencing it firsthand, not without the evidence of his own eyes.

"So what now?" he asked. "Why come out of the shadows?"

"Because the situation has escalated," Rivera replied. "Your little reconnaissance mission today stirred up a hornet's nest. Dr. Marsh knows a Morgan has resurfaced. She's mobilizing resources, calling in members from other cities. And she's accelerated the timetable for the ritual."

"How do you know this?"

"Because I was in the emergency meeting she called after your escape. Along with Katherine Bishop and Emma Nazari." Rivera's expression darkened. "They're preparing for the final stages. Gathering the bloodlines. Testing potential vessels."

"When?" Alex demanded.

"The spring equinox," Caleb answered. "When the natural thinning of the veil aligns with astronomical conditions they've been waiting decades to exploit."

"That's less than three weeks away," Alex said, the urgency of the situation hitting him anew.

"Which is why we need to accelerate your training," Caleb replied. "No more gradual acclimation. No more theory before practice. You need to learn everything your mother knew, and more, in a fraction of the time it took her to master it."

"And if I can't? If I'm not strong enough or fast enough?"

The silence that followed was answer enough.

"Rivera," Alex said, focusing on the immediate problem. "You said they put something in my apartment. Watching. Waiting. What exactly are we dealing with?"

"A Hunter," Rivera replied, his voice grim. "Nasty piece of work. Looks human to ordinary eyes—just a man sitting in a chair. But it's a construct, a puppet controlled by something on the other side. It won't leave until its target returns or it's forcibly dispatched."

"And how exactly do we dispatch it?"

Rivera glanced at Caleb, who nodded almost imperceptibly. The detective reached into his jacket and removed a small velvet pouch.

"With this," he said, emptying the contents into his palm. A silver amulet on a chain, inscribed with the now-familiar threshold symbol surrounded by smaller glyphs. "Cold iron and silver, forged at the crossroads during an eclipse. One of the few materials that can disrupt the connection between puppet and puppeteer."

"You have to get close enough to touch it," Caleb warned. "Physical contact is essential. The amulet disrupts the connection, but only within a very limited range."

Alex looked from the amulet to Rivera's steady gaze. "And you're just going to walk in there? The Hunter knows you work for the Threshold, right? Won't it be suspicious?"

"That's why I'm not going alone," Rivera replied, handing the amulet to Alex. "You're coming with me."

"That's insane. They're looking for me. That thing is literally there to capture me."

"Exactly. You're the bait." Rivera's expression

was deadly serious. "We need to deal with the Hunter before we can retrieve what you left behind."

"I didn't leave anything—" Alex began, then stopped as understanding dawned. "My mother's necklace. The one in the photo. I kept it in my bedside drawer."

Caleb nodded grimly. "A physical connection to her. To her abilities. We need it for what comes next."

"And we need your apartment as a base of operations," Rivera added. "Can't plan a counter-offensive from a bookshop."

Alex stared at the amulet in his palm, the weight of it seeming far greater than its actual mass. This was really happening. All of it. The supernatural war his mother had died fighting. The legacy he'd inherited without knowing. The choice that wasn't really a choice at all.

"How do we do this?" he asked finally.

"I bring you in as if I've captured you," Rivera explained. "The Hunter will be suspicious, but it won't act immediately. They want you alive, remember? It will wait for instructions, which gives us a window of opportunity to strike first."

It was a terrible plan with a dozen ways to go wrong. But looking at the determination in Rivera's eyes, the grim certainty in Caleb's, Alex knew it was the only option they had.

"Fine," he said. "But I want a gun. My gun, from the lockbox under my bed. If this goes sideways, I want a backup plan that doesn't involve magic jewelry."

Rivera nodded. "Fair enough. We go in, neutralize the Hunter, retrieve what we need, and get out. Simple."

"Nothing about this is simple," Alex muttered.

"One more thing," Caleb said, opening the metal box he'd retrieved earlier. Inside was a small glass vial containing what appeared to be water. "When the Hunter is neutralized, pour this around the perimeter of your apartment. Every threshold—windows, doors, even air vents. It will establish a temporary barrier against further incursion."

"What is it?" Alex asked, taking the vial.

"Water from the lake where you nearly drowned," Caleb replied, his mismatched eyes unreadable. "Where your abilities first awakened. Your blood is still in that water, metaphysically speaking. Still connected to you."

Alex thought of his recurring nightmares, of the sense of presence he always felt in those dreams. Of something waiting in the dark water, watching him. The vial suddenly felt much heavier in his hand.

"Let's do this," he said, pushing aside his unease. "Before I have time to think about how crazy it is."

"One last thing," Caleb said, placing a hand on Alex's shoulder. "The threshold sight can be a tool, a window, a weapon. But it's also a beacon. The more you use it, the more visible you become to what waits on the other side. Use it sparingly from now on. Only when absolutely necessary."

"I understand," Alex replied, though in truth, he was only beginning to grasp the implications of his abilities.

They left the underground chamber, climbing back to the familiar confines of the bookshop. As they prepared to depart, Rivera checking his service weapon, Alex steeling himself for the confrontation ahead, Caleb handed him one last item: a small, leather-bound journal.

"Your mother's field notes," he explained. "For after. When you're ready to understand the full extent of what you are. What you can do."

The bell above the shop door jingled as they stepped out into the night. Boston slept around them, its citizens unaware of the war being waged in their midst, of the ancient hungers stirring in the shadows between worlds.

Alex Morgan took a deep breath of cold night air, feeling the weight of his heritage, his destiny, settling onto his shoulders like a mantle he'd been measured for his entire life without knowing.

He was a Watcher. A guardian of the threshold.

And it was time to start acting like one.

In Alex's apartment, the thing calling itself a Hunter sat motionless in the darkness. To human eyes, it would have appeared to be simply a man. Middle-aged, unremarkable, dressed in nondescript clothing. Only the utter stillness of its posture, the absence of even the small movements of breathing or blinking, would have suggested something was amiss.

But behind its human eyes, something else watched. Something ancient and patient that had hunted the Morgan bloodline for generations. Something that sensed its prey drawing near and prepared for the moment of capture.

It didn't know that it, too, was being hunted.

CHAPTER 8

Courage isn't the absence of fear. It's the decision that something else is more important.

Alex Morgan's wrists hurt. Rivera had insisted on making the handcuffs look convincing. Tight enough to leave marks, loose enough that Alex could slip free if necessary. A necessary charade for what was to come.

They stood in the darkened hallway outside Alex's apartment, the building quiet in the small hours of the morning. Most of his neighbors were asleep, unaware of the confrontation unfolding just feet from where they dreamed their ordinary dreams.

"Remember," Rivera whispered, his breath fogging in the unheated corridor, "let me do the talking. Keep your head down. Look defeated. And whatever you do, don't activate the sight until I give the signal."

Alex nodded, pulse racing. The silver amulet hung cold and heavy around his neck, hidden beneath his shirt. In his pocket, the small vial of lake water seemed to pulse with its own subtle energy. He thought of his mother, of the photograph in Caleb's underground chamber. Had she stood like this once, preparing to confront something beyond human understanding? Had she felt this same mixture of terror and resolve?

Rivera checked his service weapon one last time, then positioned himself behind Alex, one hand gripping his captive's arm in a show of control. With his free hand, he inserted Alex's key into the lock and turned it slowly.

The door swung open onto darkness, the apartment beyond a well of shadows. Rivera reached for the light switch, flicking it on.

Nothing happened.

"Power's out," he muttered. "Or it cut the lines."

"Wonderful," Alex breathed, trying to suppress the instinct to flee. Something waited in that darkness. Something that had come a very long way to find him.

Rivera pushed him forward gently but firmly, maintaining the pretense of captor and captive. They stepped over the threshold, and immediately Alex felt it. A drop in temperature, a pressure in his ears like descending in an airplane, a subtle wrongness that had nothing to do with ordinary physical sensations.

In the dim light filtering through the windows from the street below, he could make out the familiar contours of his living room. The couch where he'd fallen asleep so many nights. The desk piled with case files and unpaid bills. The kitchen doorway beyond.

And sitting in his reading chair by the window, a figure. Motionless. Watching.

"Detective Rivera," said a voice that sounded almost but not quite human, as if the speaker was trying to remember how vocal cords worked. "We didn't expect you so soon."

"Found him trying to catch a bus to New York," Rivera replied, his voice casual despite the tension Alex could feel in the hand still gripping his arm. "Thought the boss would want him delivered immediately."

The figure in the chair didn't move, not even to turn its head toward them. "How fortunate. Dr. Marsh will be pleased."

"She wants him at the center, or should I hold him somewhere else?"

The Hunter, for that's what it was, Alex reminded himself, not a man but a puppet controlled from somewhere beyond the threshold, seemed to consider this. The silence stretched, becoming increasingly uncomfortable.

Finally, it spoke again. "Bring him closer. I want to see what all the fuss is about."

Rivera hesitated almost imperceptibly, then nudged Alex forward. They took three steps into the apartment, enough to clear the door but still maintaining distance from the Hunter.

"Close enough," Rivera said. "I've been chasing this guy for days. Don't want him getting any ideas about running."

The Hunter's head turned then, the movement too smooth, too mechanical. In the dim light, its face was ordinary, middle-aged, unremarkable, forgettable. But its eyes, its eyes were wrong. Too still. Too empty. Like looking into the eyes of a mannequin.

"The last Morgan," it said, its voice now layered with something else, something older and colder than the human form it wore. "Do you know how long we've been searching for you?"

Alex kept his head down, playing his part, though every instinct screamed at him to run. The silver amulet against his skin seemed to grow colder, responding to the presence across the room.

"Not much of a talker, is he?" Rivera observed, maintaining his casual tone. "Anyway, I should get him to the center. Dr. Marsh will want to begin preparations."

"Dr. Marsh is otherwise occupied." The Hunter rose from the chair, its movements fluid yet somehow wrong, like watching a film played at slightly the wrong speed. "I will take custody of the Morgan."

Rivera's grip on Alex's arm tightened fractionally—the signal they'd agreed upon.

"That wasn't the arrangement," Rivera said, his free hand drifting toward his holstered weapon. "My orders came directly from Katherine Bishop. I deliver him to the center, I get paid."

The Hunter took a step forward, then another. Its face remained placid, but the air around it seemed to warp slightly, reality bending in its proximity.

"Plans change, Detective," it said. "As do loyalties."

It knew. Somehow, it knew Rivera wasn't what he claimed to be.

Alex felt Rivera tense beside him, ready to draw his weapon. But they both knew bullets wouldn't stop what stood before them. Only the amulet could disrupt the connection between puppet and puppeteer, and only with direct contact.

Time slowed as the Hunter took another step toward them. Alex could feel his heart hammering against his ribs, could sense the wrongness emanating from the thing wearing a human shape growing stronger with proximity. The handcuffs around his wrists suddenly felt like an unacceptable restriction.

"Now!" Rivera shouted, shoving Alex to the side as he drew his weapon in one fluid motion.

The Hunter moved with impossible speed, crossing the distance between them in the blink of an eye. One moment it was several feet away; the next, its hand was around Rivera's throat, lifting the detective off his feet as if he weighed nothing.

"Disappointing," it said, voice now completely inhuman, a chorus of whispers overlapping. "We had such hopes for you, James Rivera."

Alex scrambled to his feet, wrenching his wrists to slip free of the handcuffs as Rivera had shown him. The metal bit into his skin, drawing blood, but adrenaline dulled the pain to a distant concern.

In the struggle before him, Rivera was turning purple, his feet kicking uselessly as the Hunter's grip tightened. The detective's gun had fallen to the floor, useless.

There was no time for subtlety, no room for the careful plan they'd devised. Acting on instinct, Alex charged forward, fingers closing around the silver amulet, tearing it from his neck as he launched himself at the Hunter's back.

The contact was like touching a live wire. Energy surged through Alex's body, blue-white and cold as Arctic seas. The Hunter's form went rigid, its grip on Rivera loosening enough for the detective to break free and collapse to the floor, gasping for breath.

"You," the Hunter hissed, turning its head 180 degrees to look at Alex, the movement sickeningly unnatural. "What have you done?"

The amulet in Alex's hand was glowing now, ice-blue light spilling between his fingers. The Hunter's form began to shimmer, reality warping around it as whatever connection tethered it to the other side fluctuated.

"Now, Morgan!" Rivera croaked from the floor. "Complete the circuit! Think of the threshold closing!"

Alex had no idea what that meant, but something deeper than conscious thought responded to Rivera's words. He pressed the amulet harder against the Hunter's back, focusing his mind on the image Caleb had shown him, the threshold as a membrane, a barrier that could be strengthened, sealed.

The effect was terrifying. The Hunter's human form began to unravel, flesh sloughing away like wax melting under intense heat. But what was revealed beneath wasn't bone or muscle or anything recognizably organic. It was absence. A void in the shape of a man, a hole in reality itself.

And through that hole, for just an instant, Alex could see what waited on the other side. A vast darkness teeming with half-glimpsed shapes. Eyes. So many eyes, all turning toward him at once, all seeing him seeing them.

Morgan, whispered a multitude of voices directly into his mind. *We found you.*

Then the Hunter collapsed, its form imploding as the connection was severed, leaving nothing behind but a puddle of foul-smelling liquid that sizzled on Alex's hardwood floor.

The sudden silence was as shocking as the confrontation had been. For several heartbeats, Alex and Rivera remained frozen; the detective on his knees still gasping for breath, Alex standing over the remains of what had once been a man-shaped puppet controlled from beyond the threshold.

"Holy shit," Alex breathed finally. "Did we... is it dead?"

"Not dead," Rivera managed, rubbing his bruised throat. "Banished. Temporarily." He staggered to his feet, leaning against the wall for support. "The amulet severs the connection between worlds, forces whatever was controlling it back to the other side. But they can always find another vessel, create another Hunter."

Alex looked down at the silver amulet in his hand. The glow had faded, leaving it looking like an ordinary piece of jewelry once more. But the metal was warm now, almost hot to the touch.

"The vial," Rivera prompted. "We need to secure the perimeter before they send something else."

With shaking hands, Alex retrieved the small vial of lake water from his pocket. Following Rivera's instructions, he moved methodically around the apartment, placing drops at each entrance, doors, windows, even the heating vents. The liquid seemed to shimmer briefly when it touched each threshold, then disappeared, absorbed into the structure itself.

"Will it work?" he asked when they'd completed the ritual. "Will it keep them out?"

"For a while," Rivera replied, collapsing onto Alex's couch. "Long enough for us to regroup, at least."

Alex retrieved two glasses from the kitchen and a bottle of whiskey he kept for particularly difficult cases. He poured generous measures for both of them, his hands steadier now that the immediate danger had passed.

"You knew," he said, handing Rivera a glass. "You knew it would recognize you weren't loyal to them."

Rivera took a long swallow before answering. "I suspected. They've been watching me more closely lately. Questions about my reports. Assignments that felt like tests." He shrugged. "Occupational hazard of being a double agent."

"So, our careful plan was doomed from the start."

"Plans rarely survive first contact with the enemy," Rivera said with a grim smile. "Especially when the enemy can literally see through someone else's eyes from another dimension."

Alex settled into his reading chair, the same one the Hunter had occupied minutes earlier. He tried not to think about that as he took a sip of whiskey, letting the burn ground him in the physical world.

"What did it mean?" he asked. "'We found

you.' Like they'd been looking specifically for me, not just any Morgan."

Rivera's expression darkened. "They probably were. Your mother hid you well, changed your name, kept you medicated to suppress your abilities. But they never stopped searching." He leaned forward, elbows on knees. "The Morgan bloodline is special, Alex. Even among Watchers. Your family has always been, more. Stronger. More dangerous to them."

"Caleb said something similar. That I could repair breaches in the threshold. Close doorways they're trying to open."

"It's more than that." Rivera hesitated, choosing his words carefully. "The Morgans don't just see across the threshold or push back against incursion. Under certain circumstances, they can reshape it. Alter the very nature of the barrier between worlds."

Alex frowned. "What does that mean, exactly?"

"It means you're not just a threat to their plans. You're the only one who could potentially undo everything they've accomplished over centuries." Rivera met his gaze steadily. "That's why they want you alive. Why they need you as a vessel. Your power turned to their purpose would guarantee their success."

The weight of this revelation settled over Alex like a shroud. Not just a participant in some cosmic game of chess, but a key piece that could determine the outcome for both sides.

"Okay," he said finally. "So, what's our next move?"

Rivera drained his glass before answering. "We need intelligence. The Threshold has accelerated their timetable, which means they're gathering the bloodlines now, preparing the vessels. We need to know who they've already taken, who they're still looking for."

"And how exactly do we get that information? I'm pretty sure my cover is blown at Threshold Wellness."

"Mine too," Rivera agreed. "But there's another way in. A more direct approach."

"What did you have in mind?"

"Infiltration," Rivera said simply. "Not as employees or clients, but as what they're looking for. Bait."

Alex stared at him. "You want me to walk right into their headquarters? After we just killed or banished whatever one of their Hunters? That's suicide."

"Not you," Rivera clarified. "Someone else they're seeking. Someone whose bloodline is on their list but who hasn't been identified yet. Someone who could pass their initial screening."

Understanding dawned. "You have someone in mind."

"I do." Rivera pulled out his phone, scrolling through contacts. "Her name is Maya Weber. Graduate student in anthropology at Boston

University. Specializing in death rituals and funerary practices across cultures."

"Weber," Alex repeated. "Like the bloodline Caleb mentioned. The name I used at Threshold Wellness."

"Exactly. She doesn't know what she is, what she can do. But she's been experiencing episodes. Seeing things. Hearing voices." Rivera's expression softened slightly. "Sound familiar?"

All too familiar. Alex thought of his own years of confusion and fear, the medication that never quite worked, the constant sense that something was wrong with him. The isolation of seeing what others couldn't.

"Does she know about any of this? The threshold, the bloodlines, what's hunting her?"

"No. She thinks she's having stress-induced hallucinations. Been to three different psychiatrists looking for answers." Rivera's tone was matter of fact but not unkind. "She's vulnerable. Searching. Exactly the kind of person the Threshold targets for recruitment."

Alex didn't like where this was going. "You want to use her as bait. Send her into the lion's den."

"With proper preparation and backup, yes." Rivera held up a hand to forestall Alex's objection. "She's already on their radar, Alex. It's only a matter of time before they approach her. Better she goes in knowing the danger, with us watching her back, than alone and unaware."

It was ruthlessly logical, but it still felt wrong. Using someone else's confusion and vulnerability, putting them directly in harm's way.

"There has to be another way," Alex insisted.

"If there was, don't you think I'd prefer it?" Rivera's voice hardened. "We're at war. An invisible, silent war that most of humanity doesn't even know is happening. And we're losing. Badly." He leaned forward, his expression intense. "Every vessel the Threshold secures brings them one step closer to the crossing. Every bloodline they collect weakens the barrier a little more."

Alex knew Rivera was right, but the thought of deliberately placing someone else in danger, someone who, like him, had never asked for any of this, sat like a stone in his stomach.

"I want to meet her first," he said finally. "Talk to her. Make sure she understands what she's getting into."

"Fair enough." Rivera checked his watch. "We can arrange that. But we need to move quickly. The equinox is coming, and with it, their ritual."

Alex nodded, then remembered something. "Wait. We came here for my mother's necklace. In the bedside drawer."

He moved to the bedroom, opening the drawer where he kept the few mementos of his mother that had survived his childhood. The silver locket was there, exactly where he'd left it. Small and unassuming, its surface engraved with what he now recognized as a simplified version of the threshold symbol.

As his fingers closed around it, a jolt of recognition passed through him, not mental but physical, as if his body remembered something his mind had forgotten. For an instant, he could smell his mother's perfume, feel the brush of her hand against his forehead, hear her voice murmuring words he couldn't quite make out.

Then the sensation was gone, leaving him holding just a locket, just a piece of silver shaped by human hands.

"Found it?" Rivera called from the living room.

"Yeah," Alex replied, slipping the locket into his pocket. "Got it."

They spent the next hour gathering what they needed. Clothes, toiletries, Alex's service weapon from its lockbox, and the case files related to Eliza Bishop's death. The apartment was temporarily safe thanks to the lake water wards, but neither of them wanted to spend any more time there than necessary.

"We'll set up at a safehouse Caleb maintains," Rivera explained as they packed. "Old brownstone in the South End. Off the grid in all the ways that matter."

Alex didn't ask how a rare book dealer had come to own a safehouse. At this point, nothing about Caleb Morgan would surprise him.

As they prepared to leave, Alex paused at his desk, looking at the scattered case files. What had begun as a simple murder investigation had become something so much larger, so much stranger. Yet the detective in him, the part that had existed before all this supernatural business entered his life, couldn't let go of the original mystery.

"Eliza Bishop," he said aloud. "She was trying to escape them. Trying to expose what they were planning."

"And they killed her for it," Rivera agreed. "Made it look like an overdose. Standard procedure when dealing with potential whistleblowers or defectors."

"But why did she turn against them in the first place? Caleb said she saw something that changed her mind. What could be so terrible that a loyal cult member would suddenly risk everything to stop it?"

Rivera zipped his duffel bag before answering. "The Threshold doesn't just recruit anyone, Alex. They specifically target those with sensitivity to the threshold. People with trace amounts of the bloodlines they need, people who have glimpsed beyond the veil occasionally but don't understand what they're seeing."

"Like Maya Weber," Alex noted. "Like I was before all this."

"Exactly. They promise answers, community, purpose. For people who've spent their lives feeling different, feeling crazy, it's incredibly seductive." Rivera's expression darkened. "But only a select few are allowed into the inner circle. Only those with strong bloodline connections are shown the truth."

"And Eliza was one of those."

"She had Bishop blood. Old blood, connected to the threshold for generations. Not as powerful as the Morgans, but significant. They'd been grooming her for years, preparing her to serve as a vessel for the crossing." Rivera hefted his bag. "My guess? She saw what that really meant. What happens to the human host when something ancient moves in."

Alex thought of Dr. Marsh, of her face shifting between human and something else, of the many voices that had spoken through her. A chill ran through him at the thought of that fate.

"And now they want me for the same purpose," he said quietly.

"You, Maya Weber, others with the bloodlines they need. All to be sacrificed in one form or another during the equinox ritual." Rivera's voice was grim but determined. "Unless we stop them."

They left the apartment in silence, careful to secure the door behind them. The lake water wards would hold for now, but nothing was permanent when dealing with forces that existed beyond ordinary reality.

Outside, Boston was waking up, the eastern

sky lightening to pearl gray as dawn approached. Office workers hurried past, clutching coffee cups, checking phones, utterly unaware of the war being waged in their midst. Alex envied them their ignorance. How simple life had been when his biggest concerns were unpaid bills and difficult clients.

"One more thing," Rivera said as they loaded their bags into his unmarked sedan. "Something you should know about Maya Weber."

"What's that?"

"She's not just any Weber. Her grandmother was Victoria Weber." Rivera glanced at Alex to see if the name registered. It didn't. "Victoria Weber was your mother's closest friend. They worked together, fought together. Until Victoria disappeared in '88."

The implications were clear. "You think Maya might know something? About my mother, about what happened?"

"I think the connections between the bloodlines are rarely coincidental," Rivera replied. "And I think Maya Weber is as much a part of this story as you are."

As they drove through Boston's awakening streets, Alex turned his mother's locket over in his pocket, feeling the engraved pattern beneath his fingertips. So many secrets. So many connections he was only just beginning to understand.

And somewhere in the city, Dr. Evelyn Marsh

was gathering her forces, preparing for a ritual that would change the world forever. A ritual that required Alex Morgan as its centerpiece.

The hunt had entered a new phase. And this time, he wasn't just being pursued.

He was pursuing back.

In her private office at Threshold Wellness, Dr. Marsh stood motionless before a wall of monitors. Each screen showed a different location—Alex's apartment building, the exterior of Morgan's Rare Books, various street intersections throughout Boston. On one screen, Rivera's sedan moved through morning traffic, carrying Alex away from his compromised home.

Katherine Bishop entered silently, her elegant composure betrayed only by the slight tension in her shoulders.

"The Hunter is gone," she reported. "The connection severed completely."

"As expected," Dr. Marsh replied, her voice that unsettling chorus of overlapping tones. "The Morgan's abilities are developing rapidly. Faster than we anticipated."

"Should we be concerned?"

"Quite the opposite." Dr. Marsh turned, her face shifting subtly between human and something else as she smiled. "Every use of his power makes him more visible to us. Every step he takes toward mastering the threshold sight brings him closer to his true purpose."

"And the Weber girl? They're going to contact her."

"Of course they are. Predictable in their desperation." Dr. Marsh's smile widened, revealing too many teeth. "Let them. When they deliver her to us, they deliver themselves."

Katherine nodded, but a flicker of doubt crossed her features. "And my sister? Her spirit continues to... interfere. The Morgan has seen her multiple times now."

"Eliza always was stubborn, even in death." Dr. Marsh waved a dismissive hand. "She exists in a state of transition, caught on the threshold. Unable to cross fully in either direction. A nuisance, nothing more."

"And if she reveals what she knows? What she saw?"

"Then we accelerate our plans." Dr. Marsh turned back to the monitors, watching as Rivera's car disappeared into Boston's morning rush hour. "The equinox approaches. The stars align. And the last Morgan has finally awakened to his heritage."

Her form flickered more violently now, the human disguise slipping to reveal glimpses of what existed beneath. Something ancient and hungry that had worn many faces over many centuries.

"Everything," it said in that chorus of voices, "is proceeding exactly as intended."

CHAPTER 9

Trust is a fragile thing. Like glass, it can be repaired after breaking, but the cracks always show.

The safehouse was nothing like Alex had imagined. Instead of a spartan hideout with tactical gear and emergency supplies, Caleb Morgan's South End property was a meticulously maintained brownstone filled with antiques, rare books, and artwork that belonged in a museum. The place looked and felt like the home of a wealthy academic, not the secret headquarters for a supernatural resistance.

"Hiding in plain sight," Rivera explained as he secured the heavy front door behind them. "The Threshold expects safehouses to look like safehouses. This is just another property owned by a successful antiquarian book dealer."

"Who apparently does very well for himself," Alex observed, taking in the original hardwood floors and crown molding.

"The benefits of a long life," came Caleb's voice as the old man emerged from what appeared to be a library. "Very long, in my case."

He looked more tired than when Alex had last seen him, the lines in his face deeper, his movements stiffer. Whatever energy he'd expended monitoring the confrontation with the Hunter had taken a toll.

"It worked?" he asked, mismatched eyes fixed on Alex.

"It worked," Rivera confirmed. "The Hunter is banished. The apartment is secured. But they know we're working together now."

"Inevitable," Caleb sighed. "Though I had hoped for more time." He gestured for them to follow him deeper into the house. "Come. We have much to discuss."

The library they entered was a bibliophile's dream. Floor-to-ceiling shelves packed with leather-bound volumes, sliding ladders to reach the highest tiers, a massive oak table at the center scattered with open books and unrolled maps. The air smelled of paper, leather, and the faint metallic tang of old ink.

"Did you bring it?" Caleb asked.

Alex reached into his pocket and produced his mother's locket. Even in the warm light of the library, the silver seemed to possess its own subtle glow, the engraved threshold symbol catching the light in ways that made it appear to shift when not viewed directly.

Caleb accepted it with reverence, holding the locket in his palm as if weighing something far heavier than metal.

"Catherine's focus," he murmured. "She channeled much of her ability through this. A talisman, but also a tool."

"Focus? Tool?" Alex frowned. "I thought it was just a keepsake."

"Nothing that belonged to your mother was 'just' anything," Caleb replied. "She infused this with her essence, her connection to the threshold. For you to use when the time came."

He placed the locket on the table beside an old leather-bound journal that Alex recognized as his mother's. The two objects seemed to resonate with each other, an almost imperceptible vibration that Alex felt more than heard.

"Where's Weber?" Caleb asked, turning to Rivera.

"Still at her apartment in Allston. Teaching assistant duties start at noon." Rivera checked his watch. "We have a few hours to prepare before making contact."

"You're certain she hasn't been approached yet? By the Threshold?"

"As certain as I can be. I've had her under surveillance for three weeks. No unusual contacts, no unexplained absences." Rivera's expression was professional, detached. "She fits the profile. Isolated, experiencing unexplained phenomena, seeking answers from conventional sources without success."

Alex shifted uncomfortably at Rivera's clinical assessment. It hit too close to home, reminding him of his own confusion and fear before all this began.

"And you think she'll just agree to walk into a cult headquarters as an undercover agent?" he asked. "Based on what? Our word that she has supernatural abilities and is being hunted by interdimensional entities?"

"She's been seeing them for months," Rivera said flatly. "Ghosts, at first—like you. Then more complex manifestations. Glimpses through the threshold. She documented everything in journals, online forums. Looking for validation, for anyone who'd experienced similar phenomena."

"Classic recruitment target," Caleb added. "The Threshold monitors those same forums, looking for potential vessels. It's only a matter of time before they find her."

"So we're doing her a favor," Alex said, unable to keep the bitterness from his voice. "Telling her the monsters under her bed are real, but hey, at least now she knows what's hunting her."

"Would you have preferred to remain in ignorance?" Caleb asked quietly. "To believe you were losing your mind rather than glimpsing a deeper reality?"

The question struck home. As terrifying as the truth had been, it was still better than the uncertainty, the fear of inheriting his father's mental illness, the constant doubting of his own perceptions.

"Fine," Alex conceded. "But we give her a choice. Full disclosure, then she decides whether to help us or not."

"Agreed," Caleb said before Rivera could object. "We are not the Threshold. We don't manipulate or coerce. That's what separates us from them."

Rivera didn't look convinced, but he nodded reluctantly. "Your call. But if she refuses, we're back to square one with no way to infiltrate their inner circle."

"Then we'll find another way," Alex insisted.

A tense silence settled over the room, broken only when Caleb changed the subject.

"Tell me about the Hunter," he said. "What did you see when you banished it?"

Alex hesitated, trying to organize thoughts he'd been avoiding since the confrontation. "It kind of unraveled. Like watching something dissolve from the inside out. But what was underneath wasn't human. It wasn't anything."

"A void," Caleb supplied. "An absence shaped like a person."

"Yes. And for a second, I could see through it. To the other side." Alex's voice dropped almost to a whisper. "There were things there. Watching. So many eyes. And they saw me seeing them."

Caleb and Rivera exchanged a glance loaded with significance.

"What?" Alex demanded. "What aren't you telling me?"

"The veil is thinning," Caleb said gravely. "Faster than we anticipated. For you to see so clearly through a temporary breach... it suggests the threshold is becoming more permeable."

"Because of the equinox? The 'astronomical conditions' you mentioned?"

"Partly. But also because of increased activity from the Threshold. Each ritual they perform, each breach they create weakens the barrier a little more. Like stretching a piece of fabric until it begins to tear."

"And once it tears?" Alex asked, though he suspected he knew the answer.

"Then what waits on the other side comes through," Caleb replied simply. "Not just Hunters or Lurkers or the other lesser entities they've managed to squeeze through existing weaknesses, but the Ancients. The ones who have existed in that realm for millennia, gathering strength, waiting for their chance to return."

"Return? You mean they were here before?"

Caleb moved to one of the bookshelves, retrieving a volume so old its binding had cracked in several places, held together with archival tape. He set it on the table and opened it carefully to a page marked with a silk ribbon.

The illustration that covered both pages made Alex's breath catch. It depicted a massive stone structure, something like Stonehenge but larger, more elaborate, surrounded by robed figures. Above the structure, the sky appeared to be tearing open, and through that tear emerged shapes that hurt the eye to follow, forms that seemed to shift and change even in the static medium of the ancient drawing.

"The last major crossing attempt," Caleb explained. "4,632 BCE, by our calendar. What primitive humans recorded as 'the time when the gods walked among us' or 'the age of giants' or a dozen other mythological frameworks."

"Jesus," Alex breathed. "You're saying those myths were real? Based on actual events?"

"Distorted by time and human understanding, but yes. The Ancients crossed fully into our world once before, ruled for generations before they were finally driven back and the threshold sealed."

"By who? How?"

"By the first Watchers," Caleb said. "Humans who developed the ability to perceive the threshold, to manipulate it. Your ancestors, among others. They discovered that the same sensitivity that allowed perception of the other side could be weaponized against it."

Rivera, who had been silent during this exchange, finally spoke. "The Threshold cult is the modern descendant of those who worshipped the Ancients, who benefited from their rule. They've been working for millennia to bring them back, to restore what they consider the natural order."

"With humans as, what, slaves? Food?" Alex asked.

"Vessels, primarily," Caleb corrected. "The Ancients cannot maintain physical form in our dimension without a host. But unlike the crude puppetry of the Hunters, the Ancients seek full integration. A merging of their consciousness with a human host uniquely suited to contain them."

Understanding dawned, cold and terrible. "The bloodlines. They've been cultivating bloodlines with threshold sensitivity for thousands of years. Breeding us like, like livestock."

"More like cultivating prize orchids," Caleb said grimly. "Rare, valuable, requiring specific conditions to flourish. The seven bloodlines they seek; Morgan, Weber, Chin, Okafor, Bishop, Nazari, LaChance, all trace back to the original Watchers who closed the threshold."

"Poetic justice," Rivera added. "Using the descendants of those who imprisoned them as the vessels for their return."

Alex felt sick. The scope of what they were describing, the patient malevolence behind it, centuries of manipulation, of selective breeding, all leading to this moment, this generation, this equinox.

"And I'm what?" he asked. "The prize bull? The perfect vessel?"

"The Morgan bloodline has always been

the strongest," Caleb confirmed. "The most sensitive to the threshold, the most capable of manipulating it. Your mother was extraordinary, but you..." He hesitated. "Your near-death experience as a child created something unique. A direct connection to the other side that makes you not just sensitive to the threshold, but capable of reshaping it entirely."

"Which is why Dr. Marsh wants me specifically," Alex concluded. "Not just any Morgan, but me."

"Precisely. With you as the primary vessel and the other bloodlines as anchoring points, the ritual would have its greatest chance of success in millennia."

The weight of this knowledge pressed down on Alex, suffocating in its implications. Not just a random target, not just a coincidental player in someone else's game, but the centerpiece of a plan thousands of years in the making.

"So what's our counter-strategy?" he asked finally. "Besides sending Maya Weber in as a spy?"

Rivera moved to the table, pointing to one of the maps spread across its surface—a street plan of Boston with certain locations circled in red.

"Intelligence gathering first," he said. "Weber gives us access to their inner circle, helps us identify which bloodlines they've already secured and which they're still hunting. That gives us potential allies, people we can warn and protect."

"Meanwhile," Caleb continued, "we train you. Intensively. To control and direct your abilities. To strengthen the threshold rather than weaken it."

"And my mother's locket? How does that fit in?"

"Catherine created this as both focus and repository," Caleb explained. "A tool to amplify threshold manipulation, but also a vessel containing some portion of her own power. She intended it for you, when you were ready."

"And am I? Ready?"

Caleb's mismatched eyes met his, unflinching. "We're about to find out."

The conversation was interrupted by a discreet chime from Rivera's phone. He checked it, frowning.

"Traffic camera alert," he explained. "Someone's watching your apartment building, Morgan. Two men in a black SUV, parked across the street for the past hour."

"Threshold agents?"

"Most likely. Standard surveillance. They won't try to enter as long as the wards hold."

"But they know I'm not there," Alex pointed out. "So why watch the building?"

"Because they don't know if you'll return," Caleb surmised. "And because they're monitoring the effectiveness of their Hunter. They don't yet realize it's been banished."

"Which gives us a small advantage," Rivera added. "They think they have eyes on you when they don't."

Alex wasn't convinced this constituted much of an advantage, but he kept the thought to himself. Instead, he returned to the more immediate concern.

"So when do we approach Maya Weber?"

"Today," Rivera replied. "After her teaching hours. I've been observing her routine for weeks. She stops at a coffee shop on Commonwealth Avenue around four, stays for about an hour working on her dissertation."

"And you just happen to know all this because...?"

Rivera's expression remained professionally neutral. "Because it's my job to know. The same way I knew your routines before we made contact."

The reminder that Rivera had been watching him, tracking him, for who knew how long sent an uncomfortable chill down Alex's spine. Necessary or not, the surveillance felt like a violation.

"I'll make the initial approach," Rivera continued, either not noticing or choosing to ignore Alex's discomfort. "Establish baseline rapport. Then you join us, make the full explanation."

"Why me? You're the professional spy."

"Because she'll believe you," Rivera said

simply. "You've been through exactly what she's experiencing now. You can show her what's possible, what she's capable of."

It was logical, but it still felt manipulative. Using his own trauma as a recruitment tool, leveraging Maya Weber's confusion and fear to turn her into an asset.

We are not the Threshold, Caleb had insisted. *We don't manipulate or coerce.* But the line seemed to be blurring by the minute.

"Fine," Alex conceded. "But we do this my way. Honest, straightforward. No games, no half-truths."

"Agreed," Caleb said before Rivera could object. "Now, we have a few hours before the Weber meeting. We should use that time to begin your training with the locket."

Alex glanced at the silver necklace still lying on the table beside his mother's journal. Even after all he'd seen, all he'd learned, part of him still resisted this final step. This deliberate embrace of abilities he'd spent a lifetime suppressing, denying, medicating away.

But what choice did he have? The Threshold was moving forward with their plans. Innocent people, people like Maya Weber, were in danger. And something ancient and hungry was waiting on the other side of reality, patient and terrible, wearing Dr. Marsh's face like a mask while it prepared to tear the world apart.

"Alright," he said, picking up the locket. "Let's

see what this thing can do."

The training was nothing like Alex had expected. No mystical incantations, no elaborate rituals. Instead, Caleb guided him through what seemed like deceptively simple mental exercises; focusing on the locket, feeling its connection to the threshold, learning to channel his perception through it rather than directly.

"Think of it as a lens," Caleb instructed. "A way to focus the sight without the physical drain. Your mother created this after years of trial and error, finding that silver with certain properties could act as a conduit between worlds without the physiological side effects."

Alex concentrated, holding the locket between his palms, feeling its subtle warmth against his skin. When he activated the threshold sight, the difference was immediate and shocking. Instead of the usual headache and nosebleed, the transition felt smooth, controlled. The locket pulsed with blue-white light visible only to his altered perception, and the world around him transformed.

The library remained structurally the same, but now Alex could see the layers of time and memory embedded in its contents. Books glowed with the residual energy of their creators and readers. The maps on the table revealed hidden patterns; currents of power flowing beneath Boston's streets, nexus points where the threshold thinned naturally.

And Caleb... Caleb was transfigured. As before, his human form remained visible, but overlaid upon it was something ancient and powerful, with antlers branching from its head and eyes that contained galaxies. Not a possession, not a Vessel like Dr. Marsh, but something else entirely. A being that existed simultaneously in multiple realities.

"What are you?" Alex whispered, the question escaping before he could stop it.

"A Guardian," Caleb replied, his voice unchanged despite his altered appearance. "One of the few who can stand in both worlds without being consumed by either. Neither fully human nor fully Other, but something in between."

"Have you always been...?"

"No. Once I was as human as you. Ezekiel Morgan's contemporary and friend. I made a choice, long ago, to become what was needed." Caleb's expression held ancient sorrow. "A sacrifice that enabled me to watch over your family for generations, to preserve what knowledge I could for this moment."

Alex wanted to ask more, to understand what such a transformation had cost, but Rivera's voice interrupted from across the room.

"It's time," he said, checking his watch. "Weber will be at the coffee shop in twenty minutes."

The threshold sight faded as Alex's concentration broke, the locket cooling in his palm. Caleb was once again just an elderly man with mismatched eyes, the otherworldly aspect hidden from conventional perception.

"We'll continue later," Caleb promised. "You're making remarkable progress, faster than I anticipated."

"Is that good or bad?" Alex asked, slipping the locket into his pocket.

"Both," Caleb replied cryptically. "Power always is."

The drive to Commonwealth Avenue was tense and mostly silent. Alex watched the familiar streets of Boston pass by, seeing them with new eyes. How many of the people walking those sidewalks, he wondered, were actually people? How many were Hunters or other entities in human guise? How many of the buildings concealed nexus points or breaches in the threshold?

Knowledge, once gained, could never be unlearned. The world had changed, or rather, his perception of it had changed. Revealing what had always been there, hidden beneath the comfortable illusion of ordinary reality.

"When we arrive," Rivera said, breaking into his thoughts, "I'll make first contact. Casual introduction, professional interest in her research. You wait nearby, out of sight, until I signal."

"And if she freaks out? If she doesn't believe any of this?"

"Then we back off, try another approach." Rivera's tone suggested he had contingency plans Alex might prefer not to know about. "But she'll believe it. They always do once they realize it explains what they've been experiencing."

The coffee shop was a small, independent place wedged between a bookstore and a vintage clothing boutique. Through the window, Alex could see about a dozen customers, students mostly, hunched over laptops, surrounded by textbooks and empty cups.

"There," Rivera said, nodding toward a young woman sitting alone at a corner table. "Maya Weber."

Alex studied her carefully. Late twenties, with shoulder-length dark hair pulled back in a practical ponytail. Wire-rimmed glasses. Dressed simply in jeans and a BU sweatshirt. Nothing about her appearance suggested someone with supernatural abilities or ancient bloodline connections. She looked like any other graduate student, tired and focused, alternating between typing on her laptop and consulting a stack of reference materials.

"How do you know she's experiencing threshold phenomena?" Alex asked. "She looks perfectly normal."

"The dark circles under her eyes. The way she startles at nothing. Watch her, she'll look up suddenly every few minutes as if someone called her name." Rivera observed her with professional detachment. "And the medication bottles in her bag. Antipsychotics, the same ones you used to take."

It was disconcerting how much Rivera knew about both of them, how closely he'd been monitoring their lives without their knowledge. But Alex had to admit the detective's assessment appeared accurate. Even as they watched, Maya suddenly jerked her head up, looking toward an empty corner of the coffee shop with an expression of confused alarm before returning to her work.

"Seeing something that isn't there," Rivera commented. "Or rather, something most people can't see."

"Alright," Alex conceded. "Make your approach. I'll wait for your signal."

Rivera nodded and exited the car, transforming his demeanor as he walked. By the time he entered the coffee shop, he projected an entirely different persona, more relaxed, less intense, the kind of man who might strike up a casual conversation without setting off alarm bells.

Alex watched through the window as Rivera ordered a coffee, then casually approached Maya's table. Whatever opening line he used made her look up with polite but guarded interest. Rivera showed her something, his police badge, presumably, and her posture relaxed slightly. Official business was less threatening than random male attention in a coffee shop.

Their conversation continued for several minutes. Rivera pointed to one of her reference books, apparently asking about her research. Maya became more animated, gesturing as she explained something. The universal behavior of academics given an opportunity to discuss their specialty.

Then Rivera said something that made her freeze, her expression changing from engagement to shock. He continued speaking, his manner calm and reassuring. After a moment, Maya glanced around the coffee shop as if suddenly aware they might be overheard, then nodded reluctantly.

Rivera raised two fingers in a subtle gesture toward the window. The signal.

Taking a deep breath, Alex exited the car and headed into the coffee shop. As he approached their table, he could feel Maya's eyes on him, assessing, suspicious. Rivera stood to make the introduction.

"Maya, this is Alex Morgan. The person I was telling you about."

"Morgan," she repeated, the name clearly registering. "Like the bookshop owner you mentioned?"

"A relative," Alex confirmed, taking the seat Rivera vacated for him. "Though I only discovered that recently."

Up close, Maya Weber looked both younger

and older than she had from a distance. Younger in her features, older in her eyes, which held the wary exhaustion of someone who hadn't slept properly in months.

"Detective Rivera says you've been... experiencing things," she said carefully. "Like me."

"Yes. For most of my life, though I didn't understand what it was until recently." Alex decided that direct honesty was the only approach that felt right. "Visions. Voices. Glimpses of people who aren't there—or who aren't there for most people, anyway."

Maya's eyes widened slightly. "And headaches? Nosebleeds sometimes?"

"Exactly. The physical symptoms of trying to process what ordinary human perception isn't designed to handle."

She leaned forward, lowering her voice. "He says you know what's causing it. That it's not mental illness or stress or any of the things the doctors keep telling me."

"It's not," Alex confirmed. "It's an ability. A sensitivity to what exists beyond ordinary reality. Something inherited through your bloodline."

"Weber," she murmured. "He mentioned that too. That there's something special about being a Weber. Which seems insane, because it's just a name, just a German surname that thousands of people have."

"It's more than that," Alex said gently. "It's a lineage. One of seven with a particular sensitivity to what we call the threshold—the barrier between our world and another place."

Maya sat back, her expression conflicted. "This sounds completely crazy. You know that, right? If anyone else told me this, I'd think they were delusional."

"I know. I felt the same way when I first heard it." Alex met her gaze directly. "But you've seen things, haven't you? Things that couldn't possibly be there. Things that no one else notices."

She was silent for a long moment, internal struggle visible in her face. Then, almost imperceptibly, she nodded.

"The old woman in the library stacks," she whispered. "Always in the same place. And the man in the hallway of my building who walks through walls. And last week..." She hesitated, as if saying it aloud might make it more real. "Last week I saw something in my bathroom mirror that wasn't me. Just for a second. A face behind my face."

Alex felt a chill at this last description. That was new, different from the Drifters, the ordinary ghosts, he'd encountered. Something more ominous.

"We can help you understand what you're seeing," he said. "Help you control it instead of being controlled by it. But there's something you need to know first." He glanced at Rivera, who nodded encouragingly. "You're not just sensitive to these phenomena. You're being hunted because of it."

Maya's face paled. "Hunted? By who?"

"An organization called the Threshold," Rivera interjected. "They present themselves as a wellness center, a spiritual retreat. In reality, they're a cult seeking people with your specific abilities for a ritual they've been planning for generations."

"A ritual," she repeated flatly. "Right. Of course. A cult ritual." She began gathering her books. "I think this conversation is over."

"Maya, wait," Alex said, reaching into his pocket for the locket. "Let me show you something. Please."

She hesitated, hand still on her half-packed bag. "What?"

"Evidence," he said simply. "Proof that what we're telling you is real."

Against her better judgment, Maya settled back into her seat. "Fine. Show me."

Alex placed the silver locket on the table between them. To ordinary eyes, it was just an antique piece of jewelry, unremarkable except for its age and the strange symbol engraved on its surface.

"This belonged to my mother," he explained. "She created it as a tool to focus the threshold sight—the ability to see beyond ordinary reality without the physical side effects. May I?"

After a moment's hesitation, Maya nodded. Alex picked up the locket, closed his eyes briefly to center himself as Caleb had taught him, and activated the sight through the silver focus.

The change was subtle but unmistakable. To Maya, it would appear as if his eyes had changed somehow—not in color or shape, but in depth, as if suddenly seeing much further than the confines of the coffee shop would allow.

"There's a Drifter by the counter," he said quietly. "Elderly man in a tweed jacket. Died of a heart attack in this shop about six months ago. He still comes in every afternoon out of habit."

Maya's eyes widened as she turned to look at the spot Alex had indicated. "I... I can't see anything."

"Because you're not focusing your sight. It's random for you right now, unpredictable. But it can be controlled." Alex held out the locket. "Try it. Just hold this and concentrate on the idea of seeing what's normally hidden."

With trembling fingers, Maya accepted the locket. The moment it touched her skin, she gasped, nearly dropping it.

"It's warm," she whispered. "And it feels alive somehow."

"Focus," Alex instructed gently. "Look at the counter again, but with the intention to see beyond ordinary perception."

Maya obeyed, her gaze fixed on the seemingly

empty space near the barista station. For several seconds, nothing happened. Then her eyes widened, her breath catching.

"Oh my God," she whispered. "There is someone there. An old man, just like you said. He's, he's, just standing there, watching the barista make drinks. He looks so sad."

She turned back to Alex, her expression a mixture of wonder and fear. "He's really there. And he's, he's dead, isn't he? I'm seeing a dead person."

"A Drifter," Alex confirmed. "Someone caught between worlds, unable to fully cross over. Harmless, just echoing patterns from their life."

"Not like the face in my mirror," Maya said, her voice dropping. "That wasn't, it wasn't human."

Rivera and Alex exchanged a glance.

"That's what we need to talk to you about," Rivera said carefully. "The difference between ordinary threshold phenomena, ghosts, essentially, and something far more dangerous that's taking an interest in people like you and Alex."

Maya placed the locket back on the table, her hands shaking slightly. "People like us. Webers and Morgans. People who can see whatever that was."

"Yes. And others—Bishops, Chins, Okafors, Nazaris, LaChances. Seven bloodlines with inherited sensitivity to the threshold, all being actively hunted by the Threshold cult for use in their equinox ritual."

"This is insane," Maya muttered, but with less conviction than before. "Complete insanity."

"Three weeks ago, I would have agreed with you," Alex said. "Then I took a case, a suspicious death investigation, that led me into all of this. The victim was Eliza Bishop, another bloodline member. She was killed because she discovered what the Threshold was really planning and tried to stop it."

"And what exactly are they planning?" Maya asked, a note of challenge in her voice.

"To open a permanent breach between worlds," Rivera replied bluntly. "To allow ancient entities to cross over and possess specially prepared human hosts—people with threshold sensitivity like you and Alex."

"Possession," Maya repeated. "Like in horror movies."

"More complex than that," Alex corrected. "But yes, essentially. And the ritual requires representatives of all seven bloodlines as focal points, with one primary vessel—the strongest bloodline—as the centerpiece."

Understanding dawned in Maya's eyes. "You. They want you specifically."

"And they'll take you too, if they find you," Rivera added. "Which they will, eventually. They monitor forums, support groups, anywhere people might discuss experiences like yours."

Maya went very still, her face draining of color. "The message board," she whispered. "University Mental Health Resources has an anonymous forum for students experiencing unusual perceptions. I've been posting there for months, describing exactly what I've been seeing."

"Then they already know about you," Rivera said grimly. "It's just a matter of time before they make contact."

"Which is why we're here," Alex added quickly. "To warn you. To help you understand what you're experiencing and protect yourself from those who would exploit it."

"And to ask for your help," Rivera said, earning a sharp look from Alex.

"My help?" Maya frowned. "How could I possibly help with any of this?"

Intelligence gathering," Rivera explained. "The Threshold doesn't know we've made contact with you. You're still, from their perspective, an unaware potential recruit. That gives us an opportunity to place someone inside their organization, someone who can help us identify which bloodlines they've already secured and what specifically they're planning for the equinox ritual."

You want me to spy on a cult of what, demon worshippers?" Maya's voice rose slightly before she caught herself, glancing around the coffee shop.

"We want to offer you the chance to fight back," Alex said, shooting Rivera an irritated look. "But only if you choose to. You can walk away right now, and we'll still help you understand your abilities, protect yourself. No obligation."

Rivera looked like he wanted to object to this framing, but he remained silent, deferring to Alex's approach.

Maya stared at the locket on the table, her expression troubled. "You said there was a face behind my face in the mirror. What was that? One of these, um, entities trying to possess me?"

"Possibly," Alex admitted. "Or it could be a glimpse of potential. What you might become if your threshold sensitivity fully manifests. Without seeing it myself, I can't say for certain."

"And this is real," she said, not quite a question. "All of it. I'm not having a psychotic break or a shared delusion or whatever the latest psychiatrist wants to call it."

"It's real," Alex confirmed. "Terrifying, confusing, but real. And you're not alone in experiencing it."

Maya was silent for a long moment, wrestling with implications too vast to process quickly. When she finally spoke, her voice was steadier than before.

"I want to see more," she said. "Not just a ghost in a coffee shop. Show me what this threshold really is, what these bloodlines mean.

If I'm going to make any decision about helping you, I need to understand exactly what I'm dealing with."

Alex glanced at Rivera, who nodded slightly. This was progress, an opening.

"We can do that," Alex said. "There's someone you should meet. The man who helped me understand what I was experiencing. He can show you things I can't yet."

"Caleb Morgan," Maya surmised. "The bookshop owner Detective Rivera mentioned."

"Yes. He's been monitoring the Threshold for decades. Helping people like us understand what they're experiencing."

"And protecting them from this cult?"

"When possible," Rivera interjected. "Though not always successfully. The Threshold has existed in various forms for centuries. They're patient, well-resourced, and utterly committed to their goal."

Maya took a deep breath, squaring her shoulders. "Alright. Take me to this Caleb person. But I'm not agreeing to anything yet. I just want information. The truth about what's happening to me."

"That's all we're offering," Alex assured her, ignoring Rivera's slight frown. "The truth, and then your choice."

As they gathered their things to leave, Alex noticed something he'd missed earlier: a slender silver bracelet on Maya's wrist, partially hidden by her sweatshirt sleeve. The design was familiar. Interlocking circles with a central motif that resembled...

"That bracelet," he said suddenly. "Where did you get it?"

Maya glanced down, looking surprised at the question. "It was my grandmother's. Why?"

"May I see it?"

Hesitantly, Maya extended her wrist. The bracelet was old silver, tarnished in places, its pattern more visible now: a series of interconnected threshold symbols, similar to but distinct from the one on his mother's locket.

"Victoria Weber," Alex murmured. "Your grandmother. She was a Watcher too."

"A what?"

"Someone who guards the threshold," he explained. "Like my mother was. Like Caleb is. This isn't just jewelry, it's a focus, like my locket. A tool for controlled threshold sight."

Maya withdrew her hand, touching the bracelet protectively. "My grandmother said it was for protection. That I should always wear it when I was afraid. I never understood what she meant."

"She was trying to help you," Alex said gently. "In the only way she could without revealing everything before you were ready."

"She disappeared when I was five," Maya said, her voice distant with memory. "Just gone one day. No explanation. The police investigated, but they never found a body. No evidence of foul play. She just vanished."

The parallels to his own story, his mother's death, his father's lies, sent a chill through Alex. Another bloodline. Another loss. Another pattern in a design spanning generations.

"I think," he said carefully, "Caleb might know more about what happened to her. The records he keeps go back centuries, tracking the bloodlines, documenting disappearances."

Something flickered in Maya's eyes. Hope, perhaps, or the dangerous lure of answers long sought.

"Then let's go," she said, gathering her belongings with newfound determination. "I want to know everything."

As they left the coffee shop, none of them noticed the woman at a corner table, ostensibly absorbed in her phone. She wore elegant business attire, her blonde hair pulled back in a chignon, nothing about her appearance drawing attention.

Katherine Bishop watched them go, then made a call.

"Contact made," she reported. "The Morgan and Rivera have recruited the Weber girl, just as you predicted."

"Excellent," replied Dr. Marsh's layered voice. "Continue surveillance. Do not intervene."

"They're taking her to the old man."

"As expected. Let him show her the family

albums, the ancient tomes. Let him explain her heritage, awaken her abilities." Dr. Marsh's voice held cold amusement. "It saves us considerable effort."

"And when they attempt to infiltrate the center?"

"We welcome them with open arms," came the reply. "The final pieces move into position. The board arranges itself for our benefit."

Katherine ended the call and rose gracefully, leaving enough cash to cover her untouched coffee. By the time she reached the door, Rivera's sedan was already turning the corner, carrying its occupants toward a confrontation none of them fully understood.

The game was entering its final phase. And despite what Alex Morgan and his allies believed, they had never been the players.

They had always been the pieces.

CHAPTER 10

Memory is a strange thing. Not a recording but a reconstruction, different each time we access it. Unless, of course, the memory isn't entirely yours to begin with.

Maya Weber stood in the center of Caleb Morgan's underground library, surrounded by the physical evidence of a reality she'd glimpsed only in fragments. Ancient books detailing threshold phenomena, maps of nexus points where the membrane between worlds thinned, genealogical charts tracing the seven bloodlines back through centuries. Her expression cycled between wonder, disbelief, and the particular relief that comes from finally understanding one is not, in fact, losing their mind.

"So, I'm not crazy," she said, fingers trailing over a family tree that included her own name near the bottom. "None of this was hallucination or stress or overwork."

"No," Caleb confirmed, his mismatched eyes watchful. "Though many with threshold sensitivity are driven to madness by what they perceive. Without context, without understanding, the human mind struggles to integrate such experiences into a coherent worldview."

"Like my grandmother," Maya said quietly. "Before she disappeared, she used to talk to people who weren't there. Have conversations with empty rooms. My parents thought she was developing dementia."

"Victoria Weber was one of the strongest Watchers of her generation," Caleb replied. "Second only to Catherine Morgan in her sensitivity to the threshold. They worked together for years, monitoring breaches, tracking Threshold cult activities."

"Until they both vanished," Alex added, the connection suddenly clear. "Within two years of each other."

Caleb nodded grimly. "The Threshold had identified both bloodlines as particularly powerful. They made eliminating that generation their priority."

"But they failed," Rivera pointed out from his position near the door. "Both Catherine and Victoria had children first. Children who had children. The bloodlines continued."

"Yes, though diluted in the Weber case," Caleb said. "Maya's father married outside the traditional bloodlines, weakening the genetic predisposition somewhat. But clearly not eliminating it entirely."

Maya touched her grandmother's bracelet, the silver warm against her skin. "And this? You said it was like Alex's locket. A tool of some kind."

"A focus," Caleb confirmed. "Victoria created it during the same period Catherine crafted the locket. Different in design but similar in purpose. To channel threshold sensitivity in controlled ways, to see without the physical drain."

"She told me it was for protection," Maya said. "That I should wear it when I was afraid. I always thought it was just a comfort object. A psychological crutch."

"It's far more than that," Caleb replied. "It's a weapon, a shield, and a lens all in one. With proper training, you could use it to perceive the threshold clearly, to defend against entities that might seek to harm you."

"Like the face behind my face in the mirror," Maya said, her voice dropping. "What was that, exactly? You never fully explained."

Caleb exchanged a glance with Rivera before answering carefully. "Without seeing it myself, I can't be certain. But the description suggests a Hunter. An entity that uses the threshold to observe those with bloodline sensitivity, searching for potential vessels."

"A spy from the other side," Alex clarified. "Looking through the membrane between worlds, watching for specific targets."

Maya paled slightly. "It was, what, evaluating me?"

"Most likely," Caleb confirmed. "The Threshold cult works in tandem with entities from beyond. They identify potential vessels through conventional means, monitoring support groups, forums, psychiatric practices, while their allies search from the other side, looking for those with active threshold sensitivity."

"And they found me," Maya concluded.

"Yes. Which means it's only a matter of time before they make direct contact."

Alex watched Maya's expression carefully, concerned about overwhelming her with too much, too quickly. She appeared to be holding up remarkably well—processing rather than panicking, asking questions rather than retreating into denial. But the strain was visible in the tightness around her eyes, the slight tremor in her hands.

"Maybe we should take a break," he suggested. "This is a lot to absorb all at once."

Maya shook her head firmly. "No. I need to understand everything if I'm going to make an informed decision about helping you." She turned to Caleb. "You mentioned training. Like what you're doing with Alex. Teaching me to use this?" She held up her wrist, the silver bracelet gleaming in the library's warm light.

"If you're willing, yes," Caleb replied. "Though time is limited. The equinox is less than three weeks away."

"When they'll try to perform this ritual. This crossing."

"Yes. Using representatives of each bloodline as focal points, with the strongest—Alex—as the primary vessel." Caleb's expression darkened. "If they succeed, the barrier between worlds will be permanently weakened, allowing entities that have been trapped on the other side for millennia to cross over, to take form in our reality."

"Using us as what, hosts? Bodies?" Maya frowned. "Why do they need specific bloodlines? Why not just anyone?"

"Compatibility," Rivera interjected from his position by the door. "The entities can't maintain coherent form in our dimension without a suitable vessel. The bloodlines have been cultivated over generations to provide that compatibility."

"Cultivated," Maya repeated, distaste evident in her voice. "Like crops."

"More like specialized biological material," Caleb corrected. "The bloodlines possess unique neurological and genetic traits that allow perception across the threshold. Those same traits make them ideal vessels for extended occupation."

"And the Threshold cult has been breeding us for this purpose?" Maya's voice rose with indignation. "For generations?"

"Not exactly breeding," Caleb clarified. "More monitoring. Tracking. Occasionally intervening to ensure bloodline continuation while eliminating those who might pose a threat to their plans."

"Like my grandmother. Like Alex's mother."

"Yes." Caleb's voice held old grief. "Victoria and Catherine were not only powerful Watchers but actively working against the Threshold's goals. They had to be removed before they could train the next generation. Before they could warn their children what was coming."

Maya was quiet for a moment, processing. Then she straightened, a new determination in her posture. "Alright. Say I agree to help you. What exactly would that involve?"

Rivera stepped forward. "Intelligence gathering, primarily. The Threshold doesn't know we've made contact with you. You're still just a potential recruit from their perspective. That gives us an opportunity to place someone inside their organization. Someone who can help us identify which bloodlines they've already secured and what specifically they're planning for the equinox ritual."

"You want me to be a spy," Maya said flatly.

"We want to offer you the chance to fight back," Alex corrected, echoing his words from the coffee shop. "But only if you choose to. You can walk away right now, and we'll still help you understand your abilities, protect yourself."

"Walk away to what?" Maya asked, a bitter edge to her laugh. "They've found me. They're watching me. There's a face behind my face in the mirror." She shook her head. "There's no walking away from this, is there? Not really."

The question hung in the air, uncomfortable in its accuracy. None of them, not Alex, not Rivera, not even Caleb with his centuries of experience, could honestly promise safety or escape from what was coming.

"No," Caleb admitted finally. "But there are degrees of engagement. Ways to minimize risk while maximizing protection."

"And my way in is through this 'threshold sensitivity,'" Maya said. "These abilities I supposedly have but can barely control."

"The bracelet will help with that," Caleb assured her. "As will training. Even a few days of focused practice can make a significant difference in your control and understanding."

Maya was quiet again, weighing options that all carried significant risk. When she spoke, her voice was steady with newfound resolve.

"I want to know what happened to my grandmother," she said. "I want to understand what I am, what I can do. And I want to stop these people from doing to others what they did to her." She lifted her chin slightly. "I'll help you. But I need to know exactly what I'm getting into. No half-truths, no 'need-to-know' limitations."

"Full disclosure," Alex agreed before Rivera could object. "Everything we know, you know."

Rivera didn't look entirely comfortable with

this arrangement, but he nodded reluctantly. "Agreed. But we need to move quickly. The Threshold is accelerating their timetable. According to my sources inside, they've already secured representatives from four bloodlines—Bishop, Nazari, Okafor, and LaChance."

"Which leaves three," Caleb concluded. "Morgan, Weber, and Chin. The most powerful and the most elusive."

"And their plan is to what? Capture us? Convert us? Kill us?" Maya asked.

"Conversion is preferred," Rivera explained. "Voluntary vessels are more stable, more suitable for long-term occupation. But, if necessary, they'll use coercion or worse. They need the bloodlines represented in the ritual, willing or not."

Maya absorbed this grim assessment, her expression hardening rather than crumpling. Alex found himself impressed by her resilience, her ability to process cosmic horror without retreating into denial or hysteria.

"So what's our next move?" she asked.

"Training first," Caleb replied. "For both of you. Then we create a credible scenario for the Threshold to 'discover' you, A vulnerable Weber seeking answers, ripe for recruitment."

"Meanwhile," Rivera added, "we continue gathering intelligence on the other bloodlines. The Chin family has been particularly difficult to track. If we can locate and warn them before the

Threshold does, we gain another potential ally."

Alex nodded, but a thread of unease wound through him. Everything seemed to be moving too quickly, pieces falling into place with suspicious ease. Maya's immediate acceptance of her role. Rivera's convenient intelligence from inside the Threshold. The accelerated timetable pushing them toward confrontation.

It felt less like crafting a counter strategy and more like being maneuvered into predetermined positions. Like players in a game whose rules they only partially understood.

"Before we go any further," he said, "I want to try something." He turned to Maya. "You mentioned your grandmother's bracelet was for protection. I'd like to see exactly what that means. What it can do."

Maya extended her wrist, the silver bracelet catching the light. "How?"

"The same way I've been learning to use my mother's locket," Alex replied, drawing the necklace from his pocket. "Through direct connection with the threshold. Each bloodline has different abilities, different ways of perceiving. I'm curious what yours might be."

Caleb nodded approvingly. "An excellent suggestion. The Weber bloodline traditionally manifests differently than the Morgans. Where Morgans can see through the threshold, Webers often connect more deeply with memory and impressions left on objects and places."

"Psychometry," Maya said, recognition flashing in her eyes. "In my research on death rituals, I kept encountering accounts of individuals who could 'read' the history of sacred objects, perceive events that had occurred around funerary sites. Academic literature dismisses it as superstition or fraud, but..."

"But you've experienced something similar," Alex guessed. "Impressions from objects. Flashes of memory that aren't yours."

Maya nodded slowly. "In museums. Working with artifacts for my dissertation. Sometimes I'd touch something and just know things about it that weren't in any catalog or documentation. I assumed it was my subconscious making connections from research I'd forgotten."

"It wasn't," Caleb said. "It was threshold sensitivity manifesting in the way typical of your bloodline. Victoria had the same ability, extraordinarily useful in our work tracking Threshold cult activities."

"How do I control it?" Maya asked. "Make it happen intentionally rather than randomly?"

"The bracelet is key," Caleb explained. "Like Alex's locket, it serves as a focus, a way to channel perception consciously rather than passively. But there's another element that might accelerate your understanding."

He moved to a cabinet against the far wall, removing a small wooden box inlaid with mother-of-pearl. From it, he extracted a cloth-wrapped bundle which he placed carefully on the central table.

"This belonged to your grandmother," he said, unwrapping the cloth to reveal a small silver hand mirror, its handle and frame decorated with the same interlocking threshold symbols as Maya's bracelet. "A focus specifically designed for her particular manifestation of the sight."

Maya reached for it hesitantly, then paused. "The face in my mirror," she said. "What if?"

"This is different," Caleb assured her. "This mirror was created by Victoria herself, imbued with her essence, her protection. It's a tool for controlled perception, not a window for hostile entities."

Still tentative, Maya accepted the mirror. The moment her fingers closed around the handle, she gasped, her eyes widening.

"I can feel her," she whispered. "My grandmother. It's like... like she's right here, watching through my eyes."

"Not just a tool but a connection," Caleb explained. "Victoria, like Catherine, prepared for the possibility that she might not survive to train the next generation. She left pieces of herself behind. Knowledge, power, protection embedded in objects meant to find their way to her descendants."

Maya stared into the mirror's reflective surface, but whatever she saw there was clearly not her own face. Tears welled in her eyes, though her expression was one of wonder rather than grief.

"She knew," Maya said softly. "She knew what was coming for her. What might come for me someday. She's been waiting all this time for me to find this, to understand."

Alex recognized the expression on her face. The same overwhelming mixture of revelation and loss he'd felt upon learning the truth about his own mother, about the heritage that had been hidden from him.

"What do you see?" he asked gently.

"Not see, exactly. Feel. Remember." Maya's voice was distant, as if she was simultaneously present in the room and somewhere else entirely. "Memories that aren't mine. A lake house. Two women working together over books like these. Planning something important. Urgent."

Alex and Caleb exchanged a startled glance.

"The summer of 1989," Caleb said. "Catherine and Victoria at the Morgan lake house, preparing countermeasures against the Threshold's plans. The last time they worked together before..."

"Before they were taken," Maya finished, her eyes still fixed on the mirror. "I can see it so clearly. Feel it. They knew something was coming. Something big. The Threshold was mobilizing, preparing for a crossing attempt." Her brow furrowed. "But the stars weren't right. The alignment wasn't perfect. They'd have to wait..."

"Thirty-six years," Caleb supplied. "Until the next perfect celestial alignment coincided with the equinox. Until now."

"They were creating protections," Maya continued, her voice taking on a cadence not entirely her own. "Not just for themselves but for their children. For the next generation that would have to face the crossing." She looked up suddenly, her gaze finding Alex with uncanny precision. "For you specifically. The last Morgan. The key."

A chill ran through Alex at these words. The key. The same term Dr. Marsh had used in his vision at Threshold Wellness. The centerpiece of their ritual.

"What else?" he urged. "What were they protecting against, specifically?"

Maya's focus returned to the mirror, her expression growing troubled. "Something ancient. Something patient. Something that had tried before and failed, but never stopped watching, waiting for another chance." Her voice dropped to nearly a whisper. "A name. They kept referring to a name, but it's not clear. Something like... Mara? No, Marsh. Dr. Marsh."

"That's impossible," Rivera interjected sharply. "Dr. Evelyn Marsh didn't emerge as the Threshold's leader until 2010. She wouldn't have been on Catherine and Victoria's radar in 1989."

"Unless," Caleb said slowly, "Dr. Marsh isn't

a person at all, but a vessel. A name used by whatever entity has been orchestrating the Threshold's activities across generations."

The implication settled heavily over the room. Not a cult leader but something older, something patient enough to work across human lifespans, wearing different faces while maintaining the same purpose.

"There's more," Maya said, her voice strengthening. "Something specific about the ritual. About why they need the bloodlines. It's not just about opening a door. It's about... reshaping what comes through. Directing it. Controlling the crossing."

"The bloodlines aren't just keys," Alex surmised, pieces falling into place. "They're components of a machine. A mechanism designed to not just allow crossing but to shape how it happens, what emerges."

"Yes," Maya confirmed, the word drawn out as she processed the impressions flowing through her. "And the Morgan bloodline is the control valve. The regulator. The part that determines whether the flow is a trickle or a flood."

Alex felt the weight of this revelation pressing down on him. Not just a target, not just a vessel, but the linchpin of the entire mechanism. The piece that, properly manipulated, could maximize the breach or seal it entirely.

"That's why they want me specifically," he

said. "Not just as a vessel but as a tool. The final component that makes their plan work."

"And why your mother worked so hard to hide you from them," Caleb added. "Catherine understood what your bloodline represented. Why it had to be protected at all costs."

Maya lowered the mirror, the connection seemingly broken. She looked exhausted but exhilarated, as if she'd run a great distance and emerged stronger for it.

"That was... incredible," she breathed. "I could feel her—not just memories but her presence, her knowledge flowing into me. Is that normal?"

"For first contact with a properly attuned focus, yes," Caleb replied. "Victoria embedded a portion of her consciousness in the mirror, just as Catherine did with the locket. A way to transmit knowledge directly, bypassing conventional learning."

"So I didn't imagine it," Maya said. "She really was... is... there, somehow."

"Not there in the sense of a ghost or spirit," Caleb clarified. "More like an echo, an impression preserved in silver and intent. The essence of her knowledge and purpose, waiting for the right person to access it."

Maya turned the mirror over in her hands, examining the intricate threshold symbols engraved in its frame. "And with practice, I can use this to access memories from other objects? See impressions left behind?"

"Exactly," Caleb confirmed. "The Weber bloodline's particular sensitivity to memory and history, channeled through a proper focus, becomes a powerful tool for investigation and understanding."

"Which could be invaluable in our current situation," Rivera pointed out. "Particularly if we can get you access to objects connected to the Threshold's activities."

A plan was taking shape, roles defined by bloodline abilities and tactical necessity. Maya would use her newly discovered skills to gather intelligence from within the Threshold. Alex would continue developing his abilities to manipulate the threshold itself. Rivera would coordinate from the outside, maintaining his cover as long as possible. And Caleb would prepare the countermeasures necessary to disrupt the equinox ritual.

Yet as they discussed strategy and timetables, Alex couldn't shake his earlier sense of unease. The pieces were falling into place too neatly, the revelations too convenient, the plan too straightforward for something involving cosmic forces and ancient entities.

"There's something we're missing," he said suddenly, interrupting Rivera's outline of security protocols. "Something obvious that we're not seeing."

"Like what?" Rivera asked, frowning.

"I don't know exactly. But this feels..." Alex

struggled to articulate the sensation. "It feels like we're being maneuvered. Like we're making exactly the moves someone else wants us to make."

"Paranoia is a natural response to learning about forces beyond human comprehension," Caleb said, though without dismissal in his tone. "But your instincts are worth considering. What specifically concerns you?"

Alex paced the confines of the underground library, trying to pin down the source of his discomfort. "Everything's happening too fast. Maya accepts her role immediately. The memories in the mirror conveniently provide exactly the information we need. Rivera has perfectly placed sources inside the Threshold. It's all just... too clean. Too easy."

"Easy?" Maya echoed incredulously. "Finding out I'm being hunted by an ancient cult because of my bloodline, that the face in my mirror was something from another dimension evaluating me as a potential vessel? That's your definition of easy?"

"Not the revelations themselves," Alex clarified. "The way they're unfolding. The timing. The connections." He stopped pacing, a new thought striking him. "Eliza Bishop. It all started with her death. With Katherine hiring me to investigate a murder she herself had orchestrated."

"A setup," Rivera agreed. "We already

established that. Katherine was working for the Threshold, using the investigation to identify and observe you."

"Yes, but why that specific approach? Why not just abduct me? Or recruit me directly like they plan to do with Maya?" Alex shook his head. "They wanted me to find Caleb. To learn about my abilities. To start training. Why?"

The question hung in the air, uncomfortable in its implications.

"Because untrained threshold sensitivity is useless to them," Caleb said slowly, understanding dawning. "A Morgan who doesn't understand his abilities, who can't consciously access and direct them, is just another human. They needed you aware. Awakened."

"A weapon must be forged before it can be wielded," Rivera muttered, the idiom taking on new, disturbing significance.

"So everything—Katherine hiring me, the clues leading to Caleb, even the Hunter in my apartment—it was all designed to push me toward exactly this point," Alex concluded. "Toward understanding and controlling what I am."

"Which means they're still several steps ahead of us," Rivera said grimly. "Anticipating our moves because they're the ones creating the conditions that shape those moves."

The realization settled over the room like a physical weight. Their plan to infiltrate the Threshold, to disrupt the equinox ritual, suddenly seemed hopelessly naïve. Not a counter strategy at all, but the next predetermined step in a game whose rules they were only beginning to understand.

"So, what do we do?" Maya asked, voicing the question they were all thinking. "If they're manipulating us at this level, how do we fight back?"

"We change the game," Alex said, the answer coming to him with unexpected clarity. "We do something they won't anticipate because it doesn't fit their understanding of who we are, what motivates us."

"Such as?" Rivera asked skeptically.

Alex turned to Caleb. "You said the Morgan bloodline can reshape the threshold, not just perceive it. That with proper focus and training, I could potentially alter the membrane between worlds."

"Theoretically, yes," Caleb confirmed. "Though such manipulation requires extraordinary concentration and power. Catherine could do it to a limited degree. Your potential is greater, but you're only beginning to understand your abilities."

"What if we don't wait for the equinox?" Alex proposed. "What if instead of trying to stop their ritual, we perform our own? Something to strengthen the threshold rather than weaken it?"

"A pre-emptive strike," Rivera said,

considering the idea. "Reinforcing the barrier before they have a chance to breach it."

"It would require tremendous power," Caleb warned. "Far more than you currently command. And without the proper celestial alignment, the effect might be temporary at best."

"But it would disrupt their timetable," Alex insisted. "Force them to adapt rather than continue manipulating us. Buy us time to develop a more comprehensive counter strategy."

Caleb was quiet for a moment, weighing possibilities. "There is a way," he said finally. "A ritual Catherine and Victoria were developing before they were taken. A method to temporarily strengthen the threshold using the combined power of multiple bloodlines working in concert."

"We have two bloodlines right here," Alex said, gesturing between himself and Maya. "Morgan and Weber. Is that enough?"

"Barely," Caleb replied. "And it would require accessing a nexus point. A location where the threshold naturally thins, where the barrier between worlds is already permeable. The effect would be focused on that specific weak point rather than the threshold as a whole."

"Still better than nothing," Rivera pointed out. "And if we choose the nexus point the Threshold is most likely planning to use for their ritual, we could potentially disrupt their preparations."

"The lake house," Maya said suddenly. "The one from my vision. Where my grandmother and Alex's mother worked together. That's a nexus point, isn't it? That's why they chose it."

Caleb nodded slowly. "Yes. The Morgan family property was built on one of the strongest nexus points in New England. The lake itself is part of it. A natural thinning in the barrier that the house was designed to monitor and protect."

"And it's where they developed their countermeasures," Alex added, the pieces connecting. "Where my mother and Maya's grandmother created the locket and bracelet. There must be something there, notes, tools, something that could help us."

"Possibly," Caleb conceded. "Though the property has been abandoned for decades. After Catherine's death, Joseph Morgan wanted nothing to do with it. The Threshold likely monitored it for a time, but eventually would have concluded there was nothing of value remaining."

"Which makes it perfect for our purposes," Rivera said, warming to the plan. "An unexpected move to a location they've written off. If there's any chance the countermeasures Catherine and Victoria were developing still exist, it's worth investigating."

The sense of unease that had plagued Alex began to recede, replaced by cautious optimism. This wasn't part of anyone's script. Not the Threshold's, not even Caleb's. A genuine deviation, an authentic choice rather than a predetermined move.

"How far is this lake house?" he asked.

"About three hours north," Caleb replied. "In rural New Hampshire. Isolated, difficult to access without specific directions." He moved to a filing cabinet and extracted a folded map, yellowed with age. "I haven't been there since 1989. The last time I saw Catherine and Victoria alive."

The weight of history, of loss, was evident in his voice. This wasn't just a tactical decision but a return to the scene of profound personal tragedy.

"If we leave now, we can be there by nightfall," Rivera calculated. "Minimal preparation, minimal digital footprint. No chance for them to anticipate the move."

"I'll need to gather some items," Caleb said. "Focusing tools, protective measures. The nexus point will be active even without deliberate manipulation. Dangerous to the unprepared."

As they quickly assembled what they needed for the journey, Alex found Maya studying her grandmother's mirror again, her expression troubled.

"Second thoughts?" he asked quietly.

"Not exactly," she replied. "Just... processing. Yesterday I was a graduate student worried about my dissertation deadline and whether I was having stress-induced hallucinations. Today I'm preparing to perform a supernatural ritual using abilities I barely understand to stop interdimensional entities from possessing me because of my bloodline." She laughed softly, though there was little humor in it. "It's a lot."

"I know," Alex said, thinking of his own rapid transition from skeptical PI to reluctant guardian of the threshold. "For what it's worth, you're handling it better than I did."

"I doubt that," Maya replied. "But thanks for the vote of confidence."

"We're ready," Rivera called from the staircase leading up to the main floor of the brownstone. "Vehicle's secure, route mapped. No digital devices, no credit cards. Ghost protocol."

As they prepared to leave the relative safety of Caleb's underground library, Alex felt the weight of his mother's locket against his chest where he now wore it. Not just a keepsake but a tool, a weapon, a connection to a heritage he was only beginning to understand.

And somewhere in the city, Dr. Evelyn Marsh, or whatever ancient entity wore that name like a mask, was orchestrating the next phase of a plan millennia in the making. Watching, waiting, anticipating their every move.

Except, Alex hoped, this one.

At Threshold Wellness, Katherine Bishop entered Dr. Marsh's private office without knocking. The room was dark except for a single lamp that cast more shadows than illumination. Dr. Marsh stood with her back to the door, gazing out the window at Boston's evening skyline.

"They're moving," Katherine reported. "All four of them. The Morgan, the Weber girl, Rivera, and the old man."

"Where?" Dr. Marsh asked, her layered voice betraying no surprise at this development.

"Unknown. They disabled their phones, withdrew cash, took precautions against surveillance." Katherine's tone held grudging respect. "Rivera knows ghost protocols. They're trying to disappear."

"Interesting," Dr. Marsh murmured. "Sooner than expected. The Morgan must have sensed something amiss in our carefully constructed scenario."

"Should we be concerned? This deviation wasn't in our projections."

Dr. Marsh turned from the window, her face shifting subtly in the half-light, human features momentarily replaced by something older, stranger.

"On the contrary," she said, a smile revealing too many teeth. "It's perfect. The final test. Proof that he's exactly what we need him to be."

"And if they succeed in whatever they're planning?"

"Irrelevant. Any action they take now only serves to strengthen his connection to the threshold, to awaken his abilities more fully." Dr.

Marsh's eyes gleamed with an unnatural light. "The more he resists, the more perfectly he forges himself into the key we require."

Katherine nodded, accepting this assessment. "And the Weber girl? Should we track her as well?"

"Unnecessary. The mirror has done its work. Victoria's little time capsule of memory and knowledge, diligently preserved all these years. So thoughtful of her to prepare her granddaughter so thoroughly for us." Dr. Marsh's smile widened. "Let them run. Let them hide. Let them believe they've escaped our influence."

She turned back to the window, to the city spread out below like a circuit board of lights and movement, each element connected in ways invisible to ordinary perception.

"The threshold thins regardless of their actions," she said. "The crossing approaches. And the Morgan forges himself into our perfect instrument with every decision he believes is his own."

In the darkened glass of the window, Dr. Marsh's reflection rippled and changed, revealing for an instant what truly gazed out at the human world. Something ancient and patient that had worn many faces across millennia while waiting for this specific alignment, this perfect moment.

This final Morgan, unaware that his every act of resistance only brought him closer to his destined role in the crossing to come.

CHAPTER 11

Some places remember what happened within their walls. Not metaphorically, but literally. Events soaked into wood and stone like blood into cloth, waiting for the right person to come along and read the stains.

The Morgan lake house emerged from the darkness as Rivera's headlights swept across its weathered facade. After three hours of driving along increasingly isolated roads, the final mile on a rutted dirt track barely wide enough for the car, they had reached their destination. And it was not what Alex had expected.

Rather than the rustic cabin he'd imagined, the structure before them was a sprawling Victorian, three stories of gabled roofs and wraparound porches, its white paint gone gray with neglect, its windows dark and shuttered. In the moonlight, it loomed against the night sky like something out of a gothic novel, beautiful and forbidding.

"Home sweet home," Alex murmured, staring at the ancestral property he'd never known existed until today.

"The Morgan estate," Caleb confirmed, his voice heavy with memory. "Built in 1871 by Ezekiel Morgan after he discovered the threshold nexus in the lake. Seven generations of Watchers lived and worked here until your mother's death."

They exited the car, the night air sharp with the scent of pine and lake water. Behind the house, just visible through the trees, the moonlight caught on the still surface of water, black and depthless in the darkness.

"That's where it happened, isn't it?" Alex asked quietly. "Where I almost drowned."

Caleb nodded. "The lake is the nexus point. The place where the threshold naturally thins. You fell through ice that shouldn't have broken, given the temperature. Your mother always believed something pulled you under."

A chill that had nothing to do with the night air ran through Alex. The drowning dreams that had haunted him for decades suddenly felt less like nightmares and more like memories struggling to surface.

"Something wanted me even then," he said.

"Or was testing you," Caleb replied. "Threshold nexus points attract entities from the other side. Some merely observe. Others interfere."

Alex watched Rivera survey the property with professional wariness, his hand resting near the service weapon holstered beneath his jacket. "Place looks abandoned. No signs of monitoring equipment or recent activity."

"The Threshold would have searched it thoroughly after Catherine's death," Caleb confirmed. "Found nothing of value and moved on. They never understood the true purpose of this place."

"Which is what, exactly?" Maya asked, clutching her grandmother's mirror close to her chest, a talisman against the darkness.

"Observation. Protection. And when necessary, intervention." Caleb moved toward the front steps, his mismatched eyes reflecting the moonlight oddly. "The house itself is a tool. Designed to monitor the threshold, to strengthen it when needed, to allow controlled access under specific conditions."

"A machine disguised as a house," Alex surmised.

"More an instrument than a machine. Like a massive focusing lens built to channel and direct threshold energy." Caleb reached the front door and removed a key from his pocket, ancient iron, ornately crafted. "Your mother gave me this the last time I saw her. Just in case, she said."

The lock turned with surprising ease for something unused for decades. The door swung open on well-oiled hinges, revealing darkness beyond.

"Someone's been maintaining it," Rivera observed, instantly alert. "Recently."

"Not someone," Caleb corrected. "Something. The house maintains itself, after a fashion. Part of its design."

They stepped into a grand foyer, their flashlight beams revealing high ceilings, a sweeping staircase, and furniture draped with white sheets like patient ghosts. Despite thirty years of abandonment, there was no dust, no cobwebs, no signs of decay or animal intrusion. The air smelled faintly of lemon oil and lavender, as if the house had been cleaned that morning.

"This is impossible," Maya whispered, running a finger along a banister that should have been thick with decades of grime but was instead smooth and polished.

"Threshold physics," Caleb explained. "The house exists partially outside conventional time. A preservation effect, strongest near nexus points."

The explanation did little to diminish the uncanniness of the perfectly maintained, abandoned mansion. They moved deeper into the house, flashlights revealing a formal dining room, a library, a music room with a draped piano, all beneath their immaculate protective sheets.

"Where do we start?" Alex asked, overwhelmed by the size of the place and the strange sense that it was somehow watching them, aware of their presence.

"The study," Caleb replied. "Catherine's

workshop. If there's anything left that could help us, it would be there."

He led them down a corridor to a door that, unlike the others they'd passed, was locked. This time, Caleb had no key.

"Only a Morgan could enter," he explained. "Blood recognition. Old magic, but effective."

Alex stared at the ornate brass doorknob, which featured the now-familiar threshold symbol at its center. "What am I supposed to do? Bleed on it?"

"Essentially, yes," Caleb confirmed without a trace of irony. "Place your palm against the symbol. It will do the rest."

Somewhat skeptically, Alex pressed his hand against the cold metal doorknob. For a moment, nothing happened. Then he felt it. A sharp sting in his palm, as if dozens of tiny needles had suddenly pricked his skin. He instinctively tried to pull away, but his hand seemed temporarily fused to the metal.

Just as quickly as it had begun, the sensation stopped. Alex withdrew his hand to find a pattern of pinpricks across his palm, already beading with blood in the shape of the threshold symbol.

"Jesus," he muttered.

The lock clicked, and the door swung open.

Beyond lay a room unlike any other in the house. A circular chamber that logic insisted couldn't possibly fit within the squareness of the architecture they'd observed from outside. The ceiling soared upward into a dome, its surface painted with astronomical charts and threshold symbols. The walls were lined with bookshelves interspersed with glass-fronted cabinets containing objects Alex couldn't identify at a glance.

But it was the center of the room that immediately drew their attention. There, a large circular table of dark wood dominated the space. Embedded in its surface was an elaborate model, part astronomical orrery, part topographical map, showing what appeared to be the lake and surrounding countryside in miniature, with metallic lines representing energies or currents invisible to the naked eye.

"The Focus," Caleb breathed, approaching the table with evident reverence. "Catherine's masterwork. A three-dimensional representation of the threshold nexus and its connection to celestial alignments."

Alex followed, drawn to the intricate model as if it exerted a physical pull. At the center of the lake representation was a small silver disk that seemed to pulse with subtle light when he came near.

"What's this?" he asked, pointing without touching.

"The nexus itself," Caleb replied. "The thinnest point in the barrier between worlds.

Where you nearly drowned as a child."

Alex shivered involuntarily, remembering the cold dark water of his recurring nightmares, the sense of something waiting in the depths.

Maya had moved to one of the glass cabinets, her flashlight illuminating objects within— silver implements, crystals, what appeared to be ritual tools. "This was a working space," she observed. "Not just for study but for practical application."

"Yes," Caleb confirmed. "Catherine and Victoria spent months here, developing countermeasures against the Threshold's plans. This room was where they did their most important work."

Rivera, ever the pragmatist, was checking the room's security. The single entrance, the shuttered windows, the general layout. "No other exits," he noted. "Defensible, but also a potential trap if we're discovered."

"The study has its own protections," Caleb assured him. "More effective than conventional security."

While the others explored the circular room, Alex found himself drawn to a small writing desk positioned near one of the shuttered windows. Unlike the other furniture in the house, it wasn't draped with a protective sheet. On its surface lay a leather-bound journal, open as if its owner had just stepped away momentarily and would return at any moment to continue writing.

The page displayed handwriting he recognized from his mother's other journal, the same tight, elegant script documenting observations and theories. But the content of this entry made his blood run cold.

April 16, 1990 – They've found us. Despite everything, despite all our precautions, they've tracked us to the lake house. V. believes we still have time to complete the countermeasure, but I'm not certain. The signs are unmistakable; threshold thinning beyond normal parameters, spectral activity increasing exponentially, the dreams becoming more vivid, more directed.

Alex dreamed of drowning again last night, the third time this week. He speaks of voices in the water calling his name. They're reaching for him specifically, using the nexus to bypass our protections. We cannot remain here much longer.

If we fail to complete the work, this record must survive. The sealing ritual requires three elements: the blood of a Morgan freely given; the focused will of a Weber to direct it; and a sacrifice to power it. V. and I have prepared ourselves for the latter requirement. One life to save countless others. A fair exchange.

Joseph refuses to accept what's coming. He loves Alex too much to imagine giving him up, even temporarily. But there is no other way. The Morgan bloodline is both lock and key. Only Alex can complete what we've begun. When he's ready. When he returns.

If you're reading this, my son, know that everything was for you. Not to burden you with an unwanted legacy, but to preserve your choice. Your freedom to decide. The locket contains what remains of me. Use it wisely. Trust Caleb. Find Victoria's granddaughter. Complete our work.

They're coming now. I can feel them at the perimeter. No more time

The journal ended there, the final words trailing off as if the writer had been interrupted mid-thought. April 16, 1990—the day before his father had recorded his mother's death in the other journal. The day everything changed.

"She knew," Alex said aloud, drawing the others' attention. "She knew they were coming for her. For us."

Caleb moved to his side, reading the journal entry over his shoulder. His expression darkened with old grief.

"Catherine always had a gift for seeing what approached," he said quietly. "Even when the rest of us were blind to the signs."

"She mentions a sealing ritual," Alex continued, focusing on the practical aspects to keep his emotions in check. "Something she and Victoria Weber were developing. A way to strengthen the threshold permanently."

"Yes," Caleb confirmed. "Their final project.

They believed they had found a method to not just temporarily reinforce the threshold but to fundamentally alter its structure. To make breaches nearly impossible for generations to come."

"But they never completed it," Rivera said, joining them at the desk. "They ran out of time."

"They were interrupted," Caleb corrected. "By what, I never knew for certain. By the time I reached the lake house, they were gone. The study sealed. No signs of struggle, yet no trace of either woman."

Maya approached last, her grandmother's mirror clutched in her hands. "My grandmother disappeared the same way," she said. "Just... gone one day. Her body ever found."

"Because what took them wasn't interested in their physical forms," Caleb said grimly. "Only in removing them as obstacles."

"Dr. Marsh," Alex said, remembering Maya's vision from the mirror. "Or whatever wears that name now."

"Most likely," Caleb agreed. "Though in 1990, it would have been wearing a different face, using a different identity."

Alex returned his attention to his mother's final journal entry, focusing on the requirements for the ritual she'd described. "Blood of a Morgan freely given. Focused will of a Weber. And a sacrifice." He looked up at Caleb. "What kind of sacrifice?"

"Life energy," Caleb replied quietly. "A soul, essentially, volunteered rather than taken. The ultimate offering to power a working of that magnitude."

"That's what she meant," Alex realized. "'V. and I have prepared ourselves for the latter requirement. One life to save countless others.'" He felt a cold certainty settle in his gut. "One of them planned to die to make the ritual work."

"Both, actually," Caleb corrected, his voice heavy with memory. "They argued about which of them it would be, each insisting it should be herself rather than her friend. In the end, they agreed to let circumstance decide, if it came to that."

"But they never got the chance to complete the ritual," Maya said. "They were taken before they could implement it."

"Which means the theoretical framework may still exist," Rivera pointed out, ever practical. "The preparations, the method. Even if they didn't perform it, they would have documented it."

"The question is where," Alex said, scanning the circular room with dozens of cabinets and bookshelves. "This place is enormous, and we don't have much time."

"Perhaps Maya could help with that," Caleb suggested, nodding toward the silver mirror she still clutched. "Victoria Weber was deeply involved in developing the ritual. Her mirror might retain impressions, memories of where the documentation was stored."

Maya looked down at the antique looking glass, uncertainty crossing her features. "I'm not sure I can control it that precisely. Before, the memories just... flowed into me. I didn't direct them."

"Intent matters," Caleb said. "Focus on what you're seeking. The mirror responds to need as much as ability."

Still hesitant but willing to try, Maya held the mirror before her, staring into its reflective surface. Her expression shifted as she concentrated, eyebrows drawing together with effort.

"I'm trying to see her working here," she murmured. "To find where they kept their notes on the ritual."

For several long moments, nothing seemed to happen. Then Maya gasped, her eyes widening as the mirror's surface appeared to ripple like disturbed water, though no one else could see the effect.

"There," she whispered. "I can see them. Both of them, working at that table." She nodded toward the central orrery. "They're arguing about calculations, about alignments. Victoria keeps saying they need more time, that the stars aren't right. Catherine insists they won't get more time."

Maya turned slowly, the mirror guiding her

movements as she followed the path of a memory only she could perceive. She stopped before one of the glass-fronted cabinets, this one containing what appeared to be astronomical instruments and silver tools of various designs.

"This cabinet," she said with growing certainty. "There's a hidden compartment. Behind the back panel. That's where they hid the final documentation. In case they were discovered, in case they couldn't complete the work themselves."

Rivera stepped forward, examining the cabinet with a professional eye. "I don't see any obvious mechanism. No seam or latch that would indicate a false back."

"It wouldn't be obvious," Caleb said. "Catherine was meticulous about security."

Alex joined them at the cabinet, studying its contents through the glass front. Among the silver instruments and tools, something caught his eye, a small disk similar to his mother's locket, bearing the threshold symbol.

"There," he said, pointing. "That matches my mother's focus."

Caleb unlocked the cabinet with a key from the ring he carried, then stepped back. "Only Morgan blood will activate it," he explained. "Like the study door."

Understanding what was required, Alex reached for the silver disk. The moment his fingers touched it, he felt the same stinging sensation as before. Tiny needles sampling his blood, confirming his heritage. The back panel of the cabinet clicked and swung open on hidden hinges, revealing a narrow space behind.

Within lay a slender leather portfolio, sealed with a silver clasp in the shape of the threshold symbol. Alex carefully removed it and brought it to the central table, where they gathered around as he broke the seal.

Inside were papers covered in his mother's handwriting, interspersed with diagrams, astronomical calculations, and ritual instructions. The top sheet bore a title in bold lettering: THE SEALING WORKING – FINAL PROTOCOL.

"This is it," Alex breathed. "The ritual they were developing. The countermeasure against the Threshold's plans."

They pored over the documents, trying to make sense of the complex instructions and theoretical framework. Much of it employed specialized terminology Alex didn't recognize, but the general outline became clear as they read.

"It's a reversal," Caleb explained, his centuries of experience allowing him to interpret what the others could not. "While the Threshold seeks to weaken the barrier between worlds, to create permanent breaches, this ritual would do the opposite. Strengthen the membrane, make it resistant to manipulation for decades, perhaps centuries."

"Using the same components the Threshold needs for their ritual," Rivera observed. "Morgan blood, Weber will, and a soul-level sacrifice."

"Fighting fire with fire," Maya murmured. "Using their own methodology against them."

Alex focused on the practical aspects, the specific requirements. "It needs to be performed at the nexus point itself," he noted, pointing to a diagram that clearly showed the center of the lake. "During a specific astronomical alignment."

"The new moon," Caleb confirmed, checking the calculations. "Which is... tonight." He looked up, realization dawning. "Whether by coincidence or design, we've arrived at precisely the right moment."

"That's impossible," Rivera objected. "The odds against that kind of timing—"

"Are irrelevant when dealing with threshold mechanics," Caleb interrupted. "Time moves differently near nexus points. Synchronicity is common, expected even. Catherine and Victoria designed this to be discovered and implemented when the conditions were right."

"Regardless of how we got here, the question is: do we attempt this?" Alex asked, looking around at his unlikely allies. "The ritual requires blood, focus, and sacrifice. Are we prepared to provide those?"

"The blood is simple enough," Caleb said. "A Morgan freely offering it—that would be you, Alex."

"The focus is clearly Maya's role," Rivera added. "Using her grandmother's mirror and the Weber bloodline's particular affinity for direction and memory."

"But the sacrifice," Alex said, voicing what they were all thinking. "It calls for a life. A soul. Who exactly is volunteering for that part?"

A heavy silence fell over the group. The ritual promised a powerful countermeasure against the Threshold's plans, a way to protect the world from the crossing for generations to come. But the cost was steep. Prohibitively so.

"There may be an alternative," Caleb said finally, his voice tentative in a way Alex hadn't heard before. "Something neither Catherine nor Victoria had access to, but which I can provide."

"Which is what?" Rivera asked skeptically.

"My essence," Caleb replied simply. "What I am. Neither fully human nor fully Other, but something in between. A Guardian, existing simultaneously in multiple realities."

"You're saying you can be the sacrifice?" Alex clarified, troubled by the implication. "That you would die to power this ritual?"

"Not die, precisely," Caleb corrected. "Transform. Return to what I was before I chose this form, this role. Discorporate might be a more accurate term."

"You'd cease to exist in our reality," Maya surmised. "You'd be gone from this world."

"Yes," Caleb confirmed. "But my essence

would power the sealing working more effectively than a conventional human sacrifice. My nature as a Guardian makes me particularly suited to reinforcing the threshold."

The offer hung in the air, shocking in its self-sacrifice yet practical in its application. Caleb had lived for centuries, watched over the Morgan bloodline for generations. His willingness to end that vigil, to transform his existence into pure energy for the ritual, was both profound and terrifying.

"There has to be another way," Alex insisted, uncomfortable with the thought of losing the mentor who had guided him into understanding his heritage, his abilities.

"If there was, Catherine would have found it," Caleb replied gently. "She was the most brilliant threshold theorist I've ever known. If she determined a sacrifice was necessary, then it is."

"But—"

"This is why I exist, Alex," Caleb interrupted. "Why I chose this form, this role, all those centuries ago. To stand as the final guardian when needed. To make the sacrifice others cannot."

Before they could discuss it further, a sound broke the silence. The distant but unmistakable crunch of tires on gravel. Someone had arrived at the lake house.

Rivera moved immediately to the study's

single window, carefully parting the shutters to peer out without being seen. "Black SUV," he reported tersely. "Just pulled up at the main entrance. Can't see how many occupants from this angle."

"The Threshold," Alex said, certainty cold in his gut. "They followed us somehow."

"Or were waiting for us to lead them here," Rivera corrected grimly. "If they've been monitoring this place all along..."

"Irrelevant now," Caleb said decisively. "We don't have time to debate. The ritual must be performed immediately, while the astronomical alignment is correct. Minutes matter."

"How? They're between us and the lake," Maya pointed out.

"There's another way to the water," Caleb replied, moving to what appeared to be a solid section of bookshelf. He pressed a specific sequence of carved threshold symbols, and a hidden door swung open, revealing a narrow staircase descending into darkness. "Servants' access, originally. Leads to a boathouse at the water's edge."

From the front of the house came the sound of the main door opening, followed by footsteps in the entrance hall. Multiple sets, moving with purpose.

"Go," Rivera said, drawing his service weapon. "I'll hold them here as long as I can."

"James—" Alex began, but the detective cut

him off.

"This is what I signed up for," Rivera said firmly. "What I've been preparing for since I first infiltrated the Threshold. Just make it count."

There was no time for further argument. Alex, Maya, and Caleb gathered what they needed from the study; the ritual instructions, their respective focusing tools, and a small silver bowl for the blood component. As they slipped through the hidden door, Rivera took up position behind the study's heavy wooden desk, gun trained on the only entrance.

The narrow staircase wound downward, deeper than seemed possible given the house's visible structure. The air grew cooler, damper, with the distinctive scent of lake water growing stronger with each step. After what felt like hundreds of feet, they emerged into a small boathouse built directly over the water.

Moonlight filtered through gaps in the wooden walls, reflecting off the still surface of the lake visible through an open bay where a rowboat waited, moored to a small dock.

"Perfect timing," Caleb observed, checking the night sky visible through the open bay. "The new moon is at its apex. The alignment is optimal."

"What exactly do we do?" Alex asked, unfolding the ritual instructions on a workbench near the boat. "The technical details were clear enough, but the practical application..."

"We take the boat to the center of the lake, to the nexus point itself," Caleb explained, already climbing into the small craft. "There, we establish a triangle of power. Morgan blood as the catalyst, Weber will as the director, Guardian essence as the fuel. Together, they create a sealing effect that works from inside the threshold rather than outside it."

"Like repairing a dam from the water side rather than the air side," Maya suggested, helping Alex gather the remaining items they needed.

"Precisely," Caleb confirmed. "More effective, more lasting, but requiring direct contact with the threshold itself."

The sound of gunshots echoed from the house above. One, two, three in rapid succession. Rivera, engaging the intruders. Buying them time with his life, possibly.

"We need to hurry," Alex said, helping Maya into the boat before joining her. "How far to the nexus point?"

"About two hundred yards," Caleb replied, taking up the oars with surprising strength for his apparent age. "The exact center of the lake. You'll know it when we reach it."

They pushed off from the small dock, gliding silently across the mirror-smooth surface of the lake. Despite the urgency of their situation, there was something eerily beautiful about the scene.

The star-filled sky above, the perfect reflection below, the sense of suspension between worlds.

As they approached the center of the lake, Alex began to feel it. A subtle vibration in the air, a pressure in his ears similar to what he'd experienced at threshold thinning points before, but stronger, more insistent. The water around them seemed to darken, not with physical shadow but with depth beyond physical understanding.

"Here," Caleb said, shipping the oars as they drifted to a stop at what appeared to be the exact center of the lake. "The nexus point. The threshold is thinnest here, barely a membrane rather than a barrier."

Looking down into the water, Alex could almost see it. Not with his physical eyes but with the threshold sight he'd been developing. A place where reality itself seemed stretched to transparency, where what lay beyond was separated by the merest film of existence.

And beneath that film, something watched. Something waited. Something that had been watching and waiting for a very long time.

"I know this place," Alex said quietly, memories surfacing from decades of nightmares. "This is where I fell through the ice. Where I drowned."

"Where you died, briefly," Caleb corrected. "Six minutes without pulse or respiration before your mother pulled you back. Six minutes on the other side, seen by what waits there. Marked by it."

"I remember," Alex whispered, the suppressed memory finally breaking through. "There was something in the water. Something with eyes. So many eyes. It spoke to me. Called my name."

"The Ancient that the Threshold serves," Caleb confirmed. "The entity that would use Dr. Marsh and the other vessels to anchor itself in our reality. It sensed your bloodline, your potential. It has been waiting for you specifically, Alex. For decades."

The knowledge should have been terrifying, but instead, Alex felt an odd calm settle over him. Understanding at last the nature of what had haunted him all his life. The shape of the enemy they faced.

"Let's begin," he said, looking up from the darkened water to his companions. "Before it's too late."

Following the ritual instructions, they arranged themselves in the small boat. Alex at the bow, Maya at the stern, Caleb between them. From his pocket, Alex removed a small silver knife that had been part of the tools they'd gathered from the study.

"Morgan blood freely given," he recited, drawing the blade across his palm where the doorknob had already marked him with the threshold symbol. Blood welled from the wound, dripping into the silver bowl he held. "Catalyst for change, lineage of watchers, guardians of the veil."

Maya raised her grandmother's mirror, holding it so that it reflected both the night sky and the dark water beneath their boat. "Weber will, focused, true," she continued the ritual words. "Direction and purpose, memory and intention, to guide what comes."

Caleb placed his gnarled hands on the gunwales of the boat, his mismatched eyes beginning to glow with an inner light that had nothing to do with the moon or stars. "Guardian essence freely offered," he completed the trinity. "Neither one world nor the other, but the bridge between, the balance maintained."

As their voices joined in the final invocation, the air around them seemed to thicken, to pulse with energy that existed just beyond ordinary perception. The water beneath the boat began to move, not with waves or current but with something else. A rippling of reality itself, as if the surface tension of existence was being manipulated.

Alex felt the change first in his blood, a warmth that spread from the wound in his palm up his arm and throughout his body. The threshold sight activated without conscious intention, showing him what was happening on levels beyond physical understanding.

The nexus point was responding to their

working, the thin spot in reality flexing, reshaping itself according to the pattern established by their combined energies. Morgan blood providing the blueprint, Weber will providing the direction, Guardian essence providing the power to manifest the change.

Above them, the stars seemed to shift, aligning in patterns that human astronomers had never cataloged. Below, the darkness of the lake became something else entirely, a window into a place that existed alongside but separate from their world, a realm of ancient intelligences and patient hunger.

And from that realm, something reached back. Something vast and cold and impossibly old, sensing the changes being wrought in its pathway to the human world.

Morgan, whispered a voice directly into Alex's mind, bypassing his ears entirely. *Last of the line. Keeper of the key. You cannot seal what is already opening.*

The voice was accompanied by a pressure—mental rather than physical—as the entity on the other side pushed against the working they had begun. Alex felt his concentration waver, his blood seeming to slow in his veins as the Ancient exerted its will against him.

"It's resisting," he gasped, clutching the silver bowl as if it were a lifeline. "It knows what we're attempting."

"Hold firm," Caleb instructed, his own voice

strained as his essence began to transform, his physical form becoming increasingly translucent as his energy fed the working. "Focus on the seal, on closing rather than opening. Your bloodline gives you that power specifically."

Maya's hands were steady on her grandmother's mirror, but her face had gone pale with effort. "Something's coming through," she warned. "Something's using the thinning to reach for us."

From the dark water below, tendrils of what appeared to be shadow but was something far more substantial began to rise. Probing extensions of an entity too vast to comprehend, searching for purchase in their reality. They coiled around the small boat, seeking entry, seeking vessels.

"Now, Caleb!" Alex shouted, feeling the working begin to falter under the Ancient's assault. "We need the final component!"

Caleb Morgan, or the being that had worn that name and form for centuries, nodded once, his mismatched eyes now blazing with power that had nothing to do with human limitation.

"Remember what I taught you," he said, his voice echoing strangely as his physical form began to dissolve into pure energy. "Remember why we fight. Remember that the threshold is not just a barrier but a balance."

With those final words, Caleb's form collapsed inward, transforming from solid matter to pure light in an instant. The energy that had been the Guardian surged through the working they had established, amplifying it exponentially, turning what had been a theoretical framework into physical reality.

The effect was immediate and overwhelming. The shadow tendrils recoiled, retreating into the depths as the nexus point began to close. Not with physical movement but with a restructuring of reality itself. The thin spot in the threshold thickened, solidified, becoming resistant to the pressure exerted from the other side.

NO! screamed the voice in Alex's mind, fury and frustration echoing across dimensions. *YOU CANNOT DENY ME! YOU ARE MINE! YOU HAVE ALWAYS BEEN MINE!*

"I belong to no one," Alex replied, speaking directly to the entity with a confidence he hadn't known he possessed. "Least of all to you."

The working reached its crescendo, power flowing through the triangle they had established, blood, will, and sacrifice united in common purpose. The nexus point sealed with a sound that wasn't a sound at all but a fundamental shift in the structure of reality itself.

And then, as suddenly as it had begun, it was over. The air returned to normal pressure. The water below became just water again, reflecting the night sky above. And where Caleb had been, there was only empty space, a absence that felt simultaneously like loss and like completion.

Maya lowered the mirror, her hands shaking with exhaustion. "Did it work?" she asked, her voice hoarse with effort. "Did we seal it?"

Alex could feel the difference in the threshold, the restructuring they had accomplished. "Yes," he confirmed, though the victory felt hollow in the wake of Caleb's sacrifice. "This nexus point is sealed. And if the theory is correct, the reinforcement will spread to other thin spots as well, strengthening the entire barrier."

They sat in silence for a moment, processing what they had accomplished and what it had cost. Caleb was gone—not dead in the conventional sense but transformed. Discorporate, his centuries of existence converted to pure energy to power their working.

"What now?" Maya asked finally. "The Threshold will still try to perform their ritual at the equinox. They have the other bloodlines. They'll find another nexus point."

"But not as powerful as this one," Alex replied. "And without a Morgan, their working will be fundamentally flawed. We've bought time, if nothing else. Time to prepare, to counter."

Maya nodded, accepting this assessment. Then her eyes widened as she looked past Alex toward the shore. "The house," she said. "It's on fire."

Alex turned to see orange flames illuminating the night, consuming the Morgan lake house with unnatural speed. Whether set deliberately by the Threshold agents or accidentally during their confrontation with Rivera, the result was the same—the ancestral home of the Morgan bloodline, with all its knowledge and history, was being destroyed.

"Rivera," Alex said, the detective's fate suddenly front and center in his mind. "He could still be alive."

They rowed back to shore with desperate speed, but even as they approached the boathouse, they could see it was too late. The fire had engulfed the entire structure, flames reaching high into the night sky, consuming wood and memory alike with insatiable hunger.

As they watched from the safety of the water, a section of the house collapsed inward with a sound like thunder. And with it collapsed any hope that Detective James Rivera might have survived the confrontation.

"I'm sorry," Maya said quietly, placing a hand on Alex's arm. "He died protecting us. Giving us time to complete the ritual."

"Like Caleb," Alex replied, grief and guilt warring in his chest. "Like my mother. Like your grandmother. How many more sacrifices does this war demand?"

Maya had no answer for that. None existed that could make sense of the cost, that could balance the ledger of lives given in secret battle against forces most of humanity would never know existed.

As the Morgan lake house burned against the night sky, Alex felt something fundamental shifting within him. The reluctant initiate was gone, replaced by something harder, more determined. The weight of legacy, of blood ties generations deep, settled onto his shoulders not as a burden now but as armor.

"Let's go," he said finally, turning away from the conflagration that was consuming generations of Morgan history. "There's nothing more we can do here."

They beached the small boat on the shore opposite from the burning house, then made their way through the woods toward the rural road beyond the property. The Threshold agents would be searching for them, but in the darkness and confusion, they had a chance to escape undetected.

"Where will we go?" Maya asked as they pushed through underbrush, her grandmother's mirror clutched protectively against her chest. "They'll be watching your apartment, my place. Caleb's safehouse might be compromised."

"We need to regroup," Alex replied, thinking through their limited options. "Assess what we've accomplished and what comes next. But first, we need transportation."

They emerged onto a narrow country road about a mile from the lake house. In the distance, they could hear sirens as local fire departments responded to the blaze. Soon the area would be crawling with emergency personnel, which could either help or hinder their escape.

"There," Maya said suddenly, pointing down the road where a pair of headlights had just rounded a bend. "Maybe we can flag them down, ask for help."

As the vehicle approached, an older model pickup truck driven by what appeared to be a local farmer, Alex made a split-second decision. They stepped into the road, waving their arms to attract attention.

The truck slowed, then stopped beside them. The driver, a weathered man in his sixties, rolled down his window, eyeing them suspiciously.

"You folks all right?" he asked. "You're a long way from anywhere out here."

"Car trouble," Alex lied smoothly. "Broke down a couple miles back. We were hoping to get a ride to the nearest town, maybe find a mechanic or a place to stay for the night."

The farmer studied them for a moment, then nodded toward the back of his truck. "Hop in the bed. I'm headed to Milton. That work for you?"

"Perfect," Alex said with genuine relief. "Thank you."

As they settled among hay bales in the

truck bed, the distant glow of the burning lake house was just visible through the trees. Alex felt a pang of loss, not just for the physical structure but for what it represented. Generations of Morgans had lived and worked there, maintaining their vigil over the threshold. Now it was gone, another casualty in a war most would never know existed.

"We sealed the nexus," Maya said quietly as the truck carried them away from the scene. "That matters. It would have been the focal point for their ritual at the equinox."

"But at what cost?" Alex replied, thinking of Caleb's sacrifice, of Rivera presumably dead in the burning house. "Two more lives. Two more names added to the list of those who died protecting a world that doesn't even know it's in danger."

Maya had no answer for that. They rode in silence for several miles, each lost in their own thoughts, processing what they had experienced and what it meant for the battles still to come.

The small town of Milton appeared on the horizon. A collection of modest buildings arranged around a main street, most dark at this late hour. The farmer dropped them at a 24-hour diner with peeling paint and flickering neon, the only establishment showing signs of life.

"Thanks again," Alex said, pressing some cash into the man's weathered hand despite his protests.

"You folks be careful," the farmer replied, studying them with sharper eyes than Alex had initially credited him with. "Strange things happen around that lake. Always have."

As he drove away, Alex wondered briefly if the local man had seen more than he let on. If living near a threshold nexus point had given him his own form of sensitivity to what existed beyond ordinary perception.

Inside the diner, they claimed a booth in the corner, away from windows and with clear sightlines to both entrances. The waitress —middle-aged and tired-eyed—brought coffee without being asked, then retreated to give them space.

"What's our next move?" Maya asked once they were alone. "The Threshold will regroup. Adjust their plans. We've disrupted their preferred method, but they'll have contingencies."

Alex nodded, thinking through the strategic implications of what they'd accomplished. "The sealing affected this nexus point directly, but according to the theory, it should strengthen the threshold as a whole. Make all breaches more difficult to create or maintain."

"Which buys us time," Maya concluded. "But doesn't end the threat."

"No," Alex agreed. "They still have four bloodlines secured; Bishop, Nazari, Okafor, and LaChance. They'll be hunting for the Chin family more aggressively now that we've removed the Morgan component from their equation."

"And they'll come after us with everything they have," Maya added grimly. "We've proved ourselves to be more than just potential vessels. We're active threats to their plans."

The weight of their situation settled heavily between them. Two people against an organization centuries old, with resources and reach beyond ordinary understanding. Without Caleb's guidance, without Rivera's inside information, their options were severely limited.

"We need allies," Alex said finally. "People who understand what we're facing. Who know about the threshold, the bloodlines, the Threshold's plans."

"Who? The authorities?" Maya's laugh was bitter. "Try explaining interdimensional entities and ancient bloodlines to the Boston PD and see how far that gets you."

"Not the authorities," Alex agreed. "But there must be others like us. People with threshold sensitivity who've been hiding, living under the radar. Caleb wasn't the only Guardian, surely."

"How do we find them? It's not like there's a support group for people who can see ghosts and perceive parallel dimensions."

"Actually," Alex said slowly, a memory surfacing from his initial research into Eliza Bishop's death, "there might be. Or something close to it."

He borrowed Maya's phone, his own long since abandoned as a security precaution. He searched for the website he vaguely remembered. After several attempts, he found it: The Threshold Experience, an online forum dedicated to "those who have glimpsed beyond the veil."

"This could be monitored by the Threshold cult," Maya warned, glancing at the site over his shoulder. "A recruiting tool."

"Almost certainly," Alex agreed. "But it's also our best chance to find others who might help us. We just need to be careful about how we approach it."

Using the diner's free Wi-Fi, Alex created a new account with an anonymous username. Then, drawing on his investigative experience, he crafted a message that would be meaningful to those with genuine threshold sensitivity while appearing as harmless speculation to anyone else:

Seeking others who have seen what waits at the lake's center. The Morgan property has fallen, but the water remembers. The Ancient is denied but not defeated. Seven bloodlines, three now hidden. If you understand, if you are Weber, Chin, or know of them, respond with "the mirror reflects both ways."

"Cryptic enough to avoid obvious detection, specific enough that someone who knows about the bloodlines might recognize it," he explained to Maya. "And the response phrase is something only someone connected to your grandmother would know."

"The mirror reflects both ways," Maya repeated. "That's inscribed on the back of my grandmother's mirror. How did you know that?"

"I didn't," Alex admitted. "But it's the kind of phrase a Weber would use, based on what we know about your bloodline's particular abilities. If someone responds with that exact phrase, it suggests genuine knowledge rather than lucky guessing."

Maya looked impressed. "You'd have made a good anthropologist. That's exactly the kind of cultural shibboleth we study to identify authentic group membership."

They posted the message to several subforums, then settled in to wait. It could be hours or days before anyone responded, if anyone did at all. Meanwhile, they needed rest, resources, and a plan for immediate survival.

"We should find a motel," Alex suggested. "Somewhere we can clean up and get a few hours of sleep. Pay cash, use false names."

Maya nodded wearily. The events at the lake house had taken a physical and emotional toll on both of them. Threshold work, real manipulation rather than passive perception, drained energy in ways ordinary exertion didn't.

As they prepared to leave the diner, the phone pinged with a notification. Someone had responded to their forum post already—far sooner than either had expected.

The message was brief: *The mirror reflects both ways. Chin family compromised yesterday. Three taken. One remains hidden. Face-to-face only. Lake Street Bridge, Boston, tomorrow, noon. Come alone or not at all.*

Alex and Maya exchanged a look of mingled hope and suspicion.

"Could be a trap," Maya pointed out.

"Almost certainly is," Alex agreed. "But they knew about the Chin family. Specific information we can verify if Rivera had contacts in Chinatown."

"Rivera is presumed dead," Maya reminded him gently.

"Yes, but his network might not be. We need to try, at least." Alex stared at the message, weighing risks against desperate need. "We'll take precautions. Scout the location first. Have an escape route planned."

"We," Maya repeated, eyebrow raised. "The message specifically said to come alone."

"I'm not letting you go alone, and you're not letting me go alone," Alex said firmly. "We're in this together now. Blood ties of a different sort."

Maya smiled faintly at that, the first real smile he'd seen from her since the events at the lake house. "Partners, then."

"Partners," Alex confirmed.

They left the diner and found a small motel on the outskirts of Milton the kind of place that asked no questions when they paid cash and gave obviously false names. The room was basic but clean, with two beds and a bathroom that had seen better days but served their immediate needs.

While Maya showered, Alex took stock of what they'd salvaged from the lake house: his mother's locket, now more firmly tied to his bloodline after its use in the sealing ritual; Maya's grandmother's mirror, similarly enhanced; the silver knife used for the blood component; and a few pages of notes on threshold theory they'd brought for reference during the working.

Not much to show for centuries of Morgan research and preparation. Not much to stand against an enemy as old and patient as the Threshold cult and the Ancient it served.

But they had accomplished something significant. The nexus point was sealed, the threshold strengthened. The Threshold's original plan for the equinox crossing was disrupted beyond repair. They would adapt, find another approach, but they would be working from a position of disadvantage now rather than strength.

And somewhere in Boston, someone with knowledge of the Chin family, the last unaccounted for bloodline, was willing to meet them. An ally, potentially. Or another enemy. Either way, a next step when they had thought all paths closed to them.

After Maya emerged from the bathroom, Alex took his turn, washing away the physical remnants of the night's events while his mind continued to process their implications. Under the hot spray, he found himself thinking of those they'd lost, Caleb, Rivera, his mother. All sacrificed to a war fought in shadows, a war most of humanity would never know existed.

When he returned to the room, Maya was examining her grandmother's mirror, turning it over in her hands with a contemplative expression.

"It feels different now," she said without looking up. "After the ritual. More... connected to me. Like it's not just a tool anymore but an extension of myself."

"I feel the same about the locket," Alex replied, settling onto the edge of his bed. "As if the working bound it more firmly to my bloodline, to my specific resonance with the threshold."

"Resonance," Maya repeated, testing the word. "That's a good way to describe it. Like tuning a musical instrument to a specific frequency."

"Caleb would have appreciated the metaphor," Alex said, a pang of loss hitting him anew. "He was always looking for better ways to explain threshold mechanics in terms ordinary people could understand."

They were quiet for a moment, honoring the memory of the ancient Guardian who had guided them, protected them, and ultimately sacrificed himself for their cause.

"Do you think he knew?" Maya asked finally. "That the ritual would require his sacrifice? That he wouldn't survive it?"

"He knew," Alex said with certainty. "Maybe not when we first arrived at the lake house, but definitely once we found my mother's instructions. He understood what was required and chose it anyway."

"Like your mother would have. Like my grandmother." Maya's voice held wonder rather than sorrow. "What kind of commitment does that take? To give everything for a fight most people don't even know is happening?"

Alex had no answer for that. The depth of dedication shown by Caleb, by Catherine Morgan, by Victoria Weber, it existed beyond ordinary human understanding, beyond conventional morality or self-interest. A recognition that some threats transcended individual life, that some principles were worth any sacrifice.

"We should try to get some sleep," he said finally. "Tomorrow will be challenging enough without exhaustion complicating matters."

They turned out the lights but didn't sleep immediately. In the darkness, their conversation continued, moving from strategy and survival to more personal matters; Maya's academic career now derailed by cosmic war, Alex's investigative background that had led him unwittingly into his birthright, the shared experience of growing up "different" without understanding why.

"Do you regret it?" Maya asked as the first hints of dawn began to lighten the motel curtains. "Learning the truth? Becoming involved in all this?"

Alex considered the question carefully. Three weeks ago, he had been a struggling private investigator with a history of mental health issues and a bleak future. Now he was a key player in a supernatural conflict that threatened the very fabric of reality. By conventional standards, his life had taken a dramatic turn for the worse.

And yet.

"No," he said finally. "I don't regret it. For the first time in my life, I understand what I am. Why I experience the world differently. That alone is worth whatever comes next."

Maya was quiet for so long that Alex thought she might have fallen asleep. Then she said softly, "I feel the same way. Terrified, overwhelmed, grieving for what we've lost. But not regretful. Never that."

As sleep finally claimed them, Alex's last conscious thought was of the lake, of the nexus point now sealed against the Ancient's influence. Of blood freely given, will focused true, and sacrifice offered without reservation. The components of a working more powerful than any he'd imagined possible.

The components, perhaps, of whatever came next in their fight against the Threshold and the crossing still to come.

At Threshold Wellness in Boston, Dr. Evelyn Marsh stood motionless before the wall of monitors, watching as the feed from the Morgan lake house went dark. Beside her, Katherine Bishop waited silently for a reaction, for instructions, for any indication of how this apparent setback would be addressed.

When Dr. Marsh finally spoke, her voice held no anger, no frustration, only a cold, patient amusement that was somehow more terrifying than rage would have been.

"The Guardian sacrifices himself," she observed. "As expected. As required."

"Required?" Katherine asked, confusion evident in her voice. "The sealing working they performed has closed the primary nexus point. Our ritual cannot proceed as planned."

"Plans evolve," Dr. Marsh replied, her form flickering slightly in the dim light, human features momentarily replaced by something far older. "The Morgan and Weber bloodlines have done exactly as we anticipated. Better, in fact. Their working has bound them more firmly to the threshold, enhanced their connection, their resonance."

"But the nexus—"

"Is one of many," Dr. Marsh interrupted. "Lesser, yes. Less ideal for our purposes. But serviceable, especially with the enhanced vessels now available to us."

Understanding dawned in Katherine's eyes. "You wanted this," she said. "You wanted them to perform the sealing."

"Want is such a limited concept," Dr. Marsh replied, her smile revealing too many teeth. "I anticipated. I allowed. I observed as pieces moved themselves into optimal positions, believing all the while they were disrupting my design rather than fulfilling it."

She gestured to one of the monitors, where security footage showed the burning Morgan lake house from a different angle. In the flames, patterns emerged that ordinary human perception would dismiss as coincidence or trick of light. But to those with threshold sight, they formed distinct symbols, doorways opening rather than closing, barriers thinning rather than strengthening.

"The Ancient is patient," Dr. Marsh said, her voice now layered with others, older and colder than human vocal cords should be able to produce. "It has waited millennia for this alignment, this convergence of bloodlines and celestial position. What are a few more days when the prize is so perfectly prepared?"

"The Morgan believes he has won a victory," Katherine noted. "Struck a blow against our plans."

"Yes," Dr. Marsh agreed, her smile widening impossibly. "And that belief will sustain him through what comes next. Keep him fighting, keep him developing his abilities, keep him connecting ever more deeply with the threshold itself."

She turned from the monitors, her form now shifting more dramatically between human and something else. Something ancient and hungry that had worn many faces across centuries while waiting for this specific bloodline, this perfect vessel.

"Let them celebrate their imagined victory," she said, moving toward the door with a fluid grace that was distinctly inhuman. "Let them believe they have disrupted our grand design, forced us into desperate countermeasures."

At the threshold of the room, she paused, looking back at Katherine with eyes that now held galaxies of ancient malevolence.

"Meanwhile, we prepare for the true crossing. Not at the lake, but here. Not at the new moon, but at the equinox as always intended. Not with just any Morgan, but with this specific one, awakened, trained, connected to the threshold in ways none before him has ever been."

"And the Weber girl?" Katherine asked. "What role does she play now?"

Dr. Marsh's laugh was a sound no human throat should produce. Layered echoes of countless voices speaking in unison across dimensional barriers.

"The role she has always been destined for," she replied. "The final component. The willing sacrifice that powers the crossing not just for me, but for all who wait beyond the threshold."

As she left the room, reality itself seemed to warp around her, as if the woman called Dr. Marsh was merely a placeholder for something far vaster struggling to maintain human form for just a little while longer.

Just until the equinox.

Just until the last Morgan came willingly into their hands, believing himself the victor rather than the prize.

CHAPTER 12

There's a specific kind of courage required to walk knowingly into what might be a trap. Not the adrenaline-fueled bravery of immediate danger, but the cold, deliberate resolve to face potential destruction because the alternative is worse.

Alex Morgan had been contemplating this particular flavor of courage for the past hour as he watched the Lake Street Bridge from the relative safety of a café across the Charles River. It was five minutes to noon. Five minutes until their mysterious correspondent, potential ally or clever enemy, was scheduled to appear.

"Any movement?" Maya asked through the disposable phone they'd purchased that morning along with fresh clothes and basic supplies.

"Nothing obvious," Alex replied, scanning the pedestrians crossing the bridge. "But the lunch crowd makes it hard to identify surveillance. How's your position?"

"Clear sightlines to both ends of the bridge. If they bring friends, I'll see them coming." Maya was stationed in a bookstore at the opposite end, positioned to observe without being easily observed. "Still think we should meet them together rather than separately?"

"Yes," Alex said firmly. "Whatever they claim about the Chin family, we're stronger as a pair than divided. Bloodlines are more effective in concert, that's what my mother's notes emphasized."

They had established this plan during the three-hour bus ride from Milton to Boston that morning. Approaching the meeting point from different directions, establishing observation posts, communicating via burner phones. Basic tradecraft that Rivera had begun to teach them before his presumed death at the lake house.

The thought of the detective still caused a pang of grief and guilt. Another name added to the growing list of those who had sacrificed themselves in this shadow war. Another debt that could never be repaid except through victory.

"It's time," Maya said, her voice tight with tension. "I'm moving to the rendezvous point."

"Understood. I'll approach from the south end. Keep the connection open."

Alex left the café, pocketing the phone with the line still active so Maya could hear any confrontation. His mother's locket hung heavy around his neck, a reassuring weight with an almost imperceptible warmth against his skin. Since the ritual at the lake, his connection to the focus had deepened, as if the silver had somehow become attuned specifically to his bloodline, his unique threshold resonance.

The Lake Street Bridge was modest as Boston bridges went. A utilitarian span across the narrower portion of the Charles, connecting residential areas rather than tourist destinations. At noon on a weekday, it carried a steady stream of pedestrians and cyclists enjoying the unseasonably warm spring day, along with the occasional car.

Alex approached casually, maintaining the relaxed posture of someone on a lunch break rather than a man potentially walking into an ambush. His threshold sight remained dormant, too conspicuous to activate in public, too draining to maintain for extended periods. But the locket gave him a heightened sensitivity even without fully engaging the sight. He could feel subtle currents in the air, places where reality seemed slightly thinner or more flexible than it should be.

The bridge, he realized as he stepped onto it, was one such place. Not a nexus point like the lake, but a natural thinning in the threshold. The flowing water beneath, perhaps, or its position along ley lines he couldn't perceive without proper study. Whatever the cause, it made strategic sense as a meeting place for those with threshold sensitivity. Easier to slip between worlds, if necessary, easier to perceive threats from the other side.

Alex spotted Maya at the midpoint of the bridge, leaning against the railing as if admiring the view of the river below. To casual observers, they would appear to be strangers, having no obvious connection. Only someone watching very carefully would notice their occasional glances toward each other, the subtle synchronization of their movements.

As the church bells in the distance struck twelve, Alex scanned the bridge again. No one approached Maya directly. No one signaled or made contact. But something had changed in the atmosphere. A tensing, a gathering of energy that had nothing to do with the physical world and everything to do with threshold mechanics.

"Something's happening," he murmured into the phone. "Not visual. Something at the threshold level."

"I feel it too," Maya confirmed. "Like static electricity, but not quite. The air feels... stretched."

A figure materialized at the opposite end of the bridge, a young Asian woman in her early twenties, dressed in ordinary jeans and a university sweatshirt, but moving with the hyperaware caution of someone expecting trouble. She wasn't there, and then suddenly she was, as if stepping out of a blind spot in reality itself.

Alex blinked, certain he must have simply

overlooked her, that she had been there all along. But the subtle ripple in the air around her suggested otherwise. Not quite invisibility in the conventional sense, but something adjacent to it. A manipulation of perception, of attention.

"I see her," he said quietly. "Northwestern end. Asian woman, early twenties. Blue MIT sweatshirt."

"Got her," Maya confirmed. "She's scanning the bridge, looking for someone. For us, presumably."

The woman continued her careful progress along the bridge, eyes constantly moving, posture suggesting she was prepared to flee at the slightest provocation. When she reached the midpoint where Maya waited, she paused, not looking directly at her but clearly aware of her presence.

"Weber," she said, just loudly enough to be heard over the ambient noise of traffic and river.

Maya straightened slightly. "Yes. And you are?"

"Chin," the woman replied simply. "Last of my line, as far as I know. The rest were taken yesterday. My parents, my sister."

Alex began moving toward them, maintaining a casual pace while closing the distance. If this was indeed a member of the Chin bloodline—one of the seven families with threshold sensitivity the Threshold cult sought—then she represented both a potential ally and a critical intelligence source.

The woman tensed as she noticed Alex's approach. "You were told to come alone," she said to Maya, her voice sharpening.

"We work as a team," Maya replied. "This is Morgan."

The name had an immediate effect. The woman's eyes widened, darting to Alex with new intensity. "The Morgan bloodline was reported destroyed," she said. "The lake house burned. The nexus sealed."

"Reports of my destruction were exaggerated," Alex said, stopping a few feet away to give her space. "Though the rest is accurate enough. The nexus is sealed, the lake house gone."

The woman, Chin, studied him with unconcealed suspicion. "Prove it," she challenged. "Prove you're Morgan bloodline."

Alex hesitated, aware that they were in public, surrounded by ordinary people going about their day, oblivious to the supernatural confrontation unfolding in their midst.

"Not here," he said. "Too exposed."

"Here is safe precisely because it's exposed," Chin countered. "They won't risk revealing themselves to ordinary perception. The bridge creates a natural blind spot in their surveillance."

She had a point. The Threshold operated through secrecy and manipulation, avoiding direct action that might expose the supernatural realities they exploited. A public confrontation in broad daylight wasn't their style.

Carefully, Alex withdrew his mother's locket from beneath his shirt, holding it where Chin could see the threshold symbol engraved on its surface.

Chin's posture relaxed fractionally. "And Weber?" she asked, turning to Maya.

In answer, Maya produced her grandmother's silver mirror, angling it so that only Chin could see its reflective surface. Whatever she saw there, something invisible to ordinary perception, seemed to satisfy her.

"All right," she conceded. "You're who you claim to be. Which means we have a lot to discuss and very little time to do it. Follow me."

She turned abruptly, heading back the way she had come. Alex and Maya exchanged a glance, then fell into step behind her, maintaining enough distance to avoid looking like a group while staying close enough for conversation.

"Why did you contact us?" Alex asked, cutting to the heart of the matter. "What do you know about what's happening?"

"I know that the Threshold is accelerating their timetable," Chin replied without turning. "I know they've captured representatives of four bloodlines already, Bishop, Nazari, Okafor, and LaChance. And as of yesterday, most of mine as well."

"How did you escape?" Maya asked.

"Family tradition," Chin said with grim humor. "The Chin bloodline has been evading the Threshold for generations. We have methods. Abilities that help us hide when necessary."

That explained her strange materialization on the bridge, not teleportation or invisibility in the conventional sense, but some form of threshold manipulation that affected perception, that created blind spots in ordinary observation.

"And your family knew about all of this?" Alex pressed. "About the bloodlines, the threshold, the Threshold cult's plans?"

"We've known for centuries," Chin confirmed. "Unlike your bloodlines, which tried to fight directly, the Chin strategy has always been evasion, misdirection, survival. We keep our heads down, stay off their radar, preserve the line at all costs."

They had reached the end of the bridge, where Chin led them into a small park adjacent to the river. She chose a bench positioned under a large oak tree, partially screened from casual observation while still public enough to deter direct confrontation.

As they settled onto the bench, Alex studied their mysterious contact more carefully. She was perhaps twenty-two or twenty-three, with the intense focus of someone who had lived with heightened awareness her entire life. Not the confusion he and Maya had experienced, the sense of mental illness, of hallucinations, but the clear-eyed vigilance of someone raised to understand exactly what she was seeing and why.

"You have questions," she observed. "Many, I assume. I'll answer what I can, but first my name is Grace. Grace Chin. MIT graduate student in quantum physics, which is more relevant to our situation than you might initially think."

"I'm Alex Morgan. This is Maya Weber."

Grace nodded, acknowledging the introduction. "I know who you are. The Morgan bloodline has always been central to the Threshold's plans. The strongest connection to threshold mechanics, the most direct line to what waits on the other side. And the Weber line, with its affinity for memory and impression, has always worked closely with the Morgans. History repeats, it seems."

"You said your family was taken yesterday," Maya said, steering the conversation back to immediate concerns. "What exactly happened?"

Grace's expression tightened with barely controlled grief. "A coordinated strike. Multiple locations simultaneously. My parents' home in Quincy, my sister's apartment in Cambridge, my uncle's restaurant in Chinatown. Threshold agents backed by what my family calls Hollow Ones, humans emptied of will and identity, controlled by entities from the other side."

"We've encountered them," Alex confirmed. "At Threshold Wellness. Like puppets with the strings pulled from beyond."

"Exactly." Grace's hands clenched in her lap. "I was at the laboratory when it happened. My father managed to warn me. One text message before they took him. Our family emergency code. I followed protocol, abandoned my apartment, my research, everything that could be traced. Activated the family defensive measures."

"Which are what, exactly?" Maya asked.

"Threshold manipulation focused on perception and attention," Grace explained. "Not true invisibility, but something adjacent. A way of sliding between the cracks of ordinary observation. The Chin bloodline specialty."

Alex thought of their work at the lake, the sealing ritual they had performed. "We disrupted their plans," he said. "Sealed the primary nexus point they intended to use for the equinox ritual. Why are they still collecting bloodlines if their crossing attempt has been compromised?"

Grace's laugh held no humor. "You think they only had one approach? One nexus point? One ritual site?" She shook her head. "The Threshold has been planning this crossing for centuries. Generations. They have contingencies for their contingencies."

The implication sent a chill through Alex. Their victory at the lake suddenly felt hollow, insufficient. A battle won while the larger war continued unabated.

"But the Morgan lake house was special," he argued. "The nexus point there was particularly powerful. Caleb said—"

"Caleb Morgan," Grace interrupted. "The Guardian. The one who exists in both worlds simultaneously." Her expression shifted to concern. "Where is he? Why isn't he with you?"

The question reopened the fresh wound of Caleb's sacrifice. "He's gone," Alex said simply. "He transformed his essence into energy to power the sealing ritual at the lake. Discorporated, he called it."

Grace's reaction was unexpected, not sympathy or sorrow, but alarm bordering on panic. "That's not possible," she said, voice dropping to a harsh whisper. "A Guardian cannot simply cease to exist. Their essence is... different. Fundamental to threshold mechanics itself."

"That's what he told us," Maya confirmed. "That he would transform rather than die in the conventional sense."

"Yes, transform," Grace emphasized. "But into what? Where? Guardians don't just end. They change state, change form, but remain part of the equation."

Alex and Maya exchanged troubled glances. In the chaos and urgency of the lake house confrontation, they hadn't questioned Caleb's explanation of his sacrifice. Hadn't considered implications beyond the immediate tactical necessity.

"What are you suggesting?" Alex asked, a new unease spreading through him.

"I'm not suggesting anything," Grace replied. "I'm telling you that something about your 'victory' doesn't add up. A Guardian's essence can be used to power a working, yes, but it doesn't simply disappear afterward. It reconstitutes, reshapes, finds new expression."

"Unless it was captured," Maya realized, horror dawning. "Unless someone, something, intercepted the energy, prevented the reconstitution."

"Which would require extraordinary power," Grace confirmed. "And intimate knowledge of Guardian nature. The kind of knowledge few possess."

"Dr. Marsh," Alex said, the pieces connecting in his mind. "Or whatever entity currently uses that name and form."

Grace nodded grimly. "The Ancient, as my family calls it. The one that has worn many faces across centuries while orchestrating the Threshold's activities. The one that seeks the crossing above all else."

A sickening possibility began to take shape in Alex's mind. "What if the sealing ritual didn't work as intended? What if instead of strengthening the threshold, we somehow..."

"Altered it in ways you didn't

anticipate," Grace finished for him. "Created vulnerabilities rather than reinforcements. It's possible. Threshold mechanics are notoriously unpredictable, especially when manipulated by those still learning their abilities."

The weight of this suggestion, that their desperate effort at the lake might have actually furthered the Threshold's plans rather than disrupted them, settled over Alex like a physical burden. Had they been manipulated from the start? Had Dr. Marsh anticipated their every move? Turned their resistance into unwitting assistance?

"We need to verify what actually happened at the lake," he said finally. "Confirm whether the nexus point is truly sealed or if something else occurred. Without Caleb's guidance..."

"I might be able to help with that," Grace offered. "The Chin bloodline has different abilities than Morgan or Weber, but our particular affinity for perception extends to threshold states as well. With the right preparation, I could potentially sense whether the sealing was successful."

"How?" Maya asked. "The lake house is three hours away, and presumably under Threshold surveillance now."

"Physical distance is largely irrelevant to threshold mechanics," Grace explained. "With proper focusing tools and a direct bloodline connection to what we're trying to perceive, I can extend my senses across conventional space."

"You'd need something connected to the nexus point," Alex pointed out. "Some physical link to the location."

"Like Morgan blood used in the sealing ritual?" Grace suggested, looking pointedly at Alex's hand where the faint scar from the lake house door's sampling mechanism was still visible. "Blood freely given in a threshold working creates a permanent connection, a pathway that can be followed by those with the right abilities."

The prospect was both promising and unsettling. Allowing a virtual stranger access to his bloodline connection, to the intimate link established during the ritual. But their options were limited, their need for accurate intelligence critical.

"What would you need?" he asked. "Besides the blood connection?"

"Privacy. Security. A place where we won't be interrupted or observed." Grace glanced around the park, her expression uneasy. "This is too exposed for deep threshold work."

"We don't exactly have a safehouse at the moment," Maya pointed out. "Caleb's brownstone might be compromised. Our apartments are definitely watched."

Grace considered this. "My family maintained several emergency locations throughout the city. Places warded against threshold observation, stocked with necessary supplies. The closest is in Cambridge, near the university."

"Can you guarantee it hasn't been compromised?" Alex asked. "If they took your family yesterday..."

"No guarantee," Grace admitted. "But the locations operate on a rotating security protocol. This particular safehouse wasn't scheduled for use in the current cycle. It might have escaped their notice."

It wasn't ideal, but it was the best option available to them. Alex nodded his agreement. "Lead the way. But we approach carefully, verify security before committing."

They left the park separately, reconvening a block away before taking a circuitous route to Cambridge. Grace led them through side streets and alleyways, occasionally pausing to perform what appeared to be ordinary actions, retying a shoelace, checking her phone, but which Alex suspected were threshold manipulations designed to obscure their trail.

The safehouse, when they reached it, proved to be a modest apartment above a Chinese grocery store in a busy commercial district. Nothing about its exterior suggested anything unusual. Just another residential unit in a mixed-use building, unremarkable in every visible way.

Grace approached cautiously, examining the doorframe with heightened attention. "Wards intact," she reported. "No signs of disturbance or surveillance."

Inside, the apartment was spartanly furnished but well-equipped for their purposes. A central room contained a table surrounded by chairs, its surface inlaid with what Alex recognized as threshold symbols, similar to but distinct from those at the Morgan lake house. Bookshelves lined the walls, filled with volumes in Chinese and English, many focused on theoretical physics and metaphysics.

"My grandfather's research material," Grace explained, seeing Alex's interest in the books. "He was trying to reconcile threshold mechanics with quantum theory. To explain in scientific terms what our bloodlines experience as supernatural phenomena."

"Any success?" Maya asked, examining the threshold symbols on the table.

"Some," Grace replied, moving to a cabinet against the far wall. "He developed theoretical frameworks that bridge conventional physics and threshold mechanics. Models that explain how parallel realities can interact under specific conditions."

She removed several items from the cabinet, a small ceramic bowl, a silver knife similar to the one they'd used at the lake, various herbs and powders in glass vials, and a circular bronze mirror with Chinese characters engraved around its rim.

"The Chin family focus," she explained, placing the mirror in the center of the table. "Similar in purpose to your locket and mirror but attuned specifically to perception across barriers. Seeing what is hidden, sensing what exists beyond ordinary awareness."

Alex watched as she efficiently arranged the items in a pattern around the mirror, measuring herbs and powders with practiced precision. This was clearly a familiar ritual to her, something she had performed or observed many times before.

"What exactly are we attempting here?" he asked as she worked.

"A perception working," Grace replied without looking up. "Using your blood connection to the lake nexus as a pathway, my bloodline abilities as the sensing mechanism, and Maya's focus to stabilize and interpret what we perceive."

"And this will tell us whether the sealing ritual worked as intended?"

"It should reveal the current state of the nexus point, yes." Grace completed her preparations and looked up at them. "But I should warn you, threshold perception isn't like ordinary observation. It can be disorienting. Disturbing, sometimes. Especially when perceiving locations where significant threshold manipulations have occurred."

"We understand," Maya assured her. "After

what we experienced at the lake, I think we're as prepared as we can be."

Grace nodded, accepting this assessment. "Then let's begin. Alex, I'll need a small amount of your blood—just a few drops in the bowl. Maya, place your mirror adjacent to mine, touching at the edges to create a combined focusing field."

They followed her instructions, Alex wincing slightly as the silver knife reopened the barely-healed cut on his palm, allowing several drops of blood to fall into the ceramic bowl. Maya positioned her grandmother's mirror as directed, creating a connection between the two focusing tools.

"Now we join hands," Grace instructed, extending hers toward them. "A triangle of intention, with the mirrors at the center. Focus on the lake, on the nexus point. On the moment of the sealing ritual."

As their hands connected, Alex felt an immediate shift in perception. Not the full activation of threshold sight, but something adjacent to it. A heightening of awareness, a thinning of ordinary reality. The room around them remained visible but seemed less substantial somehow, as if they were partially disconnected from conventional space-time.

"I see it," Grace whispered, her eyes fixed on the mirrors' reflective surfaces, which had begun to shimmer with an inner light invisible to ordinary perception. "The lake. The nexus point. The working you performed."

Images formed in the mirrors. Not reflections of the room around them but windows into somewhere else. The lake at night, viewed from above as if from a great height. The small boat at its center where they had performed the ritual. The energies they had unleashed shown as visible currents of light and shadow, interweaving in complex patterns as the working took effect.

"It worked," Maya said with relief, watching the images unfold. "The sealing took hold. The nexus is closed."

But Grace's expression remained troubled, her brow furrowed in concentration. "Wait," she murmured. "There's something else. Something beneath the surface pattern."

The mirror's image shifted, diving beneath the lake's surface to reveal the true nexus point, the thin spot in reality where the threshold between worlds was at its weakest. And there, where they had performed their working to strengthen and seal that barrier, something unexpected was taking shape.

"That's not a sealing," Grace said, horror creeping into her voice. "That's a redirection. A reconfiguration."

The energies they had unleashed—Morgan blood, Weber will, Guardian essence—hadn't sealed the nexus as intended. Instead, they had altered it, changed its fundamental nature in ways none of them had anticipated. The threshold remained thin at that point, but instead of allowing passage in either direction, it now appeared to function like a one-way valve.

"Outflow only," Grace whispered. "You've created a pathway that allows energy to flow from our side to theirs, but prevents intrusion from their side to ours."

"How is that possible?" Alex demanded, struggling to understand what he was seeing. "The ritual was specifically designed to seal the nexus completely."

"Unless someone altered the parameters," Maya suggested. "Changed some element of the working without our knowledge."

A chilling possibility occurred to Alex. "Caleb," he said. "When he offered his essence as the sacrifice. What if he wasn't, what if he wasn't who we thought he was?"

The image in the mirror shifted again, focusing now on the moment of Caleb's transformation, the Guardian dissolving into pure energy to power their working. But viewed through Grace's threshold perception, new details became visible. As Caleb's essence dispersed, it didn't simply fuel the ritual as intended. It shaped it, directed it, altered its fundamental nature in subtle ways they hadn't detected at the time.

"He wasn't just powering the working," Grace

confirmed, voicing what they were all seeing. "He was changing it. From the inside."

"But why?" Maya asked. "Why would he sabotage his own sacrifice? What purpose would that serve?"

"It wouldn't serve his purpose," Alex realized, a cold certainty settling in his gut. "It would serve theirs. The Threshold's. The Ancient's."

"You think Caleb was working for them all along?" Maya sounded incredulous.

"Not Caleb himself," Alex clarified. "But something wearing his form. Using his identity. A perfect infiltration."

"A Vessel," Grace supplied. "Like Dr. Marsh. A human form occupied by something from the other side." She studied the mirror intently. "It's possible. Guardians are unique entities. Neither fully of our world nor fully of theirs. If one were somehow compromised, corrupted..."

The implications were staggering. If Caleb, or whatever had been presenting itself as Caleb, had been working for the Threshold all along, then everything they thought they knew, everything they had been taught about their abilities and heritage, was potentially compromised. Every action they had taken based on his guidance might have been serving the enemy's agenda rather than opposing it.

"We need to break the connection," Grace said suddenly, urgency in her voice. "Now. Something's noticed our observation.

Something's looking back."

The images in the mirror were changing, distorting, as if something on the other side had become aware of their perception and was reaching toward it. The surface of the lake in their vision began to roil, not with wind or current but with movement from below, something vast and ancient rising toward the threshold they had inadvertently reconfigured.

Alex felt it before he saw it. A pressure in his mind, a presence pushing against his consciousness. The same entity he had sensed during the ritual, the Ancient that waited beyond the threshold, patient and hungry and inconceivably old.

Morgan, it whispered directly into his thoughts. *Last of the line. Keeper of the key. We see you seeing us. Again.*

With a sharp motion, Grace broke the connection, sweeping the ritual components from the table with one arm while using her other hand to shield her family's mirror. The pressure in Alex's mind vanished immediately, leaving behind a dull headache and the metallic taste of fear in his mouth.

"It sensed us," she gasped, her face pale with exertion. "It traced our perception back along the connection. It knows where we are now."

"We need to move," Alex said immediately, helping Maya to her feet. "If it could sense us, it can direct its agents to this location."

Grace was already gathering essential items, her family's mirror, several books from the shelves, a small wooden box whose contents remained unknown. "There's another safehouse," she said. "Deeper in the city. More heavily warded. We might be able to reach it before they mobilize."

But as she spoke, the lights in the apartment flickered, then died completely. Outside, the normal sounds of the busy commercial street fell silent, not gradually but all at once, as if a switch had been thrown on urban activity itself.

"Too late," Grace whispered. "They're already here."

Alex moved to the window, carefully peering through the blinds without disturbing them. The street below was impossibly, unnaturally empty—no pedestrians, no traffic, no movement of any kind. As if reality itself had been paused around their location.

"What is this?" he asked. "What are they doing?"

"Isolation protocol," Grace replied, her voice tight with controlled fear. "They're separating this location from ordinary space-time. Creating a pocket where they can operate without witnesses, without interference."

"Can we break through it?" Maya asked, clutching her grandmother's mirror protectively against her chest.

"Not without understanding its parameters

first," Grace answered, moving quickly to the apartment's small kitchen area. From beneath a cabinet, she retrieved what appeared to be an ordinary fire extinguisher, but which Alex suspected was anything but ordinary. "Defensive measures first. Then we look for weaknesses in their containment."

The building shuddered suddenly, as if struck by a localized earthquake. Dust filtered down from the ceiling, and the floorboards creaked ominously.

"They're coming through the store below," Grace surmised, hefting the fire extinguisher with practiced ease. "Standard approach. Cut off conventional exits, then enter from the most accessible point."

"What do we do?" Maya asked, looking to Alex for direction.

He reached for his mother's locket, feeling its warmth intensify at his touch. Since the lake ritual, his connection to the focus had deepened, become more intuitive. The threshold sight activated smoothly as he directed his attention toward it, showing him what ordinary perception couldn't reveal.

The apartment was surrounded by a shimmering barrier. Not physical but metaphysical, a manipulation of reality itself that separated this small pocket of space from the world around it. Within that barrier, darker energies were gathering below their feet, concentrating in preparation for assault.

"They're not just coming from below," he reported. "They're surrounding us completely. Creating a containment field with no conventional exit."

"Then we create an unconventional one," Grace replied, her expression shifting from fear to determined focus. "The Chin bloodline specialty, finding paths where others see only walls."

She turned to the mirrors on the table, her family's bronze focus and Maya's silver one, still touching at the edges where they had placed them for the perception working. "We need to combine our abilities," she said urgently. "Morgan to reshape, Weber to direct, Chin to perceive. Together, we might be able to punch through their containment field."

Another shudder ran through the building, stronger this time. From below came the sound of splintering wood, the floor giving way as something forced its way upward. Something that moved with inhuman purpose and strength.

"Whatever we're going to do, we need to do it now," Alex said, drawing the silver knife they had used in the blood ritual. "What exactly are you proposing?"

"A doorway," Grace replied simply. "Not a physical one, but a threshold passage. A temporary tear in reality that leads somewhere else. Somewhere beyond their containment field."

"You can do that?" Maya asked, incredulous.

"Theoretically," Grace admitted. "The Chin bloodline has been exploring the possibility for generations. We've never attempted it practically because the energy requirements are prohibitive and the risks significant."

"Risks such as?" Alex pressed.

"Failing to properly target the exit point. Landing somewhere unintended." Grace's expression was grim. "Potentially on the wrong side of the threshold itself."

The floor beneath them groaned as something massive pressed against it from below. Plaster cracked along the walls, and the lights, still without power, began to sway on their fixtures.

"I think we're out of options," Maya pointed out. "Whatever the risks of Grace's doorway, they're preferable to capture by the Threshold."

She was right, and Alex knew it. Being taken by the Threshold meant becoming vessels for the crossing. Their bloodlines, their abilities, turned against everything they had fought to protect. Death would be preferable to that fate. Even an uncertain escape through a threshold tear held better odds than surrender.

"What do you need from us?" he asked Grace, decision made.

"Blood from both of you, freely given," she

replied, already arranging the mirrors in a new configuration. "Combined with mine as a triangulation point. Focus your intentions on escape, on passage, on finding safety beyond their reach."

As Grace prepared the working, the pressure from below intensified. The floorboards began to splinter in the center of the room, revealing glimpses of something moving in the darkness beneath. Something that wasn't human hands or tools, but writhing, tentacle-like appendages that probed the opening with cold purpose.

Lurkers, like the one Alex had encountered in the janitor's closet at Threshold Wellness. But larger, more numerous, apparently serving as the advance force for whatever was orchestrating this assault.

Working quickly, they completed Grace's preparations, three drops of blood from each of them in the ceramic bowl, the mirrors positioned to reflect each other in an infinite regression, the focusing tools of three bloodlines united in common purpose.

"On my mark," Grace instructed, her hands positioned above the arrangement. "Focus everything you have on the intention of passage, of doorway, of escape."

The floor gave way with a tremendous crack, a gaping hole appearing in its center through which the Lurkers began to flow—a mass of writhing limbs and cold, inhuman purpose surging upward into the apartment. Behind them, visible in the chaos of the broken floor, human figures moved in the darkness—Threshold agents, coming to claim what their otherworldly allies had cornered.

"Now!" Grace shouted.

They pressed their bleeding palms to the mirrors simultaneously, focusing their combined bloodline abilities on the single, desperate intention of escape. The effect was immediate and overwhelming. A surge of power unlike anything Alex had experienced before, even during the lake ritual. Three bloodlines working in concert, amplifying each other's natural affinities, creating something greater than the sum of their parts.

Reality tore.

There was no other way to describe it. A visible rending in the fabric of existence itself, opening like a jagged wound in the air before them. Through that tear, Alex glimpsed somewhere else. Not another physical location in conventional space, but a place between places, a fold in reality where the normal rules of physics and dimension didn't apply.

"Go!" Grace urged, her face strained with the effort of maintaining the tear. "I'll hold it as long as I can, but you need to go first!"

"We're not leaving you," Alex insisted, even as the Lurkers surged closer, their cold alien presence brushing against his mind like decomposing fingers.

"One of us has to anchor the exit point," Grace explained through gritted teeth. "I've done this before, in training. I know how to follow once you're through. Go!"

There was no time for further argument. The Lurkers were almost upon them, and behind the otherworldly advance force came human figures in tactical gear. Threshold agents armed and ready to take prisoners rather than kill. To secure the bloodlines they needed for the crossing.

Maya went first, clutching her grandmother's mirror as she stepped into the tear in reality. For a heart-stopping moment she seemed to hang suspended between states of existence, neither fully here nor fully elsewhere. Then she was gone, vanished into the fold between worlds.

"Your turn," Grace gasped, blood now trickling from her nose with the strain of maintaining the tear. "I'll be right behind you."

Alex hesitated, unwilling to abandon an ally to uncertain fate. But the Lurkers were reaching for him now, cold pseudopods brushing against his legs, seeking purchase. And the Threshold agents were shouting orders, preparing some kind of containment protocol.

With a final glance at Grace, her face set in determined concentration despite the blood now streaming from her nose and ears, Alex stepped into the tear she had created.

Reality warped around him, stretching and

compressing simultaneously. His perception fragmented, reassembled, fragmented again in nauseating succession. For an eternal instant, he existed everywhere and nowhere, caught between states of being that human language had no words to describe.

Then, with jarring abruptness, he was elsewhere.

Alex stumbled forward onto solid ground, disoriented and gasping. His surroundings resolved slowly, an alleyway between brick buildings, ordinary urban architecture, but eerily devoid of sound or movement. Twilight, although it had been early afternoon when they'd entered Grace's safehouse. Either they had traveled through time as well as space, or they were somewhere with a different relationship to Earth's day/night cycle.

Maya was there, leaning against a wall, her face pale but composed. "We made it," she said. "Wherever 'it' is."

"Grace?" Alex asked, turning back towards where they had emerged.

There was nothing there. No tear in reality, no sign of passage, no indication that fundamental laws of physics had been momentarily suspended. Just brick wall and empty alleyway.

"She hasn't come through yet," Maya confirmed. "But she said she needed to anchor the exit point. Maybe it takes time to follow."

Alex wasn't convinced. The strain on Grace had been visible, extreme. Maintaining a tear in reality while Lurkers and Threshold agents closed in, it might have been too much even for someone with her training and bloodline abilities.

"We need to figure out where we are," he said, focusing on immediate practicalities rather than worrying about what they couldn't control. "And when. And whether we're actually safe or just in a different kind of danger."

They moved cautiously toward the end of the alleyway, where it opened onto what appeared to be a city street. The buildings were familiar, brownstones and older commercial structures typical of Boston's historic districts. But the street itself was unnervingly empty, without pedestrians, traffic, or the ambient noise of urban life.

"It looks like Boston," Maya observed. "But not occupied Boston."

Alex nodded, the same unease prickling at his awareness. The city around them seemed physically intact but devoid of life. As if everyone had suddenly vanished, leaving the urban infrastructure perfectly preserved.

"I don't think we've traveled in conventional space," he said slowly. "I think we're in a fold, a pocket dimension. Somewhere adjacent to Boston but not quite part of it."

Maya shivered. "Like being caught inside

the isolation field they created around Grace's apartment? But on a larger scale?"

"Something like that." Alex tried to orient himself based on the surrounding architecture. "This looks like Beacon Hill. That building there," he pointed to a distinctive church spire visible above the rooftops, "is Old North Church. So, we're still in Boston geographically, just a version of it."

"A threshold state," Maya suggested. "Not fully our world, not fully the other side. Something in between."

That description resonated with what Alex was sensing. With his threshold sight partially active, a state that had become his new baseline since the lake ritual, he could perceive subtle differences in the reality around them. The air seemed thinner somehow, colors slightly muted, shadows deeper than they should be.

"Grace sent us somewhere she thought would be safe from the Threshold," he reasoned. "Somewhere they couldn't easily follow."

"But where she could," Maya added. "That was the plan. She anchors the exit, then follows once we're through."

Alex wasn't convinced Grace would be able to follow, but he kept that concern to himself. Instead, he focused on their immediate situation. "We should find shelter, figure out our next move. If this is a threshold state, there might be inhabitants. Entities indigenous to this state of reality."

Drifters, perhaps, the ordinary ghosts that were his first experience with threshold entities. Or something more complex, more dangerous. The thought of the Ancient that had reached for him during the lake ritual sent a chill through him. If they were closer to the threshold here than in ordinary reality, such entities might have more influence, more presence.

They moved cautiously down the empty street, alert for any sign of movement or life. The buildings around them were intact but had an abandoned quality. Dusty windows, faded signage, plantings that had grown wild with neglect. As if this version of Boston had been empty for years rather than minutes or hours.

"Look," Maya said suddenly, pointing ahead where the street opened into a small square. "The Public Garden."

The familiar park was recognizable in outline, but transformed in this threshold state. The trees were taller, more ancient-looking than their ordinary reality counterparts. The iconic pond at the center was larger, its surface black and still as obsidian. And at the garden's center, where the George Washington statue should have stood, was something else entirely. A structure that resembled a gazebo but constructed of materials that shifted and changed when viewed directly, as if refusing to settle into a single state of reality.

"I think..." Maya hesitated. "I think that might be where Grace was trying to send us specifically. A landmark she knew would exist in this threshold state."

It made sense. If Grace had trained for this kind of emergency passage, she would have targeted a known location, something stable enough to serve as a destination across the complex topology of threshold states.

They approached the garden cautiously, the unnatural stillness setting Alex's nerves on edge. No birds sang. No insects buzzed. No breeze stirred the too-tall trees with their too-dark leaves. The silence was absolute in a way that felt deliberately maintained rather than simply empty.

As they neared the strange gazebo structure, its appearance stabilized somewhat. Still alien in design, with spiraling supports that defied conventional geometry, but no longer actively shifting before their eyes. It seemed to be constructed of a material like mother-of-pearl, iridescent under the muted twilight, with symbols etched into its surface that resembled the threshold markings they had encountered before but more complex, more numerous.

"It's a waypoint," Alex realized, recognizing the fundamental pattern beneath the elaborate variations. "A threshold crossroads. A place where different states of reality intersect."

"Like Grand Central for parallel dimensions?"

Maya suggested.

"Something like that." Alex approached one of the support pillars, studying the symbols etched into its pearlescent surface. "These are navigational markers. Coordinates or addresses for different threshold states."

"You can read them?" Maya asked, surprised.

"Not exactly read," Alex clarified. "But I can sense their meaning. Since the lake ritual, my connection to threshold mechanics has deepened. Become more intuitive."

He traced a finger along one sequence of symbols, feeling a resonance with what lay behind them. A state of reality adjacent to their own but fundamentally different in ways he couldn't fully articulate.

"Grace sent us to a nexus point," he said. "A place where we could potentially choose our destination rather than being trapped in a single threshold state."

"Choose to go where, exactly?" Maya asked, examining the strange structure with scholarly interest despite their precarious situation. "Back to our Boston? To yet another variant?"

"That depends on what our goal is now," Alex replied. "We've confirmed that the lake ritual didn't work as intended. The nexus point wasn't sealed but reconfigured. And Caleb, or whatever was presenting itself as Caleb, was working for the Threshold all along."

"Which means everything we thought

we knew, everything we thought we'd accomplished, is compromised," Maya concluded grimly. "We haven't disrupted their plans. We might have actually advanced them."

Alex nodded, the weight of this realization settling heavily on his shoulders. "The equinox is still coming. They still have four bloodlines secured, Bishop, Nazari, Okafor, and LaChance. And now most of the Chin family as well. They'll proceed with the crossing as planned, just with adjustments for the reconfigured nexus point."

"And they'll be hunting us more aggressively than ever," Maya added. "The Morgan and Weber bloodlines, needed to complete their set."

The direness of their situation was inescapable. Two people against an organization centuries old, with resources beyond ordinary understanding and allies from beyond the threshold itself. Without Caleb's guidance, false though it might have been, without Rivera's inside information, without even Grace's family knowledge, they were desperately outmatched.

"We need to regroup," Alex said, thinking aloud. "Find a way to verify what's happening in ordinary Boston. Determine whether there are any allies left we can trust. And then…"

"And then what?" Maya asked. "Even if we could somehow free the other bloodlines, disrupt the ritual site, we're still just people with abilities we barely understand against an enemy that's been planning this for centuries."

It was the fundamental question, and Alex had no ready answer. What could they possibly do against odds so overwhelming? What strategy could two people employ against an organization with such reach and resources?

Before he could respond, a sound broke the unnatural silence of the garden, a tearing, ripping noise like fabric stretched beyond capacity, followed by a human gasp of pain and exertion.

They turned to see a jagged opening appearing in the air near the edge of the pond. A tear in reality similar to the one Grace had created in her apartment. Through it, they glimpsed chaos, the safehouse in disarray, Lurkers swarming through the broken floor, Threshold agents in tactical gear searching methodically.

And then Grace herself tumbled through the opening, bloody and battered but alive. The tear sealed itself behind her with a sound like a thunderclap, leaving them once again isolated in the empty threshold state of Boston.

"Grace!" Maya rushed to the fallen woman's side, helping her to a sitting position. "We thought you might not make it through."

"Almost didn't," Grace gasped, blood still trickling from her nose and ears. "They got a tracer on me... had to shake it before I could follow... complex route..."

Her speech was disjointed, her eyes

unfocused. Whatever she had endured to escape and follow them had taken a severe toll on her system. Threshold work of that magnitude, tearing holes in reality itself, carried physical consequences that couldn't be ignored or powered through indefinitely.

"Save your strength," Alex advised, examining her for visible injuries. Besides the blood from her nose and ears, typical signs of threshold overexertion, she had what appeared to be burns along her left arm and side. Not conventional thermal burns but something more abstract, as if reality itself had scorched her during her desperate passage.

"No time," Grace insisted, her voice strengthening with effort. "They're recalibrating. Tracking the resonance signature of our combined bloodlines. Won't take them long to find this waypoint."

"Can they reach us here? In this threshold state?" Maya asked.

"Eventually," Grace confirmed grimly. "Threshold states aren't separate realities. Just different vibrational frequencies of the same fundamental existence. With enough power, enough precision they can align their frequency to ours."

"Then we need to move," Alex concluded. "Choose a destination from this waypoint and continue on before they can track us here."

Grace shook her head weakly. "Not that

simple. Each threshold state has its own dangers. Its own inhabitants. Some worse than what hunts us."

"What are our options?" Maya asked, helping Grace to a more comfortable position against one of the waypoint's pearlescent pillars.

With visible effort, Grace gestured toward the symbols etched into the structure's surface. "Each sequence represents a different state. Different proximity to the primary threshold. Some closer to our reality, safer but easier for them to reach. Others, deeper into the threshold territories more dangerous but harder to follow."

Alex studied the symbols with new focus, his threshold sight allowing him to perceive something of what lay behind each sequence. The fundamental nature of the reality state it connected to. Some felt almost like their own Boston, with only subtle differences in vibrational frequency. Others were drastically alien, their fundamental physics and metaphysics rearranged in ways that might be instantly fatal to human physiology.

"This one," he said finally, indicating a sequence that felt appropriate. Not too different from their reality to be survivable, but distinct enough to make pursuit difficult. "It feels like a reasonable compromise between safety and security."

Grace studied the sequence, her specialized Chin bloodline perception allowing her a deeper understanding of what Alex had selected. "Interesting choice," she murmured, strength gradually returning to her voice. "That's a mirror state. Everything physically identical to our Boston, but with fundamental differences in consciousness. In awareness."

"What does that mean exactly?" Maya asked.

"It means the physical environment will be familiar. Buildings, streets, geography all the same. But whatever consciousness inhabits that state, whatever beings evolved or emerged there, they'll perceive reality differently than we do."

"Perceive how?" Alex pressed.

Grace shook her head. "Unknown. Each threshold state develops its own perceptual framework. Its own relationship to existence. We won't know until we're there."

It was a risk, but every option available to them carried risk. Stay in this empty threshold state and eventually be found by the Threshold's agents. Return to their own reality and face immediate pursuit. Or venture into an unknown variant with unfamiliar rules and potential dangers, but where their pursuers would have more difficulty following.

"How do we activate the waypoint?" Alex asked, decision made. "How do we access this specific threshold state?"

"Blood," Grace replied, struggling to her feet with Maya's assistance. "Always blood. The currency of threshold mechanics. Three bloodlines in concert will create a stronger passage. More stable."

She approached the central column of the waypoint structure, where the symbols formed more complex, interwoven patterns. From her pocket, she produced a small folding knife, emergency equipment she'd grabbed during their hasty escape from the safehouse.

"Here," she said, indicating a shallow depression in the pearlescent surface. "Each of us contributes. Three drops. No more, no less. While focusing on the specific sequence you selected."

They followed her instructions, each adding precisely three drops of blood to the depression while concentrating on the symbol sequence Alex had chosen. As the blood of three distinct bloodlines—Morgan, Weber, Chin—pooled together in the waypoint's receptacle, the entire structure began to resonate with a tone just below the threshold of human hearing, felt more in the bones and teeth than heard.

The symbols etched into the pearlescent surface began to glow with inner light, first the specific sequence they had selected, then spreading outward to encompass the entire structure. The twilight around them deepened, as if reality itself were holding its breath in anticipation of the transition to come.

"Remain in physical contact," Grace instructed, taking Maya's hand in her left and

Alex's in her right. "The passage is about to open. We must enter together or risk being separated across threshold states."

The resonance intensified, building toward some critical threshold. The gazebo-like structure was now pulsing with light that shifted through colors no human language had names for, illuminating the empty garden around them with impossible radiance.

And then, between one heartbeat and the next, the waypoint activated.

There was no tear in reality this time, no jagged rending of existential fabric. Instead, the world around them simply... shifted. Like the turning of a kaleidoscope, reality rearranged itself into a new pattern that was simultaneously familiar and utterly alien.

They were still in Boston's Public Garden, but it was no longer empty and abandoned. The transition had been so smooth, so seamless, that for a moment Alex thought they had simply returned to their own reality. The garden was vibrant with life, trees in full leaf, flowers blooming, the pond reflecting a bright summer sky.

But something was wrong. Fundamentally, catastrophically wrong.

The people moving through the garden, dozens of them, going about what appeared to be ordinary activities, weren't people at all. At least, not as Alex understood the term. They had human form, human proportions, human clothing. But where faces should have been, there was nothing. Smooth, blank expanses of skin without eyes, nose, mouth, or any facial features whatsoever.

Yet they moved with purpose, with awareness. They carried bags, read books, walked dogs, conversed with each other through some method Alex couldn't perceive. They were clearly sentient, clearly social creatures with complex behavior. They just weren't human. Not in any way that matched his understanding of humanity.

"What the hell," he whispered, instinctively keeping his voice low despite the fact that these beings presumably couldn't hear in any conventional sense. "What are they?"

"Native consciousness," Grace replied, her voice equally hushed. "The dominant species of this threshold state. Physically identical to humans but with a completely different perceptual framework."

"They have no faces," Maya observed, scientific curiosity temporarily overriding fear. "No sensory organs that we would recognize. How do they perceive the world? How do they communicate?"

"Unknown," Grace admitted. "But they clearly do both. Just not in ways our consciousness can readily understand."

The faceless beings showed no sign of

noticing their arrival, continued their activities without interruption or special interest in the three blood-spattered humans who had suddenly appeared in their midst. Either the waypoint transition was a common enough occurrence in this threshold state to merit no special attention, or they couldn't perceive the travelers at all.

"Are we ghosts here?" Alex wondered aloud. "Invisible to them?"

"Not invisible, I think," Grace replied. "Just irrelevant. Outside their perceptual framework. Like how most humans don't notice threshold phenomena in our reality unless they have bloodline sensitivity."

It was deeply unsettling to be surrounded by beings that looked almost human but fundamentally weren't. Uncanny valley territory that triggered instinctive revulsion. But it also offered a strategic advantage. If the native consciousness of this threshold state couldn't readily perceive them, it provided a layer of concealment beyond what their pursuers might expect.

"We should move," Grace advised, still weak from her ordeal but regaining strength. "Find shelter, assess our situation, plan our next steps. The Threshold will eventually track us to the waypoint, figure out which threshold state we entered. But it will take time and resources."

"Time we can use to figure out how to counter

their plans for the equinox crossing," Alex agreed. "Now that we know the lake ritual didn't work as intended, that Caleb was compromised, we need a new strategy."

They moved cautiously through the garden, navigating around the faceless beings who continued their incomprehensible socializing without acknowledging the human intruders in their midst. Beyond the garden, the city appeared to be a perfect replica of Boston. The same buildings, same streets, same geographic layout. Just populated by an entirely different form of consciousness.

"We need intelligence," Maya said as they walked. "We need to know exactly what the Threshold is planning now, which nexus point they're targeting for the equinox ritual, how they intend to use the bloodlines they've captured."

"And whether there are any allies left we can trust," Alex added, thinking of Rivera's presumed death, of Caleb's betrayal. "Any resources we can access."

"My family maintained caches throughout the city," Grace offered. "Emergency supplies, focusing tools, threshold references. If the physical geography of this state matches our Boston exactly, those caches should exist here too."

"Would they be accessible? Usable?" Maya asked.

"Depends on how closely this threshold state

mirrors our reality," Grace replied. "The buildings should exist in the same locations. Whether the specific apartments or storage units were created identically, whether the security systems function the same way, well that's less certain."

It was a chance worth taking. Without resources, without information, they were just three exhausted, injured people hiding in a reality that wasn't their own while an enemy with vastly superior numbers and knowledge hunted them across threshold states.

They needed weapons, both conventional and metaphysical. They needed focusing tools beyond what they currently possessed. And most of all, they needed a plan that accounted for the new intelligence they had gained about the Threshold's true capabilities and the compromised nature of what they thought they had accomplished.

"Lead the way," Alex told Grace. "Show us where to find these caches. Then we start figuring out how to strike back."

As they moved through the uncanny mirror version of Boston, surrounded by faceless beings going about incomprehensible lives, Alex felt something shifting within him. A hardening of resolve, a clarity of purpose that transcended fear or doubt. The Threshold had taken everything from him. His parents, his chance at a normal life, his understanding of his own nature and abilities.

They had manipulated him from the beginning, using Katherine Bishop to set him on a path they had designed, using false guidance from a compromised Guardian to shape his development in ways that served their purposes. Every victory he thought he had achieved had been orchestrated to further their agenda.

No more. Whatever happened next, whatever desperate measures they had to employ, he would not be their puppet any longer. Not their vessel, not their key, not their unwitting accomplice in bringing about the crossing they had planned for centuries.

The Ancient that waited beyond the threshold, patient and hungry and inconceivably old, would have to find another way into the world. Another bloodline. Another Morgan.

This one was going to burn their plans to the ground.

CHAPTER 13

Time moves differently near threshold boundaries. Not just subjectively, but objectively—minutes stretching to hours or collapsing to seconds depending on how reality happens to be folded at that particular moment.

In the faceless version of Boston, three days passed in what felt like both an eternity and an instant. Three days of hiding, planning, and preparation while their pursuers inevitably narrowed the search parameters, tracing their dimensional signature across threshold states.

Grace led them to three of her family's emergency caches, hidden within ordinary-seeming locations that mirrored their counterparts in the Boston they had left behind. A storage unit in Dorchester. A safe deposit box in a Chinatown bank. A hidden compartment beneath the floorboards of what would have been her grandfather's restaurant, now occupied by faceless beings selling what appeared to be food, though nothing any human would recognize as edible.

The caches yielded practical treasures: weapons both conventional and esoteric, focusing tools designed for specific threshold manipulations, notebooks filled with Chin family research and observations spanning generations. Most valuable were the maps—not of physical geography but of threshold topography, showing nexus points throughout the Boston area where reality naturally thinned, where the barrier between worlds was most vulnerable.

"There," Grace said, indicating a location on the western edge of the city. "That's the most likely alternative site for their ritual. Former Masonic temple, constructed on a natural fissure in the threshold. Not as powerful as the lake nexus, but significant."

They had established a temporary base in an abandoned apartment building, abandoned in this threshold state, at least. Either the faceless beings had no use for the structure, or they perceived it differently than human senses did. Whatever the reason, it remained empty and secure, a place where they could plan without observation.

"Would they still proceed with the equinox ritual?" Maya asked, studying the threshold map spread across a dusty table. "Now that they know we're aware of their plans, that we've discovered the lake ritual was compromised?"

"They have no choice," Grace replied. "The

celestial alignment only occurs once every thirty-six years. The Ancient (the entity that currently wears Dr. Marsh's form) has been working toward this specific convergence for centuries. They can't simply postpone."

"But they're still missing three bloodlines," Alex pointed out. "Morgan, Weber, Chin. Without us, the ritual is incomplete."

"Incomplete but not impossible," Grace corrected. "The seven bloodlines at full strength would create an optimal crossing; stable, controlled, precisely directed. With only four, the result would be messier, more chaotic, with higher risk of containment failure. But still possible."

The implications were disturbing. Even without capturing them, the Threshold could still proceed with their plans. The crossing would still occur, just with less control, less precision. Potentially more dangerous in its unpredictability.

"So they don't actually need us," Maya concluded.

"They want us," Grace clarified. "The ritual would be far more effective with all seven bloodlines. But they'll proceed without us if necessary."

Alex studied the threshold map, tracing the ley lines that connected various nexus points throughout the city. The patterns were becoming more intuitive to him, the underlying structure of threshold mechanics more comprehensible as his abilities continued to develop.

"We need to disrupt the ritual itself," he said. "Not just keep ourselves out of their hands but actively prevent the crossing from occurring."

"How?" Maya asked. "We're three people against an organization with centuries of preparation, resources we can barely imagine, and allies from beyond the threshold itself."

It was the fundamental question they had been circling for three days, seeking an answer that wasn't suicide or futility. How could they possibly counter a conspiracy so vast, so ancient, so deeply entrenched in the fundamental structure of reality itself?

"Asymmetric warfare," Alex said finally. "We can't match their strength directly, but we might be able to target specific vulnerabilities. Critical components without which their ritual can't function."

"Such as?" Grace prompted.

"The bloodlines they've already captured," Alex replied. "If we could free even one or two, Bishop, Nazari, Okafor, or LaChance, it would further degrade the ritual's effectiveness. Potentially to the point of failure."

Grace considered this, her expression thoughtful. "Possible, but extremely high risk. They'll have the captured bloodlines heavily guarded, probably at the ritual site itself. Direct assault would be challenging."

"What about the physical components?" Maya suggested. "Ritual tools, focusing mechanisms, whatever material elements they need for the working."

"Harder to determine," Grace admitted. "Each crossing attempt has its own specific requirements based on the nexus point being used, the particular alignment of celestial bodies, the entities involved. Without inside intelligence..."

The problem always came back to information, what they didn't know, couldn't know without direct access to the Threshold's plans. They were operating on educated guesses, historical patterns, and bloodline intuition. Their enemy held almost all the cards.

Almost.

"We do have one advantage," Alex said, an idea beginning to take shape. "They think they know what we're going to do. They've been manipulating us from the beginning, anticipating our moves, turning our resistance into unwitting assistance."

"How is that an advantage?" Maya asked skeptically.

"Because what they can't anticipate is us doing something completely irrational. Something that makes no sense from their perspective. Something that counters their plans without furthering their goals."

Grace studied him with new interest. "What exactly are you proposing?"

"A counter-ritual," Alex said. "Not to seal the threshold or strengthen it as they've demonstrated they can corrupt those approaches. Something different. Something unexpected."

"Such as?" Maya pressed.

Alex hesitated, aware of how extreme his emerging idea would sound. "What if, instead of trying to prevent their crossing, we initiated our own? On our terms, with our bloodlines, directed toward our purposes rather than theirs?"

The silence that followed was heavy with implications. Grace and Maya exchanged glances, equal parts shock and consideration in their expressions.

"You're suggesting we tear a hole in reality," Grace said finally. "Deliberately. To what end exactly?"

"To contact whatever exists on the other side that isn't aligned with the Ancient," Alex explained, the plan taking clearer shape as he articulated it. "There must be other entities, other intelligence beyond the threshold that isn't part of this crossing agenda. Potential allies against what's coming."

It was a desperate gambit, born of limited options and mounting pressure. They had three days at most before the equinox alignment. Three days before the Threshold attempted the ritual that would change reality itself, bringing the Ancient and whatever served it across the barrier that had contained them for millennia.

"Even if such entities exist," Grace said carefully, "what makes you think they would help us? That they wouldn't be just as dangerous, just as self-interested as what's currently trying to cross?"

"Because whatever is trying to cross now has been specifically excluded from our reality for thousands of years," Alex reasoned. "Contained, constrained, prevented from interfering. That suggests other forces, other entities or powers made that decision. Enforced that boundary."

It was a theoretical leap, but one that made intuitive sense. If the threshold was a barrier, a membrane between worlds, then it had to have been established by something, maintained by something. The Ancients and its servants were working to breach that barrier, to circumvent whatever forces had established it in the first place.

"The Guardians," Maya said suddenly, making the connection. "Like what Caleb claimed to be. Maybe there really are entities that guard the threshold, just not Caleb himself."

"Or other Ancients with competing agendas," Grace suggested. "The threshold realm isn't monolithic. There could be factions, alliances, conflicts we know nothing about."

The possibility was both terrifying and

hopeful. They were contemplating reaching blindly across dimensional barriers to contact unknown entities of unfathomable power and incomprehensible motivation. But without allies, without assistance beyond their own limited abilities and resources, they had little chance of preventing the Threshold's ritual.

"How would we even attempt such a working?" Maya asked, practical concerns asserting themselves. "We have three bloodlines, yes, but limited knowledge of threshold mechanics at this scale."

"The Chin family archives might help," Grace said, retrieving a worn leather journal from one of the cache collections. "My grandfather was researching alternative crossing methodologies, ways to initiate contact across the threshold without the specific requirements the Threshold cult uses."

She opened the journal to pages filled with diagrams, calculations, and notes in both English and Chinese. "He theorized that bloodline representatives could establish temporary controlled breaches. Small, targeted openings rather than the wide scale thinning the Threshold seeks to create."

"Like a surgical incision versus tearing down a wall," Alex suggested, examining the diagrams.

"Precisely," Grace confirmed. "Requires less power, less elaborate preparation, but also yields more limited results. A brief window of communication rather than physical crossing."

It wasn't a perfect solution, but it was something tangible. A potential action rather than continued reaction. A way to seize initiative after being manipulated for so long.

"When could we attempt this?" Alex asked.

"The threshold is already thinning in preparation for the equinox," Grace replied. "Any working we attempt would be easier, more effective as we get closer to the alignment. But that same thinning makes it easier for them to track us across threshold states, to locate us here."

"So we're in a race," Maya concluded. "Try to contact potential allies before the Threshold finds us. Before the equinox arrives."

"Yes," Grace confirmed grimly. "And they have a significant head start."

As if to emphasize this point, a subtle vibration passed through the abandoned building. Not a physical tremor but something more fundamental. A disturbance in the threshold itself, rippling through layers of reality. All three of them felt it simultaneously, their bloodline sensitivity registering the disturbance like specialized instruments detecting seismic activity.

"They're scanning," Grace whispered, moving immediately to the windows to check the street below. "Sending pulses across threshold states, looking for our resonance signature."

"Can they pinpoint our location?" Alex asked, gathering their essential supplies in case rapid evacuation became necessary.

"Not precisely. Not yet." Grace's expression was tense with concentration as she monitored the threshold fluctuations. "They can narrow it to this variant of Boston, but not specific coordinates within it. Still, it's only a matter of time."

"Then we need to move," Maya concluded, securing her grandmother's mirror in its protective wrap. "Find a more defensible location to attempt our counter plans."

Grace consulted the threshold map again, studying the patterns of nexus points and ley lines. "Here," she said, indicating a location near the harbor. "Old waterfront warehouse district. Built on reclaimed land with unstable threshold properties. Natural thinning but chaotic, unpredictable patterns that might mask our activities."

It was their best option. They gathered what supplies they could carry—focusing tools, weapons, the most critical research materials—and prepared to leave the relative safety of the abandoned building. Before departing, Grace knelt in the center of what had been their planning room, removing a small cloth pouch from one of the cache collections.

"Resonance masking," she explained, sprinkling a reddish powder in a circle around her. "Temporary disruption of our bloodline signatures. Won't hide us completely, but will make their tracking more difficult, buy us time."

The powder ignited as she completed the circle—not with conventional flame but with a cold, blue-white light that pulsed once before fading into the floorboards. Alex felt the effect immediately, a subtle dampening of his connection to the threshold, as if a blanket had been thrown over a speaker, muffling but not eliminating the sound.

"It will last six hours at most," Grace warned. "After that, our natural resonance reasserts itself."

Six hours to reach the harbor, establish a secure location, and attempt an unprecedented threshold working with minimal preparation and limited knowledge. Against an enemy with vastly superior resources, experience, and power, who had already demonstrated the ability to track them across dimensional boundaries.

No pressure.

They left the building cautiously, moving through streets populated by the faceless beings who continued their incomprehensible lives without acknowledging the human interlopers. The city around them was familiar in geography but alien in atmosphere. Boston's architecture housing a consciousness so fundamentally different from humanity that parallels became meaningless.

As they walked, Alex found himself wondering about the natives of this threshold state. Did they perceive humans occasionally passing through their reality? Did they have their own version of bloodlines, their own threshold sensitivity? Their own Ancient entities seeking crossing from yet another layer of existence?

The multiverse model that had seemed like abstract theory in his former life now felt viscerally real. Layer upon layer of realities separated by membranes of varying thickness, each with its own physics, its own consciousness, its own relationship to existence itself.

"They're coming through," Grace said suddenly, stopping in the middle of a street that would have been Congress in their Boston. "I can feel ripples in the threshold. Multiple entry points activating simultaneously."

"The Threshold agents?" Maya asked, scanning their surroundings for signs of pursuit.

"Yes. Coordinates still imprecise, but they've managed to breach this threshold state. They'll be deploying threshold tracking specialists, focusing on our bloodline resonance."

Despite the masking powder, their unique combination of bloodlines would eventually stand out against the background threshold energy of this variant Boston. Three specific patterns, Morgan, Weber, Chin, moving together would create a signature distinct enough to track with specialized equipment and abilities.

"We need to separate," Grace decided. "Not completely, but enough to confuse their tracking algorithms. Three distinct bloodline signatures moving in different directions will be harder to correlate than a single combined pattern."

It was tactically sound but emotionally difficult. After everything they had experienced together, the thought of dividing their small force felt dangerous, vulnerable.

"For how long?" Alex asked. "And how do we reconnect?"

"Two hours," Grace replied. "Enough to create tracking confusion without leaving us exposed individually for too long. We reconvene at the harbor location, specific coordinates only, no landmarks that could be intercepted if they're monitoring threshold communications."

She quickly sketched a map on a scrap of paper, marking three distinct routes to the harbor destination and specific temporal windows for arrival. "Offset schedule to further confuse tracking. Alex first, then Maya, then myself. If any of us doesn't arrive within their window, the others proceed with the working regardless."

It was ruthlessly pragmatic, acknowledging the reality that any of them might be captured en route. That the mission had to continue even if individual components were compromised.

"What if they're specifically targeting one bloodline?" Maya asked. "Prioritizing Morgan, for instance, since it's central to their ritual?"

"Possible," Grace conceded. "But dispersing still offers better odds than moving as a group. One bloodline signature is harder to track than three combined, regardless of which specific line they're prioritizing."

She was right, however uncomfortable the strategy made them all feel. After confirming the routes and rendezvous timing, they prepared to separate. Grace distributed small cloth pouches to each of them, more of the resonance masking powder for emergency use if direct pursuit was detected.

"Remember," she instructed, "the working we're attempting requires all three bloodlines for optimal effectiveness. But two can still establish contact on a more limited scale if necessary. One alone would struggle to create any meaningful breach."

The implication was clear: even if one of them was captured, the others needed to continue. The mission transcended individual survival.

"Two hours," Alex confirmed, checking his watch. "I'll make initial contact at the harbor location in two hours. Maya follows an hour later. Grace completes the triangle an hour after that."

They separated without further discussion,

each taking a different street away from their current location. Alex headed southeast, following a route that would take him through what would have been Boston's financial district in their reality. Maya went southwest, toward Beacon Hill. Grace continued eastward, directly toward the harbor but via a circuitous path designed to confuse pursuit.

Alone for the first time since their desperate escape from Grace's safehouse, Alex felt the full weight of their situation press down on him. Three people against forces that transcended conventional understanding. Three bloodlines attempting to counter plans millennia in the making. Three humans with limited knowledge and experience facing an Ancient entity that had orchestrated events across centuries.

The odds were not favorable.

And yet.

As he moved through the uncanny mirror version of Boston, surrounded by faceless beings going about incomprehensible lives, Alex felt something stirring within him. Something that had been building since the lake house ritual, since the revelation of Caleb's betrayal, since the discovery that everything he thought he knew had been carefully manipulated by forces beyond his understanding.

Anger. But not the hot, destructive anger of immediate passion. Something colder, more focused. More dangerous.

The Morgan bloodline had been hunted, manipulated, and sacrificed for generations. His mother had died protecting him from forces she knew he wasn't ready to face. His father had lived and died in fear, trying to shield him from a heritage he couldn't escape. And now they wanted to use him, his blood, his abilities, his unique threshold resonance, to further an agenda that would reshape reality itself, that would allow ancient horrors to cross into a world unprepared for their return.

No. Not this Morgan. Not now. Not ever.

Whatever working they attempted at the harbor, whatever desperate gambit they were forced to employ, Alex was determined to break the cycle of manipulation and sacrifice that had defined his bloodline for generations. To seize control of his own threshold abilities, his own destiny, regardless of what entities or organizations thought they had already determined his path.

The financial district was eerily quiet despite the faceless beings moving purposefully through its streets. Without human conversation, without the normal sounds of commerce and transportation, the city had a muted quality, as if observed through water or thick glass. The silence made it easier to detect anomalies, disturbances in the otherwise uniform background of this threshold state.

Which was why Alex immediately noticed

when the silence deepened, intensified, in a way that felt deliberately imposed rather than naturally occurring.

He paused at an intersection, threshold sight activating instinctively as his senses registered danger. The faceless beings continued their activities, apparently unaffected by whatever was causing the localized silence. But to Alex's enhanced perception, something was very wrong with the street ahead.

The air itself seemed thicker, more resistant, as if reality were being compressed or folded in ways that violated fundamental principles. A containment field, similar to what the Threshold had deployed around Grace's safehouse but more precisely targeted, more carefully calibrated.

They had found him. Not through bloodline tracking as the masking powder was still active, still dampening his resonance signature. Through some other method, some other approach he hadn't anticipated.

Alex ducked into the recessed doorway of what would have been a bank in his Boston, considering his options. The most direct route to the harbor was now blocked by whatever threshold manipulation they had deployed ahead. Alternative paths would take longer, potentially missing his rendezvous window with Maya and Grace.

Worse, if they had found him this quickly despite the masking powder, they might have located the others as well. The entire separation strategy could be compromised.

He needed to warn them, but conventional communication was impossible across threshold states without specialized equipment they didn't possess. The only option was to complete his own journey to the harbor rendezvous and hope the others managed the same.

Alex studied the street ahead, his threshold sight revealing more details about the containment field they had established. It wasn't a complete barrier, not yet. More like a net being drawn closed, designed to herd him toward a specific location where capture would be more feasible.

Standard containment protocol based on what Grace had described. First isolation, then restriction of movement, then direct confrontation once the target was sufficiently contained that escape became improbable.

But the protocol assumed conventional movement through physical space. It didn't account for alternatives that someone with threshold sensitivity—particularly Morgan bloodline threshold sensitivity—might employ.

From his pocket, Alex removed his mother's locket, the silver warmed against his palm as it recognized his bloodline resonance. Since the lake ritual, his connection to the focusing tool had deepened, became more intuitive. The threshold sight it enabled was now less a distinct state he entered and more a perceptual overlay he could maintain indefinitely, viewing both ordinary reality and threshold mechanics simultaneously.

But the locket could do more than enhance perception. As he had discovered during their three days of research and preparation in this threshold state, it could also manipulate reality under specific conditions. Not to the degree that their combined bloodlines could achieve, but enough for limited, localized effects.

Enough, perhaps, for what he was contemplating now.

Alex closed his eyes, concentrating on the unique vibrational frequency of this threshold state. The specific pattern that distinguished it from other variants of Boston across the multiversal spectrum. The faceless version existed at a particular "pitch" in the multidimensional orchestra, a specific note in the vast chord of possible realities.

And like any musician worth their salt, Alex had learned to hear adjacent notes, to sense the harmonics that existed alongside the fundamental tone.

There. Just "above" the current frequency. Another threshold state, another variant Boston, similar enough in basic parameters to be reachable without the complex apparatus of a full crossing ritual. Similar enough that a temporary, localized shift might be possible with the right focus, the right bloodline connection, the right technique.

It was risky. Threshold manipulation without proper preparation, without the stabilizing influence of multiple bloodlines working in concert, carried significant dangers. Reality shifting was not a precise science under the best conditions. Under pressure, with limited knowledge and experience, the potential for catastrophic failure was high.

But the alternative was capture. Was becoming another component in the Threshold's equinox ritual. Was having his bloodline, his abilities, his very essence turned against everything he had fought to protect.

Alex made his decision.

Holding the locket firmly in his left hand, he used the small silver knife from Grace's cache collection to make a precise cut across his right palm—not deep, just enough to draw blood. Three drops fell onto the locket's surface, momentarily obscuring the threshold symbol engraved there before being absorbed into the silver itself.

"Blood freely given," he whispered, echoing the ritual language they had used at the lake. "Catalyst for change, lineage of watchers, guardians of the veil."

The locket began to warm in his hand, then to generate heat beyond what any metal should be capable of producing without actually burning flesh. The threshold sight intensified, showing Alex not just the barrier ahead but the layered realities that existed adjacent to this one. Parallel Bostons stacked like transparencies, each with its own rules, its own physics, its own relationship to existence.

He focused on the specific variant he had identified, the one just "above" the current frequency. Focused on creating not a permanent breach but a temporary shift, a localized alteration that would allow him to step from one threshold state to another without passing through the barrier the Threshold agents had established ahead.

Reality resisted. Then bent. Then tore.

Not dramatically, not with the jagged rending that Grace had created for their escape from the safehouse. This was more subtle, more controlled. A gentle parting of dimensional fabric, a temporary permission rather than a forced entry.

Through that parting, Alex glimpsed another Boston. Not the faceless variant he currently occupied, but something different. The geography remained the same; the street layout, the buildings, the basic urban structure. But the quality of light was wrong, the color palette shifted toward blues and purples rather than the normal spectrum. And the beings that moved through this variant...

He couldn't focus on them directly. His

mind simply refused to interpret what his eyes were seeing, as if the natives of this particular threshold state existed in configurations his human brain wasn't equipped to process. Not faceless humans but something so fundamentally alien that perception itself failed when attempting to categorize them.

It didn't matter. He wasn't planning to stay in that variant, just pass through it as a detour around the Threshold's containment field. A dimensional sidestep to avoid what he couldn't confront directly.

Taking a deep breath, Alex stepped through the opening he had created, transitioning from one threshold state to another with a sensation like passing through an electrified spiderweb. Countless filaments of reality brushing against his skin, his mind, his very being as he moved between them.

For one nauseating moment, he existed in multiple states simultaneously. Partly in the faceless Boston, partly in the blue-shifted variant, partly in spaces between and beyond conventional understanding. Then reality settled around him, resolidified into a coherent state as the opening closed behind him.

The blue-shifted variant of Boston welcomed him with alien indifference. Whatever beings inhabited this threshold state either couldn't perceive him or found his presence unremarkable. They continued their incomprehensible activities without acknowledging the human suddenly standing in their midst.

Alex moved quickly, not wanting to remain in this unsettling variant any longer than necessary. The containment field the Threshold had established in the faceless Boston presumably didn't extend to this adjacent reality. At least not yet. He had a narrow window to bypass their trap, to continue toward the harbor rendezvous before they recalibrated their pursuit.

The journey through blue-shifted Boston was disorienting in ways that transcended simple visual differences. Time itself seemed to flow differently here. Moments stretching and compressing unpredictably, making it impossible to judge how long he had been walking. The air felt thicker, more resistant to movement, as if the fundamental physical constants of this reality were calibrated slightly differently than in his native state.

When he estimated he had moved beyond the likely range of the Threshold's containment field, Alex paused in what appeared to be an alley between tall structures that vaguely resembled office buildings, though their architecture followed principles no human designer would or could employ.

Again, he used the locket to sense the layered realities around him, to identify the specific frequency of the faceless Boston they had been occupying. Again, he offered three drops of blood to activate the focus, to open a temporary passage between threshold states.

The transition back was smoother, perhaps because his system was becoming accustomed to the process. The sensation of passing through the dimensional boundary was less jarring, the moment of existing in multiple states simultaneously less nauseating.

Then he was back in faceless Boston, standing in what would have been a service alley behind commercial buildings in his native reality. According to his watch, nearly forty minutes had passed since he'd made the dimensional sidestep, far longer than the actual distance travelled should have required. Time dilation effects, presumably, one of the many complications of threshold navigation that Grace had warned about.

Still, he was ahead of schedule for the harbor rendezvous. And more importantly, he had successfully evaded whatever trap the Threshold had set for him. Small victories in a conflict where every advantage, however minor, might prove critical.

Alex continued toward the harbor, more cautious now, more alert for signs of pursuit or containment. The faceless beings continued their incomprehensible lives around him, neither helping nor hindering his progress through their version of Boston. He wondered, not for the first time, what they perceived when they looked at him, if they looked at him at all. Whether humans were as alien and unsettling to them as they were to him.

The harbor district appeared as he rounded what would have been Atlantic Avenue in his Boston, a sprawl of weathered buildings and industrial structures fronting dark water. The architecture matched the geographical layout he remembered, but like everything in this threshold state, it had an uncanny quality that transcended simple visual differences.

The warehouse Grace had identified as their rendezvous point stood at the edge of a disused pier. A massive brick structure with boarded windows and a sagging roof. In his Boston, it would have been abandoned or repurposed for luxury apartments. Here, it appeared similarly neglected, though whether the faceless beings conceptualized 'abandonment' the same way humans did remained an open question.

Alex approached cautiously, checking for signs of surveillance or threshold manipulation. Nothing immediately registered to his enhanced perception. No containment fields, no reality distortion beyond the background instability Grace had described as characteristic of the harbor area.

Inside, the warehouse was cavernous and empty, dust motes dancing in shafts of blue-tinged light that penetrated through gaps in the boarded windows. The air smelled of salt and decay and something else. Something more abstract, more fundamental. The scent of a thin place, a location where reality itself had worn threadbare over time.

Alex checked his watch. Still thirty minutes before Maya's scheduled arrival, assuming she hadn't encountered similar complications during her journey. An hour and a half before Grace would complete their triangle. Time enough to prepare the space for the working they intended to attempt.

From his backpack, he removed the materials they had gathered from Grace's family caches; focusing tools, threshold references, components for the contact ritual they hoped to perform. According to Grace's grandfather's research, establishing communication across the threshold required precise arrangement of bloodline representatives and their respective focuses, forming a pattern that mirrored specific threshold geometries.

He began preparing the space according to the diagrams they had studied, marking key points on the warehouse floor with chalk, positioning focusing tools at precise intervals to create the necessary resonance pattern. The work was methodical, detailed, requiring exact measurements and careful attention to threshold symbols.

Twenty minutes into the preparation, Alex felt it. .A subtle shift in the warehouse's atmosphere, a pressure change that had nothing to do with weather or conventional physics. His threshold sight activated automatically, showing him what ordinary perception couldn't reveal: a thinning in reality itself, a localized weakening of the boundary between threshold states.

Someone was coming through. Not from another variant of Boston, but from somewhere more fundamental. Somewhere closer to the primary threshold itself.

Alex reached for the conventional weapon Grace had provided, a 9mm handgun loaded with specialized ammunition designed to affect entities that existed partially outside conventional reality. Not nearly as effective as properly focused bloodline abilities, but better than nothing if confronted with Threshold agents or their otherworldly allies.

The thinning intensified, reality stretching like plastic wrap pulled to transparency. Through that thinning, Alex glimpsed something moving, a human silhouette, female, somehow familiar despite the distortion effects of cross-threshold observation.

The warehouse air rippled, folded, parted. And through that parting stepped Maya Weber, clutching her grandmother's mirror with white-knuckled intensity, blood streaming from her nose and ears. The physical toll of threshold manipulation without proper preparation or support.

"Maya!" Alex rushed forward as she stumbled, catching her before she could collapse. "What happened? You're early."

"They found me," she gasped, her voice hoarse with exertion. "Containment field. Like at Grace's apartment. Had to use the mirror. Forced a passage. Like Grace did but smaller. Targeted."

Alex helped her to a crate where she could sit, offering water from his supplies. The bleeding had already stopped but she looked pale, drained.

"How did they find you?" he asked. "The masking powder should have hidden your resonance signature."

"Different approach," Maya replied, wiping blood from her face with a trembling hand. "They're using some kind of psychometric tracking. Focusing on impressions left on physical objects. Everything we touched in Grace's safehouse before escaping. My specialty inverted against me."

It made tactical sense. If bloodline resonance tracking was being hampered by the masking powder, they would switch to alternative methods. The Weber bloodline's particular affinity for memory and impression could be turned against Maya. Using her own specialization as a pathway to locate her across threshold states.

"Did you see Grace?" Alex asked. "Was she compromised too?"

Maya shook her head. "No sign of her. But if they found me despite the masking powder, they could be tracking her too. Different method perhaps, tailored to Chin bloodline abilities."

It was a sobering possibility. Their plan required all three bloodlines for optimal effectiveness. With only Morgan and Weber present, their options were significantly limited.

"We give her one hour," Alex decided. "Her scheduled arrival window. If she doesn't appear by then, we proceed with whatever working two bloodlines can manage."

Maya nodded grimly, her strength gradually returning as she recovered from the forced threshold passage. "What have you prepared so far?"

Alex showed her the partial arrangement he had established based on Grace's grandfather's research. The focusing points, the threshold symbols, the geometric pattern designed to create a controlled breach for communication purposes.

"It's designed for three points," Maya observed. "A triangulation of bloodlines. With only two, we'll need to adapt the configuration."

She studied the diagrams they had copied from the Chin family archives, making adjustments to accommodate their reduced capabilities. "Less stable," she concluded. "Shorter duration. More limited contact if we achieve it at all. But potentially still functional."

They worked together to modify the arrangement, creating a binary configuration rather than the triangular pattern originally intended. The changes weren't simply geometric but conceptual. Altering the fundamental approach to threshold manipulation based on their available resources.

As they worked, Alex described his own encounter with the Threshold's containment field, his dimensional sidestep through the blue-shifted variant of Boston.

"Risky," Maya commented. "Reality shifting isn't precise under ideal conditions."

"Seemed preferable to capture," Alex replied. "And it worked, more or less."

"This time," Maya said pointedly. "Continued manipulation without proper understanding of the mechanics involved the consequences compound.

It was a concept Grace had explained during their three days of preparation, the idea that reality itself kept a ledger of sorts when it came to threshold manipulation. That repeated breaches, passages, or alterations created an imbalance that eventually required correction. Sometimes catastrophically.

"One more reason to make this working count," Alex said. "We might not get another opportunity."

They completed the modified arrangement just as Maya's scheduled arrival window closed with no sign of Grace. The hour they had agreed to wait stretched into ninety minutes, then two hours, with growing certainty that the third member of their alliance had been captured or worse.

"We need to proceed," Maya said finally, voicing what they both knew. "Whatever happened to Grace, we can't wait any longer. The equinox alignment is tomorrow. The Threshold will be completing their final preparations. This is our last chance to find allies, to disrupt their ritual."

She was right. The modified working they had prepared was their only remaining option. Their final, desperate attempt to reach across the threshold to whatever entities or forces might oppose the Ancient's crossing plans.

"How do we begin?" Alex asked, taking position at one of the two focal points they had established in the warehouse floor.

"Blood, as always," Maya replied, retrieving the silver knife from their supplies. "Morgan and Weber combined, directed through our respective focuses toward a specific threshold frequency."

Together, they stepped through the opening, transitioning from the faceless variant back to their native reality with a sensation like diving into warm water after hours in the cold. A return to fundamental rightness, to proper alignment with their native dimensional frequency.

The passage deposited them in what appeared to be an alleyway in Boston's North End, not far from where the harbor warehouse existed in the threshold variant they had left behind. Night had fallen in this reality, the narrow street illuminated only by distant streetlights and the ambient glow of the city.

Alex checked his watch, surprised to find that it was nearly midnight. Time dilation effects again—what had felt like hours in the threshold state had translated to nearly a full day in their native reality. The equinox alignment was no longer tomorrow but today. Mere hours away.

"We need to move quickly," he said, orienting himself in the familiar geography of his city. "The Threshold will detect our return almost immediately. Bloodline resonance is more distinctive, more trackable in our native reality state."

Maya nodded, already scanning their surroundings for immediate threats or surveillance. "Where do we go? We can't return to any location they know about."

"We need somewhere to prepare, to rest briefly before attempting the working against Dr. Marsh's vessel," Alex replied, considering their limited options. "Somewhere they wouldn't immediately think to look for us."

The answer came to him with unexpected clarity—a location connected to his past but not his present, to his professional life before all this supernatural conflict had engulfed him. "The office," he said. "My PI agency. It's a small suite in a commercial building downtown. Hasn't been used much since I took Katherine Bishop's case, but I still have the keys."

It wasn't perfect, few places in Boston were truly secure. But it offered temporary shelter, basic amenities, and wasn't directly connected to the supernatural aspects of Alex's life that the Threshold had been monitoring and manipulating.

They moved through Boston with practiced caution, using side streets and service alleys where possible, avoiding main thoroughfares and surveillance cameras. The city felt simultaneously familiar and foreign after their time in the threshold variant. The normal human activity, the conventional sounds and smells and sights both comforting and jarring in contrast to the faceless beings they had lived among.

Alex's office was as he had left it weeks earlier. A small, somewhat shabby suite in an aging commercial building that had seen better days. Dust had accumulated on the cheap desk and filing cabinets, mail had piled up inside the door slot, and the air had the stale quality of long disuse.

"Home sweet home," he said with grim humor, securing the door behind them. "Not exactly luxury accommodations, but it should serve our purposes."

"It's perfect," Maya replied, setting her backpack on the desk and beginning to unpack the essential supplies they had brought back. "Anonymous, functional, and presumably not on the Threshold's immediate search grid."

They used the small kitchen area to prepare coffee, both desperately needed the caffeine after the physical and mental exertion of threshold manipulation, and spread their materials across the desk to review the specific working the Watchers had shown them for neutralizing Dr. Marsh's vessel.

"The timing is critical," Maya observed, studying the diagrams they had transcribed. "The working creates only a momentary vulnerability in the Ancient's control of its vessel. The actual separation must be accomplished within that window."

"And the separation itself requires physical proximity," Alex added. "We can't do this remotely. We need to be in the same location as Dr. Marsh, ideally within arm's reach."

It was perhaps the most challenging aspect of what they were attempting. Creating a vulnerability was one thing. Exploiting it, physically separating the Ancient from its vessel during the brief window they would create was another entirely. Especially given the security the Threshold would have established around their leader, the central figure in their equinox ritual.

"So we need to infiltrate the ritual site," Maya concluded. "Get close enough to Dr. Marsh to implement both stages of this working. While avoiding capture, neutralizing whatever security they've established, and not disrupting the bloodline representatives they're holding."

When she laid it out so starkly, the odds seemed impossible. Two exhausted, under-resourced individuals against an organization with centuries of preparation, supernatural allies, and the home field advantage.

"Actually," Alex said slowly, a new approach taking shape in his mind. "Maybe we don't need to infiltrate. Maybe we could bring Dr. Marsh to us."

Maya looked up sharply. "What are you thinking?"

"The Threshold wants our bloodlines," Alex explained, the strategy crystallizing as he spoke. "They've been hunting us across threshold states, committed significant resources to our capture. What if we offer ourselves as bait? Create a situation where Dr. Marsh herself would come to secure such valuable assets?"

"Deliberately getting captured?" Maya sounded skeptical. "That seems like an enormous risk. Once they have us, our ability to implement any working would be severely compromised."

"Not captured exactly," Alex clarified. "More like appearing vulnerable. Creating a scenario where they think they can take us easily, where the prize is too valuable to delegate to ordinary agents. Where Dr. Marsh would want to be present personally to secure the Morgan and Weber bloodlines she's been seeking for so long."

Maya considered this, her analytical mind working through the tactical implications. "It could work," she conceded after a moment. "The Ancient has demonstrated repeated personal interest in your bloodline specifically. If it believed it could secure both Morgan and Weber representatives in one operation, it might indeed oversee the capture directly."

"Especially with the equinox alignment mere hours away," Alex added. "The timing creates both urgency and opportunity from their perspective. Too valuable to ignore, too time-sensitive to approach with excessive caution."

The strategy was taking definite shape now. Not an infiltration into the heart of enemy territory but a deliberate lure, a calculated risk to bring their target to a location of their choosing under conditions they could at least partially control.

"We'd need to establish the right scenario," Maya said. "Something believable but not too obvious. A situation that appears to offer them advantage while actually serving our purposes."

"And we'd need to select the right location," Alex continued. "Somewhere that seems to favor their approach but actually provides us with tactical benefits. Environmental factors we can leverage if necessary."

They spent the next hour developing the specifics of their plan, refining the approach based on what they knew of the Threshold's methods and motivations. The working the Watchers had shown them would require precise preparation, specific arrangement of their focusing tools, and absolute coordination between Morgan blood and Weber sight to create the momentary vulnerability in Dr. Marsh's vessel.

As dawn approached, they finalized the last details and gathered what supplies they would need for the confrontation ahead. Both were operating on minimal sleep, maximum caffeine, and the peculiar clarity that comes from facing existential threat with limited options and no room for error.

"One last consideration," Maya said as they prepared to leave the temporary safety of Alex's office. "If we succeed—if we manage to separate the Ancient from Dr. Marsh's vessel—what happens to Eliza Bishop's ghost? The spirit that started this whole investigation for you?"

It was a question Alex hadn't considered in days, perhaps weeks. With everything that had happened since his first encounter with Eliza's ghost in his apartment, the original catalyzing event had receded in importance, overshadowed by cosmic conflict and threshold manipulation.

"I don't know," he admitted. "My understanding of threshold mechanics suggests she's caught in a state of transition. Unable to fully cross over because of the circumstances of her death, because of her connection to the Threshold's plans. If we disrupt those plans, remove the Ancient's influence from our reality then..."

"She might finally be able to complete her transition," Maya finished for him. "Find whatever awaits beyond the threshold for human consciousness after death."

The thought brought a measure of closure, of potential completion to the case that had drawn Alex into this supernatural conflict. Whatever happened in the confrontation ahead, at least one spirit might find peace as a result.

"It's time," Alex said, checking his watch one final time. The equinox alignment would reach its apex in less than twelve hours. Whatever they were going to do needed to happen soon, before the Threshold's ritual progressed to its irreversible stages.

They left the office as dawn broke over Boston, the city awakening to what its inhabitants believed would be an ordinary spring day. No one, save a select few involved in the conflict that had been unfolding in shadows and threshold states, knew that reality itself hung in the balance. That ancient entities waited beyond a thinning membrane between worlds, patient and hungry and inconceivably old.

That the veil which had protected humanity from horrors beyond comprehension for millennia was about to tear.

And that two exhausted, outmatched individuals with bloodline connections to threshold mechanics represented perhaps the only remaining obstacle to a crossing that would reshape existence itself.

As they moved through early morning streets toward the location they had selected for their confrontation, Alex felt an odd calm descend over him. The weight of legacy settled onto his shoulders not as a burden now but as armor. The Morgan bloodline had been guardians of the threshold for centuries, standing against forces that most of humanity never knew existed.

Today, that duty fell to him. Whatever happened, whatever the cost, he would not be the Morgan who failed.

CHAPTER 14

Sometimes the most important battles are fought not on vast fields with armies clashing, but in small, forgotten places—a single room, an abandoned building, a quiet corner where reality itself hangs in the balance.

The Boston Public Library seemed an unlikely place for a cosmic confrontation. Its grand McKim Building, a Renaissance revival masterpiece of limestone and marble, had stood in Copley Square since 1895, housing knowledge across centuries without any apparent connection to supernatural conflict or threshold mechanics.

But beneath its stately exterior, beneath the soaring reading rooms and carefully preserved collections, the library held a secret that few beyond dedicated researchers and staff ever discovered.

The underground stacks, a warren of narrow corridors lined with movable shelving units, existed in a kind of architectural limbo. Neither fully public nor completely private, accessible yet obscure, they represented a liminal space within conventional reality. And buried deep within those stacks, far from casual visitors or ordinary researchers, lay the Crawford Collection. A repository of texts focused on precisely the subjects that had consumed Alex Morgan's life these past weeks.

Occult philosophy. Metaphysical theory. Historical documentation of incidents that mainstream scholarship dismissed as superstition or hallucination.

In his previous life as a private investigator, Alex had occasionally used the collection for research on cases touching on historical oddities or cult activity. Now, it represented the perfect staging ground for the confrontation they hoped to engineer. A location with natural threshold resonance due to the texts it contained, with limited access points that could be monitored, and with architectural features they could leverage to their advantage.

"Are you sure they'll come?" Maya asked as they finished their preparations in a secluded corner of the stacks, hidden from casual observation by the massive shelving units that surrounded them like canyon walls of knowledge.

"They'll come," Alex replied, his voice certain despite the anxiety churning beneath his calm exterior. "The masking powder has worn off. Our bloodline resonance is fully detectable again.

And the additional working we performed..."

He glanced at the small arrangement they had established in the center of their chosen space. A modified version of a beacon ritual described in Grace's family archives. Not large enough or powerful enough to create actual threshold breach, but precisely calibrated to broadcast their specific bloodline signatures across conventional space.

Like sending up a flare that only those with threshold sensitivity could see. A beacon declaring "Morgan and Weber bloodlines here" to anyone monitoring for such signatures.

And the Threshold was definitely monitoring. With the equinox alignment mere hours away, with four bloodlines already secured for their ritual, they would be hypersensitive to any trace of the remaining three they sought. Especially the Morgan line, central to their plans for generations.

"How long?" Maya asked, checking the small silver watch that had been part of the cache collection they'd brought from the threshold variant.

"Not long," Alex replied. "Their tracking specialists will have detected our return to native reality state almost immediately. The beacon working just gives them precise coordinates, makes us too tempting a target to ignore."

They had positioned themselves carefully

within the Crawford Collection's domain. A reading alcove at the end of a narrow corridor of stacks, with only one direct approach. The temporary working they had established was hidden from casual view but would be immediately apparent to anyone with threshold sensitivity. Their focusing tools, Alex's mother's locket and Maya's grandmother's mirror were arranged according to the specifications the Watchers had shown them for creating vulnerability in the Ancient's vessel.

Everything was prepared. Everything was ready. Now they just needed their target to appear.

They didn't have to wait long.

The first indication came not as sound or sight but as a subtle change in the atmosphere. A pressure drop that affected the inner ear, a static charge that raised the fine hairs on arms and the back of the neck. The threshold thinning around them, reality stretching as someone, something, manipulated the underlying fabric of existence itself.

"They're here," Maya whispered, her hand moving to her grandmother's mirror where it lay positioned for the working they intended. "Multiple signatures based on the resonance pattern. At least five distinct entities approaching."

Alex nodded, his own threshold sight confirming her assessment. Multiple figures moving through the stacks toward their location. Some with the distinctive resonance of human consciousness, others with the cold, alien patterns he had come to recognize as Lurkers or similar threshold entities operating in human reality.

But it was the presence at the center of this approaching group that commanded his attention. A void in perception, a negative space where something ancient and vast concealed itself within human form. Not human, not Lurker, not like anything he had encountered before except in brief glimpses across dimensional barriers.

The Ancient. Wearing Dr. Marsh's face like a carnival mask, using her body like a puppet, directing this operation personally just as they had hoped.

Their gambit had worked. The prize of capturing both Morgan and Weber bloodlines simultaneously, mere hours before the equinox ritual, had proven too tempting to delegate to ordinary agents or proxies.

"Remember the sequence," Alex murmured to Maya, his hand moving to his mother's locket where it lay at the center of their prepared working. "Morgan blood initiates, Weber sight directs, focusing tools aligned during the momentary vulnerability."

Maya nodded, her expression calm despite the tension evident in the set of her shoulders.

They had rehearsed the working over and over during the hours since their return from the threshold variant, committing each step to muscle memory. The timing would be critical. The vulnerability would last mere seconds, barely long enough to implement the separation if everything went perfectly.

The approaching group reached the end of the corridor leading to their alcove. Four Threshold agents in tactical gear, human but with the hollow-eyed vacancy Alex recognized from their previous encounters, their wills subjugated to whatever consciousness directed them. Behind them, two Lurkers maintained human-adjacent forms but moved with the wrong geometry, their limbs bending at impossible angles, their features shifting like bad special effects when viewed directly.

And at the center, Dr. Evelyn Marsh. Or rather, the entity that wore Dr. Marsh's form. In ordinary reality, with ordinary perception, she would have appeared as a striking woman in her forties—steel-gray eyes, tailored clothing, the polished presentation of a successful professional. But through threshold sight, the illusion broke down at the edges. Her outline blurred, doubled, suggesting multiple entities occupying the same space simultaneously. Her eyes contained depths that had nothing to do with human anatomy, reflecting knowledge and malice accumulated across millennia.

She smiled as she saw them. A gesture that involved too many teeth arranged in patterns human jaws shouldn't be able to accommodate.

"The prodigals return," she said, her voice that distinctive chorus of overlapping tones Alex remembered from his visions. "How convenient that you should reveal yourselves now, with the alignment nearly upon us. One might almost suspect a trap."

"Would that matter?" Alex replied, keeping his tone conversational despite the adrenaline flooding his system. "You need our bloodlines for optimal ritual effectiveness. The equinox alignment happens whether we cooperate or not."

"True enough," Dr. Marsh acknowledged, stepping forward while her agents maintained position at the corridor entrance. "Though I had hoped for a more civilized acquisition. Not this desperate last stand in the bowels of a library."

She glanced around their chosen battleground, her expression suggesting amused contempt rather than concern. "The Crawford Collection. How appropriate. Old texts gathering dust, forgotten knowledge moldering in the dark. Like your bloodlines. Once significant, now reduced to two frightened specimens backed into a corner."

"If we're so insignificant," Maya challenged, "why pursue us across threshold states? Why commit so many resources to our capture?"

"Efficiency," Dr. Marsh replied simply. "Optimal ritual effectiveness, as your companion noted. The crossing will occur regardless, but with Morgan and Weber bloodlines included..." Her smile widened unnaturally. "The precision. The control. The specific outcomes we've worked toward for centuries rather than merely breaking through."

As she spoke, she continued her slow advance into the alcove, her agents and the Lurkers remaining at the corridor entrance, presumably to prevent escape rather than to assist directly. The Ancient clearly believed it needed no help to subdue two exhausted humans, regardless of their bloodline abilities.

That arrogance was central to their plan.

"You've been manipulating us from the beginning," Alex said, drawing her attention back to him as Maya subtly adjusted her position relative to their prepared working. "Katherine Bishop hiring me to investigate her sister's death. Caleb posing as a Guardian to guide my development. The lake house ritual that reshaped the nexus rather than sealing it."

"Such efforts merely accelerated what was inevitable," Dr. Marsh replied, now fully within the alcove, exactly where they needed her to be. "Your bloodline would have awakened regardless, Alex Morgan. Would have developed threshold sensitivity and ability no matter what path you followed. We simply directed that development along more useful channels."

Her casual admission of their manipulation should have stung, should have triggered the anger that had fueled Alex through recent days. Instead, he felt a strange calm descend. The clarity of purpose that comes when theory gives way to action, when planning yields to implementation.

"One question before this ends," he said, hand moving imperceptibly closer to his mother's locket. "Why? Why seek crossing at all? What does our reality offer that justifies centuries of effort, of planning, of manipulation?"

Dr. Marsh's expression shifted, something ancient and cold emerging more clearly through her human features. For a moment, Alex glimpsed what truly looked out through those steel-gray eyes. Something vast and patient and hungry that had existed long before humanity crawled from primordial oceans, that would likely continue long after the last human consciousness winked out of existence.

"Embodiment," she replied, her voice dropping to a register that seemed to bypass conventional hearing entirely. "Physical form. Sensation. Experience. Things lost to us when the threshold was established, when we were contained. Exiled. Separated from what was rightfully ours."

"This world was never yours," Maya countered, her hand now positioned directly above her grandmother's mirror, ready to activate their working.

"Child, this world was ours before it was anything else," Dr. Marsh said, genuine amusement coloring her multilayered voice. "Before your kind evolved consciousness, before you built cities or conceived gods or imagined yourselves significant. We were. We are. We shall be again."

She took a final step forward, now at the optimal distance for their working. Close enough for direct effect, not so close that immediate physical intervention could disrupt the process.

"Enough conversation," she said, her tone shifting to brisk efficiency. "The alignment approaches. Your bloodlines are required. Come willingly or not, but you will come."

It was the moment they had been waiting for. Dr. Marsh fully committed to their capture, focused on their value as ritual components rather than potential threats, positioned precisely where their prepared working could have maximum effect.

Alex met Maya's eyes across the small space, a silent confirmation passing between them. Then, with practiced synchronization, they activated the working the Watchers had shown them.

"Blood freely given," Alex recited, pressing his thumb against the small blade they had positioned beside his mother's locket, allowing three precise drops to fall onto the silver surface. "Catalyst for severance, bloodline of watchers, breaker of bonds."

"Sight truly focused," Maya continued, angling her grandmother's mirror to catch the light in a specific pattern, creating geometric reflections that had nothing to do with conventional optics and everything to do with threshold mechanics. "Direction and purpose, memory and intention, to reveal what hides within."

Their focusing tools—locket and mirror—responded instantly, generating that now-familiar warmth that transcended ordinary thermal properties. The threshold symbols they had marked on the floor around Dr. Marsh began to glow with inner light. Not visible to conventional perception but clearly apparent through the threshold sight both maintained with practiced ease.

Dr. Marsh's expression shifted from confident acquisition to shock as she realized what was happening. Not a surrender or desperate last stand but a calculated attack specifically targeting her vessel's connection to the Ancient consciousness it contained.

"No," she snarled, the word distorting as her human vocals struggled to express the fury of the entity within. "This knowledge was hidden. Suppressed. You cannot—"

But they could. And they were.

The working took effect with surprising speed, creating visible distortion in the air around Dr. Marsh's form. Reality rippling like heat waves above hot asphalt, the boundary between her physical body and the consciousness it contained momentarily revealed as distinct rather than fused entities.

For a critical second, vulnerability existed where there had been only impenetrable defense. The Ancient's connection to its vessel weakened, the quantum-level reinforcements the Watchers had described temporarily nullified by the specific combination of Morgan blood and Weber sight, focused through generational tools designed for exactly this purpose.

"Now!" Alex shouted, lunging forward to complete the working while Maya maintained the directed focus that kept the vulnerability open.

His hand closed around his mother's locket, tearing it from its position in their prepared arrangement and pressing it directly against Dr. Marsh's forehead where the threshold symbol they had drawn in their own blood still glowed with inner light.

The effect was immediate and catastrophic.

Reality itself seemed to tear around Dr. Marsh's form. Not a clean separation but a violent sundering as the Ancient consciousness that had inhabited her vessel for decades was forcibly extracted. Her body convulsed, back arching at an impossible angle, mouth opening in a silent scream as something began to emerge from her.

Not with physical movement but with a dimensional shift. Layers of existence separating like oil and water after being forcibly mixed. The Ancient revealing its true form as it was pulled from its human disguise.

What emerged defied comprehension, defied description in any human language. A shape that hurt the eyes to follow, that seemed to exist in more dimensions than human perception could process. Limbs that weren't limbs, appendages that served functions no terrestrial evolution had ever required, a face if it could be called that, composed of structures arranged in patterns that suggested sensory apparatus beyond anything biology had produced on Earth.

And eyes. So many eyes. Eyes that had watched humanity since before humanity had existed. Eyes that had seen civilizations rise and fall, species evolve and go extinct, reality itself reshape under forces beyond mortal understanding.

Those eyes fixed on Alex Morgan with ancient, cold fury as the separation completed. As the working he and Maya had implemented successfully extracted the Ancient consciousness from its carefully prepared vessel.

Morgan, it communicated directly into his mind. *Last of the line. Breaker of bonds. This severance changes nothing. The crossing comes regardless. Others wait. Others serve. Others complete what was set in motion millennia before your kind achieved consciousness.*

Then it was gone.

Not destroyed or banished, but drawn back across the threshold by forces their working had set in motion. Pulled into the realm where it had been contained for so long, where it had existed in patient exile while planning its return.

Dr. Marsh, or the human shell that had once housed that Ancient consciousness, collapsed to the floor, empty and still. Whether the woman who had originally owned that body still existed in any meaningful sense, whether any trace of her consciousness had survived decades of occupation by an entity from beyond the threshold, remained unknown.

The Threshold agents and Lurkers at the corridor entrance reacted with immediate aggression. Weapons raised, otherworldly limbs extending as they prepared to attack despite the loss of their central directing intelligence.

But another presence intervened before they could advance.

A tear appeared in reality, at the center of the alcove.

Not the violent sundering caused by the Ancient's extraction, but a controlled, precise opening between states. Through that opening stepped Grace Chin, bloodied but very much alive, accompanied by two figures Alex didn't recognize. A middle-aged Asian man and woman with Grace's distinctive features, presumably family members.

"More Chins," Maya breathed, recognition dawning. "They escaped. They found each other."

Grace assessed the situation with practiced efficiency, taking in the fallen form of Dr. Marsh, the advancing Threshold agents, the Lurkers with their impossible geometries.

"Time to go," she announced, gesturing toward the tear in reality she and her family members had created. "The extraction worked, I see. Well done. But we need to move immediately. Their ritual site is already active, the remaining bloodlines generating preliminary threshold thinning despite the Ancient's extraction."

"How—" Alex began, but Grace cut him off with a raised hand.

"Explanations later. Exit now. This location is about to become extremely hostile."

She wasn't wrong. The Threshold agents and Lurkers had recovered from their momentary confusion and were advancing down the corridor toward the alcove, weapons raised, otherworldly limbs extending with predatory intent.

"What about her?" Maya asked, gesturing toward Dr. Marsh's collapsed form. "Is she alive? Is she still... herself?"

"Irrelevant at present," Grace replied tersely. "The vessel is just biological material now. The consciousness it contained is what mattered, and you've successfully removed that from our reality. A significant achievement, but only the first step in preventing the crossing."

The urgency in her tone convinced them where prolonged explanation couldn't have. Together, they stepped through the tear Grace and her family had created, leaving behind the Crawford Collection, the advancing Threshold forces, and the empty vessel that had once housed an Ancient consciousness.

The transition was smoother than their previous threshold crossings, perhaps due to the Chin family's specialized abilities with such navigation. They emerged not in another variant of Boston but in what appeared to be an underground chamber. Concrete walls, fluorescent lighting, the institutional aesthetic of a facility designed for function rather than form.

"Welcome to the last resistance," Grace said as the tear closed behind them, sealing off pursuit. "The final line of defense against the crossing the Threshold has been planning for centuries."

Alex and Maya took in their surroundings with threshold-enhanced perception. The chamber they had entered was larger than it first appeared, a circular space perhaps fifty feet in diameter, with corridors branching off in multiple directions. The walls were covered in threshold symbols similar to but distinct from those they had encountered previously. More complex, more numerous, arranged in patterns that suggested defensive rather than offensive intent.

Most significantly, the chamber contained people. Dozens of them, moving with purpose between workstations filled with both conventional technology and focusing tools similar to those Alex and Maya carried. Some wore tactical gear suggesting paramilitary training, others the practical clothing of researchers or technical specialists.

All had the distinctive resonance signature of threshold sensitivity, though with variations suggesting different bloodlines, different abilities, different relationships to the mechanics of reality itself.

"What is this place?" Alex asked, overwhelmed by the scale of operation he was witnessing. "Who are these people?"

"The resistance," Grace repeated, leading them deeper into the chamber. "Those who oppose the Threshold's plans for crossing. Those who maintain the barriers the Ancients have been trying to breach for millennia."

"But... how?" Maya gestured at the facility around them. "How has something this extensive remained hidden? How have we never heard of this organization despite everything we've experienced?"

"Compartmentalization," replied the older Asian man who had accompanied Grace through the threshold tear. "Need-to-know protocols taken to their logical extreme. Even those with bloodline sensitivity, even those directly opposing the Threshold's activities, aren't informed of our existence until absolutely necessary."

He extended his hand formally, first to Alex, then to Maya. "Edward Chin. Grace's father. Presumed captured or killed by the Threshold, but actually extracted by our operatives and brought here to continue coordinating defense efforts."

"And I'm Helen Chin," added the woman beside him. "Grace's mother. Similarly 'captured' as part of our counter-intelligence strategy."

Alex's mind struggled to process these revelations. Not just the existence of an organized resistance with resources and personnel far beyond what he had imagined possible, but the implication that much of what they had experienced—including Grace's apparent capture—had been part of a larger strategy they hadn't been privy to.

"You let us think you'd been taken," he said to Grace, a note of accusation in his voice. "Let us attempt a desperate working with incomplete information, insufficient resources, minimal preparation."

"Yes," Grace acknowledged without apology. "Because your working needed to appear genuine to succeed. The Ancient would have detected deception if you'd known the full strategic context. Your desperation, your isolation, your belief that you were operating without support —those were essential components in creating the psychological conditions necessary for the extraction to work."

Before Alex could respond to this calculated manipulation, before he could process what it meant that even their allies had been using them as pieces in a cosmic chess game, a new figure approached from one of the branching corridors.

Tall, broad-shouldered, with a healing cut across his cheek and the watchful eyes of someone who had seen too much to ever fully relax. Detective James Rivera.

"You made it," he said simply, offering his hand to Alex. "Wasn't sure you would, after everything. Good work with the extraction. First genuine setback the Threshold has experienced in decades."

Alex stared at the detective he had presumed dead in the burning lake house, momentarily speechless with shock.

"How?" he managed finally. "The fire. We saw the house collapse. There was no way out."

"There's always a way out if you know where the doors are," Rivera replied cryptically.

"The Morgan lake house had more threshold connections than were immediately apparent. The fire itself was our creation. Necessary destruction of a compromised location after securing essential materials."

The revelations kept coming, each one forcing Alex and Maya to reconsider events they thought they had understood, experiences they believed they had interpreted correctly. The isolation and desperation they had felt while navigating threshold states, while developing their abilities, while planning their confrontation with Dr. Marsh—all had apparently occurred within a larger context they hadn't been allowed to perceive.

"So everything—" Maya began, but Edward Chin raised a hand to interrupt.

"Full explanations will have to wait," he said, his expression grave. "The extraction of the Ancient from its primary vessel is a significant achievement, but the crossing attempt continues. The Threshold's ritual site is already active, the four bloodlines they've secured generating preliminary threshold thinning despite the setback you've created."

"The equinox alignment is in less than three hours," Helen Chin added. "And while the Ancient itself has been temporarily removed from this reality state, its servants continue implementing the crossing ritual. Without the precision its direct presence would have provided, but with sufficient power to create catastrophic breaching if not countered immediately."

"What do you need from us?" Alex asked, setting aside his confusion and sense of betrayal in the face of continued existential threat. Whatever manipulations had brought them to this point, whatever deceptions had shaped their understanding, the fundamental danger remained.

"Your bloodlines. Your abilities. Your focusing tools." Edward gestured toward a large tactical display at the center of the chamber, where a holographic representation showed what appeared to be the former Masonic temple Grace had identified as the Threshold's ritual site. "We're implementing a counter-ritual at multiple locations around Boston, establishing a containment field designed to neutralize the threshold thinning they've initiated."

"Morgan and Weber bloodlines are critical components in that containment field," Helen explained. "Your specific abilities, reshaping and direction, create the structural framework within which our defensive measures operate. Without your participation, our counter-ritual will be severely compromised."

It was a request but also an assumption, that having come this far, having sacrificed and struggled against the Threshold's plans, they would naturally continue the fight regardless of how they felt about the resistance's methods or motivations.

And they weren't wrong. Whatever complications these revelations introduced, whatever questions remained unanswered, the fundamental choice remained clear. Participate in the counter-ritual or allow the crossing to proceed unimpeded.

No choice at all, really.

"Tell us what you need," Maya said, speaking for both of them. "But afterward, we want answers. All of them. No more compartmentalization, no more need-to-know limitations."

"Agreed," Edward replied without hesitation. "Assuming there is an afterward. The threshold is already thinning beyond standard parameters. We have minimal time to implement effective countermeasures."

The tactical display zoomed in on the Masonic temple, showing energy readings and threshold measurements that confirmed his assessment. The ritual site pulsed with power that had nothing to do with conventional physics and everything to do with the fundamental structure of reality itself. Even without the Ancient's direct presence, even without Dr. Marsh's vessel coordinating the efforts, the working proceeded with dangerous effectiveness.

"Where do we go? What exactly do we do?"

Alex asked, professional focus reasserting itself as he studied the tactical display.

"You'll join separate teams implementing containment measures at two of the seven focal points surrounding the ritual site," Rivera explained, indicating positions on the holographic map. "Morgan bloodline at the eastern anchor, Weber at the southern. The Chin family will coordinate from here, maintaining overall strategic direction of the counter-ritual."

"Seven focal points?" Maya noted. "Seven bloodlines. The containment mirrors their ritual structure."

"Oppositional symmetry," Grace confirmed. "Counter-force requires corresponding structure to be effective. Their working uses seven bloodlines to thin the threshold; our counter-ritual uses the same seven to reinforce it."

"But they have four bloodlines secured," Alex pointed out. "Bishop, Nazari, Okafor, and LaChance. Held against their will, channeling their abilities without conscious cooperation. How are you matching that?"

"We have representatives of those bloodlines too," Edward replied. "Some rescued from Threshold acquisition attempts, others identified and recruited before they were targeted. Not always the strongest expressions of each lineage, but sufficient for counter-ritual purposes when properly focused and directed."

The resistance was more extensive, more

organized, more resourced than anything Alex had imagined possible during their desperate journey through threshold states. The contrast with their isolated struggle, their improvised plans, their limited understanding was stark and somewhat humbling.

"Time is critical," Helen reminded them, checking a device on her wrist that displayed measurements Alex didn't recognize but assumed related to threshold stability. "The teams are prepared, awaiting only your arrival to activate their respective containment measures."

Rivera stepped forward, offering what appeared to be standard tactical communications gear—earpieces, compact radios, specialized equipment Alex couldn't immediately identify.

"These will keep you connected to central coordination," he explained. "Allow real-time adjustments based on threshold fluctuations and Threshold counter-responses. They're expecting resistance but not a coordinated operation at this scale. That's our primary advantage."

Alex and Maya accepted the equipment, making necessary adjustments with Rivera's guidance. As they prepared to join their respective teams, to take their places in this larger conflict they had only just discovered existed, Grace approached with a final piece of information.

"One thing you should know," she said, her expression softening slightly from its tactical intensity. "The extraction working you performed against Dr. Marsh's vessel? It wasn't just successful, it was unprecedented. No previous attempt to separate an Ancient from its host has succeeded without destroying both entities. What you accomplished creates new strategic possibilities, new approaches to threshold defense we hadn't previously considered viable."

It was a small validation amid overwhelming revelations, but significant nonetheless. Their desperate gambit, their improvised implementation of knowledge implanted by the Watchers, had apparently achieved something noteworthy even by the standards of an organization that had been fighting this shadow war for generations.

"The resistance has existed for centuries," Grace continued, "opposing the Threshold's crossing attempts across multiple celestial alignments, multiple generations. But we've always been reactive, defensive. Containing breaches after they occur, limiting damage rather than preventing it entirely."

"And now?" Maya prompted.

"Now, perhaps, we begin a new phase," Grace replied. "Your extraction working demonstrates that direct intervention against Ancient consciousness is possible under specific conditions. That offense, not just defense, might be a viable long-term strategy."

The implication settled over Alex and Maya as they completed their preparations. What they had achieved, what they had survived and learned and implemented, might represent more than a temporary disruption in the Threshold's plans. It might constitute a fundamental shift in a conflict that had been unfolding in shadows for millennia.

A new beginning, of sorts. If they survived the next three hours.

"Ready?" Rivera asked, checking their equipment one final time.

Alex touched his mother's locket, now restored to its place around his neck, warm against his skin as it recognized his bloodline resonance. Maya did the same with her grandmother's mirror, now secured in a specially designed carrier at her hip.

"Ready," they confirmed in unison.

As they moved toward separate corridors that would lead them to their respective teams, their respective positions in the counter-ritual about to unfold across Boston, Alex found himself thinking of where this journey had begun. A private investigator with a history of mental health issues, struggling to pay rent, taking a case that seemed straightforward enough, a suspicious death investigation for a wealthy client.

Now he stood at the center of cosmic conflict, bloodline abilities awakened, threshold mechanics becoming increasingly intuitive, part of an organized resistance against entities that had existed before humanity evolved consciousness.

The journey had cost him much. Understanding of who he was, what his heritage meant. Trust in his own perceptions, his own memories. Belief in a world where reality followed predictable, comprehensible rules.

But it had given him something too. Purpose. Connection. A sense of belonging to something larger than himself. Not just the resistance organization he had discovered today, but the lineage of Morgans stretching back generations, all standing against forces that would reshape existence itself if given the opportunity.

Whatever happened in the hours ahead, whether they successfully contained the Threshold's ritual or failed to prevent the crossing they had been fighting against since that first encounter with Eliza Bishop's ghost, Alex Morgan was no longer the man who had taken Katherine Bishop's case all those weeks ago.

He was a Watcher. A guardian of the threshold. The last Morgan, perhaps, but not the last defender of the boundary between worlds.

As he followed Rivera toward whatever awaited at the eastern anchor point of their counter-ritual, Alex felt that familiar warmth from his mother's locket intensify—not with heat but with recognition, with approval, with the sense that Catherine Morgan would have understood and supported the path her son now walked.

Behind them, at the heart of the resistance's hidden facility, the tactical display continued monitoring threshold measurements across Boston. The ritual site at the former Masonic temple pulsed with power, with potential, with the accumulated efforts of centuries of preparation now approaching its critical moment.

The equinox alignment was coming. The threshold was thinning. The veil between worlds grew increasingly permeable with each passing minute.

But this time, the forces working to maintain that barrier, to prevent catastrophic crossing, had something they hadn't possessed in previous confrontations.

Hope. Born from the unexpected success of two bloodlines working in desperate concert. From knowledge implanted by entities beyond human understanding. From the discovery that Ancient consciousness could be separated from its vessel without destroying both.

A new beginning, indeed. If they survived to see it.

In Boston's Public Library, in the shadowed

alcove where cosmic confrontation had unfolded amid ancient texts and forgotten knowledge, something stirred. Not physical movement but a disturbance in reality itself—a ripple in dimensional fabric, a momentary thinning between states.

Through that thinning, briefly visible to anyone with threshold sight, a familiar figure appeared. Eliza Bishop—or the consciousness that had once inhabited that name and form, her spectral presence more defined, more coherent than in previous manifestations.

She looked around the empty alcove, at the fallen form that had once housed an Ancient consciousness, at the threshold symbols still faintly glowing from the extraction working Alex and Maya had performed.

"Thank you," she whispered to the empty air, to the absence left behind by those who had successfully implemented what she had died trying to expose. "It wasn't human. And now, neither am I."

Then she was gone. Not dismissed or banished, but transitioning by choice. Moving beyond the threshold state that had held her since death, continuing whatever journey awaited consciousness after its physical vessel failed.

The symbols faded. The threshold stabilized. The alcove returned to ordinary reality. Just another forgotten corner in a vast repository of knowledge, unremarkable to casual observation, significant only to those who understood what had transpired there.

One battle in a war most of humanity would never know existed. One moment of cosmic significance amid the everyday flow of a city going about its business, oblivious to how close existence itself had come to fundamental restructuring.

The veil held. For now.

VESSELS OF POWER

Six weeks after containing a winter artifact that nearly froze Boston solid, private investigator Alex Morgan is still adjusting to his new reality. The elemental essence he helped capture hasn't fully relinquished its connection to him, leaving Alex with unexpected abilities that are growing stronger by the day.

When a wealthy collector steals ancient seasonal vessels and kidnaps a gifted student, Alex finds himself at the center of supernatural politics. The Winter Court views him as either a valuable asset or dangerous anomaly. The enigmatic Twilight Court pursues its own mysterious agenda. And local werewolves offer an unexpected alliance that could shift the balance of power in Boston's hidden world.

As Alex races to rescue the missing student and recover the stolen artifacts, he must navigate treacherous factions while mastering his evolving powers. But the collector's true plan goes beyond mere theft – he aims to harness the fundamental forces of nature itself. And he believes Alex's unique connection to winter essence is the key to achieving godlike power.

Vessels of Power continues the thrilling paranormal adventure that began in Hunter of Evil, and is perfect for fans of Jim Butcher's Dresden Files, Ben Aaronovitch's Rivers of London series, or John Connolly's Charlie Parker books. Dive into a world where detective work meets magical mystery, and where the boundaries between worlds grow thinner with each passing day.

Available shortly from Amazon.

Printed in Great Britain
by Amazon